THE BEASTS WE RAISE

Other books by D.L. Taylor

The Beasts We Bury

D.L. TAYLOR

THE BEASTS WE RAISE

FIRST INK

First published 2026 in the US by Henry Holt and Company

First published 2026 in the UK by First Ink,
an imprint of Pan Macmillan
The Smithson, 6 Briset Street, London EC1M 5NR
EU representative: Macmillan Publishers Ireland Ltd, 1st Floor,
The Liffey Trust Centre, 117–126 Sheriff Street Upper, Dublin 1 D01 YC43
Associated companies throughout the world

ISBN 978-1-0350-8205-6

Copyright © D. L. Taylor 2026

The right of D. L. Taylor to be identified as the author of this work has been
asserted in accordance with the Copyright, Designs and Patents Act 1988.

All rights reserved. No part of this publication may be reproduced,
stored in a retrieval system, or transmitted, in any form, or by any means
(including, without limitation, electronic, mechanical, photocopying, recording
or otherwise) without the prior written permission of the publisher.

Pan Macmillan does not have any control over, or any responsibility for,
any author or third-party websites (including, without limitation, URLs,
emails and QR codes) referred to in or on this book.

1 3 5 7 9 8 6 4 2

A CIP catalogue record for this book is available from the British Library.

Printed and bound in the UK using 100% Renewable Electricity by CPI Group (UK) Ltd
Book design by Meg Sayre and Aurora Parlagreco

This book is sold subject to the condition that it shall not, by way of trade or otherwise,
be lent, hired out, or otherwise circulated without the publisher's prior consent in any
form of binding or cover other than that in which it is published and without a similar
condition including this condition being imposed on the subsequent purchaser.
The publisher does not authorize the use or reproduction of any part of this book in
any manner for the purpose of training artificial intelligence technologies or systems.
The publisher expressly reserves this book from the Text and Data Mining exception in
accordance with Article 4(3) of the European Union Digital Single Market Directive 2019/790.

Visit **www.panmacmillan.com** to read more about all our books and to buy them.

Content warning: *This book contains animal violence*

TO MY HUSBAND, JORDAN, BECAUSE HE ACCEPTS

ALL THE MANY DIFFERENT PARTS OF *ME*

1
Mance

It's been months, but I'm still not used to the feeling I get when I step into the dungeons and my own voice echoes up from the shadowy depths to greet me, screaming.

It's like being hit with a cold blast when you walk outside, only instead of frigid air it's a rush of bleak horror. My limbs lock up. My scarred hands begin to tremble. Something a little like guilt and a lot like fear curdles inside me, right in the empty space where the screaming girl used to live before a dead man's magic allowed me to thrust her out.

Suffice it to say, I don't visit often.

Even today, I have to force myself to cross the threshold. When the pitch of her shriek makes the hair stand up on my arms, I almost turn on my heel and leave, back into the warmth and quiet of the hallway. It would be so easy to simply pull the door shut again.

But then the sound of crinkling paper snaps me back into myself and I look at the letter I've just crushed in my fist. I remember why I'm here, remember that I need to find out what the crumpled words mean.

And whether they truly have the power to bind me.

So, shoving my hands into my pockets, I put my head down

and descend, deep into the carved-out cliffside, those awful screams getting louder and louder the closer I get to the base of the wooden steps, underscored by a chorus of low growls, vicious snarls, and the scrape of claws on rock.

But when my boots hit the ground, the crack of my heel is as loud as a whip, and all the noise suddenly breaks off.

I hold still, like a mouse spotted by a hawk, my stomach in knots. My own creatures, the less dangerous ones, squirm and tremble within me, trying to burrow deeper into my guts to escape detection.

Some foolish corner of my mind hopes that she'll just leave me alone.

Then metal bars clang as a body crashes against them and the voice that sounds like mine rises again, with vigor. Instead of wordless rage, now the screeching girl flings insults, even obscenities, all cruelly tailored to cut me deep. Because she *knows* me. She came from me, and she has devastatingly intimate knowledge of the wounds I hide from everyone else. From the depths of those shadows that I refuse to look at directly, she stabs at them, ripping at their edges with her words in the hopes that she will get to watch me bleed, as her predators pace around her, howling their support.

I break into a run, covering my ears.

Because she's not the one I'm here for today, and I don't need to listen to her. I don't have to *take* this.

My boots pound the rough stone floors until their echoing beat and my own harsh breaths are all I can hear, and then right before the row of cells veers sharply to the left, I double over, panting.

I need to get it together. I cannot do what I need to do today if I'm this out of control.

Wincing, I force my fingers to unclench. I wrench my shoulders back and thrust my chin up. I wrest my features into an expression of calm. And then I hold it, mercilessly, until my breathing slows down to match and the animals inside me whimper into submission.

Then, finally, I turn the corner with a slow, easy step, feeling the prickle of the mountain's chill on my skin. Until I stand before the only other prisoner here, one who makes my stomach twist for completely different reasons.

My father.

He is seated, fingers steepled over his mouth, like he's been waiting for me. And for a moment, we just regard each other. He's lost weight and there are bags under his eyes, but he still holds himself with a military posture, as if he's sitting on his throne instead of wasting away in a prison.

I've done my best to make his cell comfortable, although I know he doesn't respect the effort. I had a nice bed hauled down, plus a table and a padded chair. Even a rug.

Nonetheless, when I study him, I see only contempt in his features.

I'm not sure what he sees when he looks at me, but I hope it's the calm I've tried to construct rather than the fear behind my eyes.

"Mancella," he says finally, lowering his arms. "To what do I owe the pleasure? It's not every day that a prisoner gets a visit from a *Prime*." He spits the last word, wrapping his disdain around it, and the last several months are a cavern between us.

He was the Prime once. If it were up to him, he still would be. But I stripped him of his power, first magically and then politically, and I took the throne for myself. Ever since then, he's been stewing in this cell.

I could have chosen to kill him instead. In fact, for a terrifying moment, I almost did.

No, *she* almost did, which is why she's locked up.

Suppressing a wince, I run my finger along the edge of the envelope, and my father's eyes flick down to it, his brow creased.

I speak loudly to force his gaze back up to mine. "Well," I say, with a boldness I don't feel, "you're not so great with the note-taking, which has left several gaps in my understanding of our relationships with other realms. Which means that I am forced to come down here and *ask* you whether you could clarify a particular point for me. Specifically, what does the Forest Realm—"

He barks out a humorless laugh, and the sound echoes around us in a mocking chorus, cutting me off. "You want me to *help* you? After everything you've done?"

A cold weight settles in my chest, and my casual facade slips.

Everything *I've* done, he says.

Like *he's* never done anything to me. Never locked me in a room with a wild beast and refused to let me out until it was dead. Never forced me to use those same beasts to kill. As though *he* isn't the person who drove me to "everything I've done" in the first place.

Irritation spikes in my rib cage and my creatures stir. I don't know what I was expecting from him. I should never have come down here at all.

I turn to leave, even as panic claws at my throat and the letter burns in my pocket, but he stops me with a word. "Wait."

Don't show weakness, I tell myself. *Don't let him know how much you need this.*

I narrow my eyes and cast a disdainful look back over my shoulder. He analyzes it carefully, as I feared, and I grit my teeth to keep it from cracking.

"A bargain," he suggests finally. "There's a certain book I'd like to peruse. I'll answer your questions if you have it sent down to me."

Slowly, I turn back around, searching his face the way he searched mine. "What do you mean, a book?" I ask. "Which book?"

"The Census. Let's say . . . Volume 36."

Alarm shoots down my spine. Not because I know what he wants the book for, but because I *don't.* I don't have so much as a guess.

What could he possibly do with a catalog of our realm's citizenry? Not a recent one, either. Volume 36 would be a few generations out of date now. I doubt anyone in it would even still be alive.

"Why?"

"I don't have much in the way of diversion down here."

"The Census is not exactly peak entertainment. It's just statistics. And why that volume?"

"You could pick a different volume if you prefer. Any one you'd like."

This only makes my confusion worse. "Why the *Census*, though?"

"What's in that letter that makes you so desperate to get answers that you'd come down here for the first time in months?" he retorts breezily. I bite my cheek to keep from replying and he smiles unkindly. "Just demonstrating that total transparency is not an aspect of our bargain."

Mentally, I curse, because he's demonstrating more than that. He's showing me that he sees my anxiety, after all. He knows I'm not in as good of a bargaining position as I'm trying to pretend.

"I *am* picking a different volume," I tell him. "And I'm going to have it searched first for any coded messages."

He waves a hand, unconcerned. "Fine."

"Fine," I repeat slowly. I don't like that I can't understand his motives. But he's not wrong that I'm desperate, and if he sees that already then the negotiations would only deteriorate from here. I pinch the corner of the envelope until my fingers go numb, and then I make a decision. "Assuming the search goes well . . . I'll have it delivered by the end of the day. But you'll have to answer my questions first. Now. Honestly and to my satisfaction."

My father leans back in his chair, pleased. "It's a deal," he says. "Ask away."

Again I hesitate, concerned about how smug he seems, how quickly he agreed. But then Silver's face flashes in my mind and I flinch. It's enough, more than enough, to make me push down the concern and cross back to stand directly in front of my father's cell. "The Forest Realm . . . ," I start again.

Our history with them is a painful one. When I was a child, my grandfather thought they were getting too strong, too close to our borders, and he started a war. In the end, that war cost him his life, and my father became Prime. But instead of taking the change of leadership as an opportunity to broker peace, he doubled down on the war efforts, enlisting almost every able-bodied citizen we had, demanding most of their lives in the fight and leaving their children to be raised by the Academy as another generation of soldiers. The Forest Realm surrendered, but neither of our realms has fully recovered from the aftermath, even though over a decade has passed.

I'm not here to question those actions today, though, so I push on. "When you negotiated the terms of surrender with them, what did they include?"

He frowns, surprised. "Not much. A ceasefire, a yearly financial tribute."

"That's all?"

"Yes. Why?"

I keep my expression schooled, ignoring the question. "And what have your relations with the Forest Realm been like since then?"

He shrugs. "Minimal. They send their tributes as required, and in turn I leave them alone."

"But then why would they—" I break off suddenly, realizing what I was about to reveal.

He raises an eyebrow, gaze drifting to the letter again before I shove it into my pocket, clearing my throat. "You're certain there are no other terms? No other promises made on either side that I should know about? Not then or at any other point in your reign?"

Something amused flashes in his eyes. "No, none. Is there a reason you're asking?"

Once again, I ignore his question, blowing out a long breath, less cautious about showing my emotions now that I have the information I need. "All right," I say. "Thank you. You've been very helpful. As promised, I will send the book down shortly."

Without another word, I turn on my heel, marching back

toward the staircase, too relieved to even say goodbye. I feel his eyes following me until I turn the corner, but it's easy to shrug them off as my mind races through the implications of what he's told me, the avenues his words have opened up.

Unfortunately, that means I'm too lost in thought to properly brace myself against my other prisoner. She's been quiet, and I let my guard slip. For a second, I forgot she was there.

When I pass by her cage, she leaps at me. Her shoulder slams into the bars so hard that it makes the magical shield glow, illuminating her furious face for one terrifying moment before I rip my gaze away and stumble back, my heart rate ratcheting up and my animals rioting.

I will never get used to the way my features look when they're distorted by hatred. The way my eyes can burn.

"You're a monster!" the girl—the severed piece of my soul—shrieks into my face. "You walk around up there in the sunshine pretending that you're perfect. That you're kind. But you can't avoid me forever. I *will* find a way to break out of this cell, and when I do, I will show everyone what you truly are. I will—"

"Can't you just be *quiet*, Livid?" I snap back at her, whirling. Still embarrassed that I was caught off guard.

It's not rage that colors my tone. I don't feel that emotion anymore.

But, unexpectedly, cutting the depths of my anger out of my core has made me more prone to the milder emotion of irritation. More likely to lose my patience.

Unsurprisingly, the girl does not oblige my request. She lashes out harder, her screams turning almost incoherent, as her predators pace the cell behind her, gnashing their teeth. I berate myself for engaging at all. Skin still crawling with the panicked wriggles of my own creatures, I turn and sprint the rest of the way up the stairs, only stopping when I've slammed the door firmly shut behind me and latched it, cutting off all sound. Wishing I could cut the emotion off just as easily.

I'm breathing hard again, my pulse pounding in my ears. But at least the hallway is quiet.

Until—

"Hey," a voice says from nearby. "Are you okay?"

I gasp, my head snapping up and my fingers scrambling behind me to make sure the lock is secured. That the awful secret I'm keeping from the world is solidly contained on the other side.

Silver, his choppy hair falling into his face as always, studies me with amber eyes full of concern. I exhale in relief, even as a jolt of guilt coils in the pit of my stomach, chased by an aftertaste of fear that he might have heard some of Livid's screaming, might have glimpsed the part of me that I so desperately want to hide from him. From *everyone*. But when his expression doesn't change, the fight drains from my body and I slump forward, almost dizzy from its loss.

Without missing a beat, he moves to catch me, gathering me securely against his chest. I lean into him, inhaling his familiar pine-smoke scent and burying my face in the crook of his neck, my chin resting on his collarbone. He skates his fingers up my spine, and my muscles turn to jelly beneath his touch.

Closing my eyes, I press even closer, attempting to chase the shadows of the dungeons away. Attempting to lose myself in his embrace completely.

"I'm fine," I assure him, perhaps too brightly. "Everything's fine.

I just . . . had to talk to my father about something, and it's left me a little . . . shaken."

His arms flex, then tighten around me. "What could you possibly need to talk to *him* about?"

Silver's history with my father is almost as difficult as my own. His parents were both conscripted in the war and died in mere weeks, leaving Silver to be raised by the Academy, which is an unforgiving place to grow up. He escaped, though, and has been living in the streets since. Oh, and a few months ago he was part of a plot to murder my father in cold blood, although he did back out of it in the end. All this to say, Silver is not exactly the former Prime's biggest fan.

I realize with a start that it's been too long since he asked a question, and I don't know what to say. I was trying to avoid telling him about Livid, but I absolutely don't want him to know what I was talking to my father about, either. Not until I can figure out what I'm going to do about the monumental decision looming before me.

One that would affect him as much as it affects me.

The letter weighs heavy in my pocket, and another wave of guilt washes over me as I stare up into his loving, unsuspicious eyes.

"Just . . . politics," I say vaguely.

He tilts his head. "You know you can tell me," he prompts. "If it's serious enough to talk to *him*, then it must be a pretty big deal. If I can help, I want to."

"I know, I just . . ." I plaster on a pained smile. "I'm sorry, but I don't have time right now. I need to hold a counsel. On something *extremely* time sensitive. But we'll catch up soon?"

He nods slowly, though I can tell he's still studying me, trying to figure out what I won't say.

So I raise onto tiptoes and press my lips to his, hoping to reassure him that we, at least, are fine, no matter what else is going on.

I only mean for it to be a quick peck, but he surprises me by deepening it, one hand cradling the back of my head, and the other pressing into the small of my back until we're melded together, his kiss slow and languid enough to make my knees buckle. To make me *want* to stay.

"Soon?" he confirms, voice husky. "You promise?"

"Soon," I repeat, startled to find my own voice breathy and faint. I clear my throat, embarrassed. "I promise."

He smirks at my bashfulness, a dimple appearing. "Okay then."

When he releases me and steps back, I only barely stop myself from swaying toward him and starting the kiss all over again. But then the corner of the envelope shifts, digging into my leg, and I straighten suddenly, the reality of my situation crashing back into the forefront of my mind.

Heart in my throat, I rush the rest of the goodbye and hurry on to my counsel room, certain Silver is going to have questions for me later.

Hopefully by then I'll have answers.

I take the steps of the West Tower two at a time before flinging open a pair of double doors at the top to reveal a simple, domed space, nothing inside but a large table in the middle and a circle of identical chairs. The room is empty, and I exhale in relief, hastily locking the door behind me and shutting the curtains until the room is lit only with the low orange glow of a wrought iron candelabra that dangles above.

I'm not expecting anyone else.

My father had advisors, of course, but when I became Prime I dismissed them all. I can't trust them. Because either they approved of my father's actions, in which case I don't want their advice, or they were simply too weak to oppose him, in which case they're no good to me. I know I'll have to gather a counsel of my own eventually, but finding the right people is difficult. It will take a little while.

In the meantime, I'll just sort through everything myself.

My mind skips back to Livid, and how she said I was pretending. She's not *entirely* wrong. I keep more secrets than I'd like.

Including the fact that she's not the only part of me I can split from the rest of my body.

She was the first. The loudest.

I named her Livid because that's what she *is*. The worst of me. Angry. Hateful. I *had* to lock her up. It was the only way to keep her from hurting anyone else. The only way to keep myself from falling into the same traps that Alect, the cousin whose death gave me this power, set for himself. He let *his* worst parts walk around unchecked, and they did awful things. Things that he as a whole person would never have considered. Ultimately, they got him killed.

I won't make the same mistakes.

But there are other parts of me that have made themselves known in the last few months of adjusting to this new power. Parts I *do* want to hear from, who have valuable thoughts and insights to add to my current dilemma.

And sometimes it's easier to tackle a problem when I can separate myself and debate it out loud.

So I stand at the head of the table, look a little to my left, and split.

It's . . . unpleasant. Like every single bit of me is ripping in half. Like something essential is torn from my soul, leaving a rupture.

But then there is a girl standing beside me, smiling softly with a mouth that looks like mine.

I call this one Heart, because that's what she leads with. She's my kindness, my belief in others. The part of me that always looks for the good. She has my face and body, but her outfit is different—a flowy dress instead of my pants and tunic. When first summoned, she wears her hair in a ponytail that matches mine, but she immediately shakes it out into loose waves. Then she draws me into a hug, and I take a moment to sink into it, cherishing her comfort.

When I pull back, she takes a seat, and I brace myself for the next one. Again, the sensation of ripping, the feeling of loss. And then there is Poise.

Poise is the embodiment of my diplomatic training. She's my most composed self, my best foot forward. Her floor-length dress is tasteful and formfitting, and she quickly turns the ponytail into a complicated-looking twist. She carries herself with dignity and strength. It makes me feel stronger just to look at her.

Summoning twice leaves me depleted, and my skin tingles as though I've just ripped off a scab that spanned my entire body.

Even so, I split again, enduring the ripping, tearing feeling one final time, until my last form, Asset, is standing by the table as well.

She's my practical side. My planner. The one who can always figure out what needs to be done and execute it before the rest of us have even started trying. She's wearing pants as well, but they're covered in pockets that are all crammed with useful things. With efficient, purposeful movements, she winds her ponytail into a tight, utilitarian bun, mouth thin and eyes focused on me.

That's all of us. We made the intentional decision to cap it at four. That way, unlike Alect, I won't split myself into such small slivers that they're barely even human anymore. I'll be smarter than that.

"So," I say, trying to focus. It can be hard to think clearly when they're all out. I feel a bit like a painting stripped of its color, only outlines and smudges left. But enough to function. "Now that we know we're not bound by any deals my father made... How do we respond to *this*?"

I take the letter out of my pocket and toss it on the table, where it lands with a quiet rustle that belies the weight of its contents.

We all look at it, grave.

There's no need for me to tell them what's in it. We share memories right up until we split. Which means they know the letter is from the Forest Realm, and they know exactly what it says.

Namely, that the Prime of the Forest Realm is dead.

That his successor, whom I have never met, will be coming to meet me at the end of the week.

And one more thing.

That he is asking for the highest demonstration of commitment to our alliance that it is possible for me, as Prime, to give.

Specifically... my hand in marriage.

2
Silver

"Mance is hiding something from me," I tell Vie, ducking under an outcropping of rock.

"Hmm," she responds indifferently. "Sounds to me like your entire relationship is doomed and you should probably just cut and run while you can."

I frown at her, annoyed. "I'm not *worried* about it. I just wonder what it is. Also, just so you know, most friends would offer sympathy in a situation like this."

"You shouldn't have sought me out right before a fight," she retorts, sidestepping a stalagmite. "It's not my most sympathetic time."

"When *is* your most sympathetic time?"

"Once a month or so I get a five-minute window."

"Ah." The stone tunnels we're walking through take a sharp dip downward, and so does the temperature. We're almost to the heart of the mountain, where illegal betting thrives. "Well, I didn't come here for you, actually."

She scoffs, like she doesn't believe me. "So what are you here for, then? Gonna place a bet?"

"Nah. I'm looking for a kid."

Her expression darkens into a scowl, and when she speaks,

her tone is no longer humorous. "Oh, right," she sneers. "I forgot you're the Academy's lapdog now."

I wince at the phrasing.

But she's not exactly wrong.

After Mance took power and rewrote the laws of the land, Rooftop, Vie, and I had the chance to go back to our original professions.

And Rooftop actually did it. He could slip back into being a baker as easily as slipping on an apron. But that's because he never really left that life. He was a chef on hiatus, but he was always a chef.

Vie, on the other hand, didn't feel right working for the only other butchers in town, since they were her parents' rivals. At least, that's what she says. But I think the truth is that she's no longer comfortable in that world. Vie *was* a butcher, but now she's something else. And I don't think she knows how to go back. Or wants to. So she still shows up for battles in the fighting rings, even though Rooftop and I beg her to stop.

And then there's me. I made candles and then I was a thief, and now neither one seems to fit at all.

To be fair, I did give being a candlemaker a go. At first. But I would fall into bed at the end of a long day with hardened wax under my fingernails and a dozen different scents clinging to my skin, feeling restless and unimportant.

So when Petrice, Mance's former Captain, finished her transformation of the Academy and approached me about helping her track down the runaways who were still missing, I leaped at the opportunity. It seemed like the perfect combination of my Outskirts skill set and my brand-new commitment to Do Good.

Only now we're running out of kids to find, and I still have no idea what's next. What else I could possibly be good for.

I shake my head, clearing the thoughts. Because none of that matters right now. I got a lead on someone in the rings telling everyone he used to be Academy, which means that at least for tonight I have a job to do. I'll worry about tomorrow tomorrow.

Vie and I reach the end of the rough stone hallway and she leans forward to knock a particular rhythm on the heavy wooden door. It swings open, and the noise and light on the other side are momentarily overwhelming.

The place is packed. Money is flowing. Fighters are going hard. Blood hits the stone to raucous cheering, and there are so many torches lining the walls that it feels like stepping into the middle of a bonfire.

We elbow our way to the moderator so Vie can check in, then find a spot near the wall, so close to the torches that I start to sweat. Vie snarls at several people along the way, and I realize she's doing her best to look tough so bettors will think her worth their money.

"There's my opponent for tonight," she says around an exaggerated glower. "You see him?"

I follow her eyes to a stocky guy at least five years older than her with the face of a pug. He spits on the ground when he notices us looking.

"He's trying to intimidate me," Vie snarls. "Help me intimidate him back?"

"Sure," I say. "What do you need me to—"

She throws a punch, and without thinking, I catch her fist in one hand.

She frowns. "You're supposed to let me hit you."

"You want me to just let you punch me in the face so you can look tough in front of someone you're probably about to wipe the floor with anyway?"

"If you wouldn't mind."

I throw her fist back at her. "Give me info on the guy I'm looking for and I'll at least fake it for you convincingly."

"Fine," she says through narrowed lips. "Who is it?"

"Goes by Ruin."

She hisses, but this time it feels genuine.

"Don't you dare say that name to me," Vie seethes.

I can't help it. I laugh. "He beat you, huh?"

"He cheated."

"By?"

"By . . . having too good of a right hook."

I smirk. "What can you tell me about him?"

"Not much, really. He kinda came out of nowhere. No one had ever heard of him, but then he showed up and climbed the ranks in a matter of days. He's a good fighter obviously, but there's something . . . off about him."

"Interesting," I say, turning that over in my mind. "Is he here tonight?"

"You're in luck," she growls. "He just walked in."

My eyes flick to the entrance to see a kid emerging from the tunnels, half obscured by shadow. He's tall and skinny, but somehow manages not to look gangly. Maybe it's because every muscle in his body is tensed, like at the slightest provocation he might snap. He has shaggy black hair that reaches his shoulders and a scowl twice as fierce as Vie's. But it's his eyes that really give me pause. They're a light green that's almost yellow, like the scales of a mamba snake. Like the magic that hangs on the horizon. And the way he swings them around the room, it feels like they're blades, cutting down every single person with one dismissive slash.

"He seems nice," I say.

And then Vie punches me in the face.

※ ✱ ※

I steal some of the ice from the fighters' bucket and hold it against my cheek as Vie takes the ring. It provides some semblance of relief against both the pain and the oppressive heat of the torches.

As I predicted, Vie takes her opponent down easily. He's big, but he's slow, in more ways than one. After a few jabs into sensitive areas that he's neither fast enough nor clever enough to cover, he crumples at her feet to the uproarious support of the crowd. As the jeering fades and her opponent hoists himself up with a glare, the cavern fills with the sound of clinking coins, and Vie slides out of the circle with a triumphant smirk.

And then it's Ruin's turn.

I sit up straighter with interest as he enters the painted circle, because the crowd gets rowdy when they see him.

He doesn't pander to them, though. Instead, he prowls around the ring like he's just waiting for someone else to enter, and he doesn't really care who it is. Finally, a freckled redhead with a scar across his nose steps up, mouth grim, and Ruin's attention locks onto him in a way that makes me lower the ice from my cheek so I won't miss what happens.

The bell has barely rung before Ruin launches himself forward, grappling his opponent and delivering his first blow to the redhead's gut. After landing the hit, I expect him to dance back, but he doesn't. He keeps going, delivering a torrent of brutal-looking jabs, with no space for even a breath between. It's like once he's started, he can't stop. And there's an unsettling burning in his snake-scale eyes, like a dog that's been abandoned by its owners and turned feral. His opponent folds and sags beneath his onslaught until he's on the ground, unmoving. And Ruin just keeps going, hitting and kicking with that cold-burning rage in his eyes.

The bell rings again to signal that his match is finished, but Ruin pretends not to hear it. He's ramming his foot into the redhead's stomach, causing him to vomit blood, when the moderator finally pulls him off and away.

Based on the reaction of the crowd, I'm the only one sickened. They stamp their feet and jingle their coins in praise as the redhead empties the contents of his stomach on the ground in front of them.

I angle my eyes toward Vie, who leans next to me on the wall. "Was he like that when he fought you?" I ask tightly.

She nods. "He broke my leg."

I hiss through my teeth and grab her arm, spinning her to face me. "Why didn't you tell me?" I demand in a low voice.

"Because I don't need a babysitter," she replies coolly, wrenching back her arm. "And Ruin's leaving, by the way, so if you want to catch him you'd better hurry up."

For a moment, I war with myself. I want to stay, want to

convince her to leave this violence behind for good.

But it doesn't seem like she's in a listening mood right now anyway. So I might as well go after the one I have an actual shot at helping.

"We'll talk about this more later," I tell Vie.

"Sure we will," she says.

Ignoring her dismissiveness, I shove my way through the mass of people, weaving through sweaty onlookers and keeping well clear of the chalk-drawn rings. Only by the time I make it into the cooler air of the tunnel, Ruin is out of sight. I hurry down the passageway, then look around the tavern when I emerge. He isn't there, either. Fortunately, when I burst through the doors I catch a glimpse of him turning at the end of the street.

Relieved, I quicken my pace to catch up to him, but wherever he's going, he's not taking a direct route. I know these streets pretty well, but Ruin is weaving through alleys seemingly at random. At one point, I lose him completely and come face-to-face with a dead end. I turn to double back and retrace my steps when someone slams me against the wall, yellow-green eyes burning and an arm braced across my throat.

"Why are you following me?" Ruin asks. His voice is gravelly, like it's overused, even though these are the first words he's spoken all night.

"I just want to talk," I say.

He narrows his eyes. "About what?"

"Mind lowering the arm so I can tell you?" I ask.

"You seem to be talking just fine with it where it is," he says, not moving a muscle. "What's your name?"

"I'm Silver," I tell him.

To my surprise, he drops me immediately, backing up a couple paces and examining me more carefully.

"Silver," he says. "I imagined you taller."

I didn't expect him to have heard of me, but I guess I should've. My proximity to Mance and my involvement with the events leading up to her Ascension aren't exactly a secret, so there are more whispers about me than I'm used to these days. Most of them don't get the story right, but they don't get it completely wrong, either. It's a mixed bag as far as what this guy might have heard.

"And I imagined you less . . ." I trail off and he raises an eyebrow. ". . . never mind."

He crosses his arms over his chest. "Well, it's about time you showed up."

I look up at him. "You've . . . been expecting me?" This is not how this usually goes. Most of the time, I have to get past defenses, make a whole pitch. Talk about the new curriculum, the better food. The lack of glass shards jutting from the walls and stones chained to ankles. But apparently, Ruin doesn't need convincing. "Well, great. Do you need to grab your stuff or anything? I could walk you to the Academy now . . ."

He jerks his head to the side, once. "No," he says. "I'm not going to the Academy."

I look him up and down, taking in the tension of his stance and the tightness around his mouth. I make a humming noise in the back of my throat as I understand.

He wasn't waiting for me to come get him. He's been expecting me because he's been prepping for a fight. Based on what I saw in the ring, I'm not eager to find out how far he'll go.

So I throw my hands up in defeat.

"Fine," I say, somewhat bitterly. "No one's dragging you back. It's all voluntary now. I was just trying to give you some other options. But if you want to spend the rest of your life punching strangers until you grow too old to survive it, then that's your prerogative."

This is not how this usually goes, either. I'm typically a lot more understanding, a lot more charming. But my conversation with Vie is still on my mind, and I realize I'm talking to her more than to him.

I shove my hands in my pockets and make to leave, but Ruin stops me with one shoulder braced against mine. "Hold on," he says.

I tense, not especially thrilled to be this close to the arms that took a kid down so viciously mere moments ago. "Something *else* I can help you with?" I ask.

"You're right," he says, surprising me. "I don't want to spend the rest of my life in those pits. I want a lot more. Just not the Academy."

I frown, backing up and taking him in again. "Then . . . what?" I ask. "And what's it got to do with me?"

"I want you to get me a job."

Once again, I'm thrown. But also a little intrigued. I tilt my head. "I . . . don't exactly have a spare," I tell him, still not sure where I come in.

"You got your start as a servant at the castle, right?" he pushes. "Get me that job."

But I shake my head. "That's not really how it went down. Also, I don't work there anymore."

He scowls, as though irritated that I'm not just agreeing without question. "I hear you're close to the Prime, though," he presses, not backing down. "You're telling me you couldn't pull some strings with her? Get me some low-ranking position in the kitchens or the stables or something? I'll do laundry if that's what it takes."

I don't like the way he said "close to the Prime," like I'm only with her for her power. But just as I open my mouth to refuse again, something desperate flashes across his face before he tucks it away.

And I soften, understanding him differently.

He's like Vie when she first started fighting, willing to do anything just to earn enough to survive. Even if it means hurting or getting hurt. But he's not like Vie today yet, unwilling to leave the ring even when better opportunities are presented. Looking at him now, with his shoulders hunched and his expression shuttered, I wonder if the persona he had on in the ring was as much of a front as Vie's. If the desperation I glimpsed in his eyes is because he feels trapped.

It's a feeling I can understand.

I press my lips together, thinking. This guy and I are not exactly setting up to be best buddies. He hurt my friend and he's muscling his way through this conversation like he's never said please in his life. It has my hackles raised.

But I *did* want to help someone tonight. And if the people I actually want to help won't let me, then . . .

I blow out a breath slowly.

"Tell you what," I say. "I'll see what I can do."

3
Heart

I don't usually go out alone. It's risky, splitting from Mance and going off in different directions, because someone might see her in more than one place and wonder. But last night left all of us so wrecked that this morning we're taking drastic measures.

Even though we argued until the candles burned down to stubs, we still haven't agreed on a plan for the proposal. Sometimes dividing ourselves makes things more balanced, all our voices getting equal weight. But sometimes, like now, it only polarizes our opinions. The crux of this particular conflict was between me and Asset. Reason and emotion. Head and Heart.

Because *Asset* refused to agree that we would definitely turn down the proposal. She argued that a political marriage was something we've always known would come, and that this is in many ways a strategically good match. That we're only just establishing our reign and we're not willing to offer the military resources our father did, so we need other methods of shoring up alliances, marriage being one obvious possibility. She wanted to at least hold off on any decisions until we could hear out the Forest Prime completely, weigh it all properly.

But there is nothing to *weigh*.

Not when we finally have a real chance to be with Silver. Not when his dimples make us melt and his kisses make our toes curl and his unfailing support has been the only thing getting us through these last few months.

Not when it would break his heart.

And *ours*.

We went at it for hours, Asset calm and measured and me pleading and tearful with Poise trying to moderate, until, finally, Mance gave up and called us all back, only for the fight to continue raging in her mind.

She didn't sleep. And in the morning, exhausted, she sent the three of us out to fulfill her duties so she could get some rest with an empty mind.

I was chosen to help with the Outskirts cleanup efforts, which has been systematized by Asset, and I'm glad. It's a cause that's important to me, and is probably one of the only things that might distract me right now.

I take a breath, trying to center myself, and look around.

Sunlight glints off the shattered glass embedded in the earth, and I can't help but think that even pain like this has a bright edge of loveliness to it. Not because the shards sparkle when they catch the light, but because there are people who managed to survive here despite those shards. Who managed to love and laugh, right here, among this tragedy and brokenness.

Today in particular there is a quiet joy interlaced with the ache, because the existence of this wasteland of sharp fragments has inspired a whole community to come together and try to fix it. In a patch of land that was once a blight on the realm, inhabited by outcasts shrinking into the shadows, today there is a redemption in progress.

I know the others think I'm naive to see the best in people. But on days like today it's hard not to.

Feeling more relaxed than I have all morning, I stand in line with everyone else and am quickly assigned a square plot and a set of tools.

At first, when I claim my area, getting on my knees in the dirt, the people around me startle and fall silent, not knowing how to act around their ruler. But I merely give them a wink and keep my head down, and eventually the cheerful chatter around me returns. I listen to it with idle satisfaction, even as sweat beads on my brow and my muscles burn.

This, right here, is what I became Prime for. This is what I envisioned. Tangible hope, visible change. Something *better*.

Shade falls across my square, and I look up, pleased to see my former Captain, Petrice, blocking the sun.

"Thank you for being willing to meet me out here," I tell her. I'd sent word this morning, wanting to talk things through with her. Even if I can't talk through everything.

"Of course," Petrice says easily. "I am at your command." She kneels down next to me, and I notice she's brought her own pair of gloves. Unbidden, she begins picking through the corner of the square I haven't gotten to yet, fishing out the largest chunks and dropping them in my bucket with a series of soft plinks.

For a moment, we work in silence, and it's not an entirely comfortable one. We haven't spoken to Petrice much in recent months outside of her reports about the Academy, and I'm not sure the others would want me to now. Once, we considered making her one of our inner circle. But that was before the argument.

Still, she's a good woman, and I have questions. Ones she may be able to answer.

When the pause stretches too long, Petrice looks over at me, and I meet her eyes. "You were there, weren't you?" I ask finally. "When we fought the Forest Realm. You were part of it."

She stills, her thumb running absently along a shard of glass with a single, perfect hawthorn leaf sprouting out of it. Although it looks smooth, its edge cuts straight through her glove, and red beads spring up on her now-exposed finger. "I was," she says softly.

I drop my sieve and pull off her glove, examining the cut. It's shallow enough that I don't need to request bandages from the makeshift medical station onsite. I have several small ones in my bag that are up to the task.

She starts to protest as I pull one out, but I give her a pointed look and she relents, letting me clean the wound with swabs and a small bottle of alcohol.

"What can you tell me about the Prime of the Forest Realm?" I ask as I dab. "I've never met him."

She inhales sharply, though it might be because of the alcohol stinging her wound. "He was a desperate man when I encountered him," she says. "I'm not sure I saw his best side."

"But perhaps his truest," I push back.

I make one last swipe against her wound before putting away the swab, but this time she doesn't flinch, either from my care or from my words. Instead she nods, understanding what I mean. "He had honor. He had loyalty to his own. He never abandoned a squadron, even if the odds were against them. But he was cruel to his enemy. To us. He took any shot he could, no matter how underhanded. Of course . . . we were doing just the same, at your father's command."

I feel a surge of grief at the pain in her voice, one that makes the creatures within me shift. When we split, our animals seem to pick favorites, dividing themselves between us. The ones that live in me are the pets. The cats and dogs and rabbits. Their soft furs brush up against the underside of my skin.

No matter how many times I hear about the war, it will never make sense to me why there had to be so much needless suffering. I press my lips together as I smooth a bandage over the pad of her finger. "That must have been hard for you. And for him. For everyone really, I suppose."

She nods, slipping the glove back on. "It was war."

I feel another stab of angst at her dismissiveness, but I don't press her on it. Instead, I clear my throat, fiddling with the rest of the bandages as I put them back in my bag.

"Did you . . . ever meet his son?"

Her eyes catch on mine, clearly detecting that this is what I really want to know. She fingers the new hole in her glove before responding. "Only once," she says. "He was extremely young, of course. Like you. So he wasn't brought out for the battles. But there was one night when Prime Merod directed us to attack deeper into the forest than we ever had before. We didn't realize until we arrived that we were attacking civilians. And . . . Reltas was there. In one of the homes we invaded. Probably hiding from us."

I let this sit with me, idly running my sieve through areas I've already cleared as I consider what that must have been like. "And . . . ?"

"I only caught a glimpse, but he was a small child, even for his age. Sort of wan and pale. Yet, for someone so young . . . he looked at me with such *burning* hatred. So fierce and so . . . hard. I've never forgotten it."

"One can hardly blame him," I say in a small voice.

"No," Petrice agrees. "One cannot."

I put my sieve down, distracted. Wondering if Reltas has healed from that day or if he still harbors that hurt and hatred close.

What has the last decade been like for him? What brought him to the point of wanting to *marry* me?

I want to ask for Petrice's opinion, but our argument still lingers between us. Besides, it feels wrong to confide in her about this when we haven't even told Silver yet. So I try to speak around it.

"I was talking to . . ."—I lower my voice—"*Asset* last night." Petrice is one of the only people who knows about my new power, so this at least is not a secret. "About the kinds of hard decisions one needs to make when ruling a realm. And . . . how to know which choice to make. Do you have any advice on that? In particular when the choice is . . . painful?" I wince, wishing I could be clearer.

Petrice lays a hand on my knee. "As Prime, you *will* have to make sacrifices," she says gently. "That's a core part of the job. But it will be up to you which ones you're willing to make, and for what purposes you are willing to make them."

"So you won't counsel me?" I ask, bitterly unsurprised. I can feel my kitten's paws kneading my insides in dismay.

"Without full information, I cannot. And besides . . . you have not always taken my counsel well."

I feel the pinpricks of my kitten's claws digging in.

She's talking about our argument.

She's talking about *Livid*.

I put my head down, lip quivering. "She's dangerous," I insist weakly. "We *had* to."

"Anyone can be dangerous if they're caged and ignored, Heart. And in my experience, no matter how hard we try, the parts that we push down have a tendency not to stay caged forever."

The force behind her words surprises me. "Do you have such parts?" I ask sincerely, lifting my head to look her in the eyes.

"I think we all do to an extent," she says. "I just told you a little of the war I waged. Do you think it left no scars on me? Do you think everything it brought out of me was good and wholesome? Mancella is right not to feed those parts and make them all of her. But she is *not* right to suppress them. It can be just as harmful."

I bow my head again, guilt a weight in my chest. "I will . . . consider your words."

"See that you do."

Swallowing, I tuck a loose strand of hair behind my ear. She rises and so I rise with her. We clasp arms, and then I watch her disappear into the crowd, back toward the towering cliffs.

Feeling like the dogs inside me are worrying at my very bones with their teeth, I return to my plot, ready to pick up the sieve and throw myself back into my task. Hoping to work through some of these complicated feelings as I do. But just as I'm about to kneel, something catches my eye.

It's a girl, about my age, with a long ponytail of hair so blond it's almost white. She's weaved leaves into it, and I can't tell if she means for them to be decoration or camouflage. They are both, turning her into a stunning creature that blends into the trees as though she is a part of them.

I don't know her, but that isn't what claims my attention. After all, I can't know everyone in my realm. But the way she's hunched over her square, almost as though she's trying to hide it, gives me an odd feeling.

Cautiously, I step closer, craning to see what she's covering with her arms.

To my surprise, it's a hole. A few feet deep. At first, I think perhaps she's trying to dig up some particularly stubborn roots, but she has no bucket for glass shards, and she seems to have little regard for the ones in the dirt, plunging her arms in up to the elbows, even though they are already peppered with red scrapes.

"Excuse me," I start, intending to offer her medical care, but before I can even finish the sentence she's on her feet, a knife drawn.

A moment of silence passes between us as she seems to realize who I am.

Only instead of being chagrined and apologetic, she grips the knife harder, her brown eyes darkening. My pulse starts hammering in my ears.

"I guess it's deep enough," she says.

It takes me a second to realize what she means, and then I glance behind her at the pit she's made. "Deep enough for what?" I ask.

She doesn't answer, only tosses something behind her into the hole. I barely get a glimpse before she kicks dirt over it, but it looks like a scroll, with some writing on it. Perhaps . . . names?

"May I ask—" I start.

"No time," she says. "You should probably run."

Then she leaps upward with impressive dexterity, grabbing

onto one of the overhanging branches and—moving so fast I can hardly keep track of her—pulls herself up and springs from one tree to the next until she's out of sight, her long white ponytail streaming in the air behind her.

I remain rooted in place, thoroughly confused.

What did she mean *run*?

When she disappears completely, I let my gaze drift to the loose earth in front of me, trying to decide whether to dig up whatever she's buried.

But before I can even begin to debate it, the ground below my feet bucks.

I lose my footing, stumbling hard to the left.

My first thought is that it's an earthquake, but the ground isn't exactly *shaking*. It's more like I'm standing on a lake instead of solid land, and something just caused a ripple at my feet. It spreads outward, the circle becoming wider and wider.

People nearby cry out, startled, as they trip over ground that used to be flat.

But it doesn't end there.

If the dirt is a lake, then whatever was in that scroll has caused a small whirlpool, spinning and churning faster than solid ground has any right to. My heart speeds up and my creatures squirm, recognizing before my brain does that things are about to get very, very bad. And then something shoots upward, right in the middle of the swirling dirt, suddenly enough to make me stumble backward in surprise.

Because it's . . . a hand.

A groping, clawing hand.

And then an arm.

And then another.

In the time it takes for my stomach to roil in horror, a multitude of human-looking arms burst forth from the ground, like wasps exploding from a nest. I gape at them, panicked, as they grab for anything in their vicinity, clenching and pulling and tearing down.

One manages to latch on to the woman next to me, dragging her viciously into the dirt.

The woman screams, scrambling to pry at the fingers, but soon more hands emerge and snatch at her until she is wrenched out of the air and into the earth, her shrieks muffled by the fresh soil that fills her mouth. I run for her, but she's buried before I even make it halfway, and several more hands shoot up between us, forcing me to dance back.

The scroll. Whatever it is, it must be doing this.

I have to get it.

"Into the trees!" I scream to the others, because the arms don't seem to have any bodies attached, so their range is limited. My voice serves to wake up those who have frozen in fear, and soon there is a mad dash for any trees that look like they might bear a load.

Meanwhile, I sprint back toward the scroll. It wasn't buried too deep, so it shouldn't be too difficult to dig up. In theory. But the hands are clustered most densely directly on top of it, which means that to get to it I will have to go through them.

I dodge one groping hand, and then another, only to skid to a stop directly in front of the heart of the horde.

Asset makes me wear a knife, and today I'm grateful for it. I draw the small blade from its sheath and fling myself into the center of the writhing flesh, aiming for the spot where the scroll was buried.

The hands grab onto me immediately. They rip at my hair, tug at my clothes, scratch at my skin, all working together to drag me deeper into their strange, squirming mass.

One goes for my throat and, wincing, I plunge my knife into the soft bones of its wrist, hoping to wound the limb enough to make it back off, or at least loosen its grip.

It doesn't seem to notice or care. It doesn't relent, and there isn't even any blood welling around the gash. It's like I've sliced into the meat of a corpse.

With dread, I realize I will have to actually cut it off me. My wince becomes a grimace, but when the bruising fingers start pulling me down, into the earth, pressing hard enough to cut off my air supply, I get over my hesitation and start sawing, the creatures within me going wild.

I hack away with hot desperation, cutting through tendons and scraping against bone, the sound of severing flesh making me sick to my stomach.

But it's not enough. The other arms are wrapping around me now, drawing me down into a bruising embrace. I slice my way through about a quarter of the wrist at my throat before I realize it's no use. Even if I were to free myself from its grip, there are dozens of hands ready to replace it. I can't cut them all.

Black spots enter my vision, but even so I switch tactics, slashing blindly in front of me. My only goal now is to maneuver my body toward where the scroll was buried and destroy it. I don't have long, but it was close. If I could just *get* there . . .

But the arms shift, enveloping me completely, and suddenly I'm not sure which way is up. Which way is the scroll. Which way is my next gasp of air. In the span of a few seconds, they have wound around me so completely that all I can see is flesh on every side.

I twist, panting and searching for a gap, only to find one and be shocked by dirt filling my mouth instead of air.

The feeling of it is so wrong, so revolting, so *terrifying* that I buck backward. In a sudden burst of horror that makes my creatures frenetic within me, I realize that I may not actually succeed. That I may *die*, and for nothing. It doesn't seem possible, but the sludge in my mouth tastes like the grave.

There's a small corner of my mind that frantically tries to figure out what that would mean. No part of me has ever died before. No part of Alect, either. Would it kill Mance? Somewhere in the castle, will she just cease to live because of my mistake?

Or would it only kill me? Would she go on without me, forced to live with no Heart? For the rest of her life, would she be unable to summon up compassion for anyone, unable to see the good in anything?

What would that do to her?

At the thought, my body is possessed by a desperate, violent need to survive, and I lash out everywhere at once. The knife gets lost hilt-deep in the crook of an elbow, but I keep going, digging my nails into bloodless skin, kicking at anything that touches me, whipping my head from side to side.

They only press in tighter.

I open my mouth in a frustrated scream, but that was a mistake. More dense, sludgy dirt pours into my throat, so thickly that my jaw feels unhinged. I try to spit it out, but a hand attaches to my face, locking the muck in. Sealing off my air for good.

I'm choking, spluttering, thrashing, panicking, crying. My

creatures feel like they're trying to claw their way right out of my body.

But the fingers only dig deeper into my flesh. The dirt only piles higher on top of me. And there's no air.

No air at all.

My chest explodes in pain as my lungs scream for oxygen.

My heart pounds so hard it feels like the inside of my rib cage is bruised.

I feel the wave of nausea that precedes unconsciousness, but I fight it. I fight everything. The arms, the way my body is shutting down, the oppressive darkness around me, the crushing weight that presses in from all sides. I fight it with an animal desperation that burns, all while my creatures fight, too, ripping at the underside of my skin.

But we can't fight forever.

All too soon, dizziness causes my movements to slow. My mind gets fuzzy. I feel . . . hopeless.

And then I can't delay the blackout any longer.

My muscles go slack and my brain goes numb, as bitter tears soak the dirt near my face.

Unconsciousness closes in, and I only have time for one last, wretchedly anguished thought.

That perhaps everyone was right about me.

Perhaps . . . I was naive, after all.

4
Silver

"The collar is itchy."

"Tell me about it."

Seeing how wrong the servant's uniform looks on Ruin's lanky frame makes me wonder if it ever looked right on me. Taking him in feels like slipping through time to the moment when all this started. When a street kid in a new, starchy collar was transplanted from the Outskirts into a palace.

At least he doesn't have to use a fake name.

Or, well, I guess. At least he's up-front about the fact that it's fake.

I thought about going back to my real name after Mance became Prime, but it didn't feel right. I'm not that kid anymore. But it's nice to have the option anyway.

"That's some kind of room for sitting in," I tell him, continuing the tour. "And that's some kind of room for eating in. They're allowed to both sit and eat in any room in the castle should they so choose, but they nonetheless feel the need to designate specific rooms for each task. Several of them, actually."

"This is a weird tour," Ruin says under his breath.

"I'm sure the Head of Staff will give you a proper one later. This is the fun one."

He gives me a look like he might disagree with that description but nods at another door anyway. "What's that one?"

I glance over my shoulder as we pass. "That's the entrance to the dungeons."

He perks up at that, craning his neck back around like he might suddenly be able to see through walls. "Are there actual prisoners down there?" he asks with a conspiratorial whisper.

"Just one," I say, a surge of anger lacing through me at the thought of the former Prime. Even now, defeated as he is, some feelings are hard to let go of. "As far as I know. But anyway, you don't need to worry about him. Kitchens are next. They're great because—"

But when we turn the corner we bump into Mance, and the sight of her derails whatever I was about to say. Ruin has a strong reaction, too, his back suddenly ramrod straight and his attention sharpening.

Mance keeps her different forms a secret from most people, but she's told me, and I like to think I'm an expert at figuring out which part of Mance I'm talking to. The easiest thing is to look at the hair. Presently it's up in a ponytail—not an elaborate updo, a practical bun, or a free-flowing mass—so this is probably the "core" Mance. But I always look at the eyes to make sure, because they're more honest. Hair can be changed, but the different sides of Mance have different ways of holding their emotions.

This one looks tired. Drained. Which both confirms that I'm talking to the core Mance and also tells me that all her forms are currently out. It's not exactly like she's empty without them, just . . . a little dimmer. Almost a little lonely.

When she notices us, she smiles vaguely in my direction, like her thoughts are too heavy and a small curling of her lips is all she can muster for me.

Without thinking, and heedless of the fact that we're not alone, I reach out and wrap her in my arms, tucking her head under my chin. She returns the embrace, laying her cheek on my chest with a sigh and sagging against me.

"I feel like I haven't seen you in days," she mumbles into my shirt.

"I saw you yesterday," I remind her. "But I agree that it wasn't for long enough." Behind me, Ruin makes some sort of noise, possibly startled or embarrassed by our affection, but I ignore him. "Seems like you've been . . . dealing with something?"

I don't know if prompting her again to share with me is a good idea with her looking as exhausted as she does, but I can't pretend it hasn't been bothering me. I know she has a lot going on. She's running a whole Realm right now. Trying to uproot all the poison that her father and grandfather planted. It's hard, and it's important, and it's time-consuming.

But it hurts when she doesn't let me be a part of it, even if my part is just this. Holding her and listening to her problems. It worries me that she thinks there's something she can't share.

She must feel it, because she pulls away and takes my face in her hands, her eyes searching.

"I'm sorry," she says. "For being distant. You're right, there's something that we should . . . that we *need* to talk about. If you have a minute now, maybe we could go—"

She's in the middle of gesturing at one of the sitting-type rooms when all of a sudden, midsentence, she inhales sharply. My eyes cut to her face.

Without any further warning, her whole body seizes up, contorted and tense.

It's so abrupt that I almost don't catch her as she pitches forward, twitching unnaturally.

"Mance?" I yell. "Mance!"

But she's not responding. Or maybe she can't. Her eyes go blank and roll into the back of her head as her body slumps in my arms. I stagger against the wall, trying to hold her up, and when we hit the stone she emits a moan that gives me goose bumps.

"Get a healer," I tell Ruin. "*Now!*"

I don't look up, but I hear his rapid footsteps retreating down the hall. I'm overwhelmingly relieved that we already covered the healers' wing on our tour. Hopefully it's one of the ones I actually described accurately.

Scooping Mance into my arms, I stumble into the nearest room, which turns out to be the larder. Rows and rows of wine greet us, and there's nowhere comfortable to set Mance down, so I lean against a cask and cradle her in my lap, the smell of sour fermentation making my head swim. It only compounds the sick feeling in my stomach.

"Mance, what's happening?" I ask desperately, combing her hair away from her face. "Talk to me."

She doesn't respond.

I slide my fingers against her jaw in a reflexive move to feel for a pulse.

Only to come up short when . . .

There isn't one.

My heart lurches and time seems to stop.

No. "Mance!"

I shake her and then immediately stop. That might not be a good idea. I might jostle something that shouldn't be jostled.

What do I do, though? Where's that healer? This can't be the end, there must be something that can be done.

Something—

Suddenly, her eyes roll forward again and she gasps. Not like she's surprised, but like she's straining for air. I feel like I am, too. I'm not sure I've actually taken a breath since the moment I felt her throat.

It's thrumming now, racing beneath my fingers, reassuring me that she *is* alive.

But alive doesn't mean okay.

As her mouth gapes, sucking in oxygen by the lungful, she starts shivering, whimpering, swatting at places on her body like she's attacking phantoms. I barely duck one swinging arm and catch the other just before it slams into a spigot, folding my fingers over hers and pressing them into my lips.

"Mance, please . . . ," I moan. I'm doing my best to stay outwardly calm, but inside I'm absolutely losing it. What is *happening* to her?

She twitches again and then goes abruptly, unnaturally still. "I . . ." The muscles of her jaw flex, like speaking is difficult. "I died, Silver."

"You—" The feeling of her flesh with no pulse surges to the front of my mind, and I press my fingertips lightly into the space below her jaw to feel it again, to find the reassuring rhythm that denies the awful thing she's just said. None of this makes sense. She clearly hasn't died, because she's right here in my arms, curled against me. I'm *not* losing her. Not today.

But then I realize what she must mean and the breath dries up in my throat as my fingers freeze in place. "Who?" I croak. "Which one?"

She swallows, then whispers brokenly, "Heart."

It feels like my own heart has been torn from my chest at the word. "No . . ."

I sag against the wood cask, winded. *Wounded.*

Not Heart. That can't be true. She's the sweetest of them. The one who always looks at me like she can see everything I'm meant to be and has no doubt at all that I'll live up to it. Even if I don't always believe that look, I need it sometimes. The idea of not having it, the thought of her being gone, cuts through me like a knife.

"*No*," I say again, louder. Mance came back to me. I refuse to accept that Heart won't. "When your animals die, you can still summon them. Right? What if it's the same? Do you think . . . Can you still summon her?"

"I don't know."

". . . Try?" Even as I say it, I almost choke on the word, terrified to know for sure.

She looks sick at the suggestion, like she's just as afraid of the answer as I am. But after a couple seconds, her gaze goes unfocused.

And . . . nothing happens.

My throat gets tight.

Usually, her splits are fairly instantaneous. She only needs to think it and it happens, like moving your arm.

But a full second goes by, and she's just lying there, staring at nothing.

Then *another* second passes, one of the slowest of my life.

By the end of the third second, tears begin to gather in the corners of her eyes, and an anguished sob starts to work its way up from the center of my chest.

But then, just before the cry leaves my lips, her body finally splits, one version peeling off the other like a mist that rises on a lake at dawn.

And then Heart is there. Standing right in front of us.

My first emotion is relief, and it's heady enough to make my head swim. A flood of tension releases from my shoulders, and Mance collapses against the cask as well, clearly feeling the same.

But then I really look at Heart, and it feels like I've been punched in the gut all over again.

There's dirt on her face, and it's tracked with tears, forming crusty paths down her cheeks. Her hair is in a ponytail like Mance's, but it looks considerably more unkempt, and she doesn't shake it out immediately like she usually would. Her mouth isn't smiling. Her eyes are wide and blank.

Worst of all, her entire body is covered with dark purple bruises. They look like . . . handprints.

Including one wrapped around her neck.

I slowly get to my feet, needing to touch her. Wanting to soothe away the hurt. Wishing I could go through time and pull her out of whatever moment she just came from.

"I thought when one of you got injured, it would heal when you merged," I say. The words sound accusatory.

"It . . . used to," Mance whispers.

And she used to be able to summon without any effort. But whatever happened today, it was powerful enough to make Mance's magic *change*. Which doesn't strike me as a particularly excellent thing.

Heart opens and closes her mouth like a fish, as though she's trying to find one of her usual cheerful quips, but she keeps coming up short. I take two steps forward and reach for her, but my hand barely skims the side of her cheek before she disappears in front of me and I am left with only dirt on the tips of my fingers.

"We have to go," Mance says, already rising and heading for the door. "Now."

I want to tell her to bring Heart back out immediately and let me hold her properly. To slow down before marching off. Because she needs comfort right now. *I* need comfort. We should be able to take a *minute*. But, gritting my teeth, I force down my objections.

Clearly, there's something going on that I don't understand. And if she has to go, then my job is to go with her. What she's looking for is support, not criticism. So I will give her that.

Inside, though . . . I'm a mess.

And Mance isn't looking much better. She takes off, hurrying through the castle with an irregular, jolting gait, like she's fighting to keep the memories from overwhelming her. All I can do is follow.

"Asset," she mutters under her breath. "I need Asset. Where is she?"

"The war room?" I guess. It's where she usually plans.

Mance turns on her heel and flies up a flight of stairs, then down a hallway, practically falling through a large gilded door.

Inside, everything is cluttered. The walls are papered with maps, so many that it's impossible to determine what color the walls themselves might be underneath them all. And the maps are covered in layers of scribbles, half in her father's scrawling hand, and half in Mance's own, neater lettering.

There's a desk in the center of the room strewn with parchment, and crouched on top of it is Asset. She's peering very closely at a globe. When we burst through the doors, however, her head snaps up. One hand half darts to a knife at her waist, but she doesn't complete the action when she sees it's us.

Her dark eyes assess our expressions in one glance.

"Tell m—" she starts in a low voice. But Mance calls her back before she even fully finishes the inquiry, and I quickly see why as a familiar stallion bursts into being in the middle of the hallway.

Asset holds all the practical animals. The sheep, the chicken. The horse.

Mance launches toward the beast, and for a second I'm afraid she'll take off without me. But once she clambers atop it, she pauses long enough to lean back and extend a hand. Her posture and expression are steadier now with Asset present, but I can tell she's still rattled. Especially with her stallion flaring his nostrils and stomping his hooves on the carpet like it's paining him not to break into a gallop.

With a stab of relief, I take her hand and haul myself up, settling in behind her and wrapping my arms around her waist. It brings back other memories, of fleeing together on this very horse, toward a boat in the woods where we spent the night curled up together in an ivy-covered room. I pull her tightly against my chest, wishing we were headed there now. She doesn't push me away, but she doesn't lean into me either.

"Are you okay?" I whisper.

She shakes her head once but says nothing, and I don't press any further. I can see that she's trying to hold it together, and the last thing I would ever want to do is undermine that. I'll be there for her later when she can fall apart in private.

For now, Mance grabs ahold of the horse's mane and he shoots forward. We thunder down the steps—which feels *incredibly* unsafe and ill-advised (and that's coming from me)—then burst through the front doors of the palace. Alarmed guards cry out and scramble to follow, but we don't wait for them. We take off, thundering down the cobblestone streets, the din of pursuit falling away behind us.

At first, everything seems normal. All the houses are where they should be. The day is bright and clear. I even hear laughter on the wind.

But before too long, people start to trickle into the streets beside us, looking frantic. As we push forward, the crowd grows more and more, like rivulets coming together to form a stream, and then a raging river. It gets harder to push through them, but Mance is forceful in urging the stallion on.

It's not until we get close to the base of the cliffs that I start to hear the wails. They blend together and rise in a chorus of anguish that gets louder and louder as we ride right toward it, and my skin feels clammy. I suddenly wonder if I'm ready to see what awaits us at the base of these cliffs. To see what caused Heart's death.

Then we round a bend, and there it is. The Outskirts.

Or . . . what used to be the Outskirts.

Mance whimpers in my arms, and I make a noise that is not far off as I struggle to comprehend what I'm seeing.

Having lived out there for almost a third of my life, I am familiar with every tree—glass or otherwise. I know the location of each beaten-down base and ramshackle home, even the ones hidden from view.

But if I thought the place was a wreckage before, it's nothing compared to the way it looks now. Houses are not only ripped apart, but they're also somehow half-submerged into the dirt, as though sinking slowly into a swamp. Trees are buried, too, and bent at odd angles. All the tent poles and ribbons from the cleanup efforts are gone.

And . . . all of the people as well.

All of them.

It doesn't feel real until Mance flings herself off the horse and onto her knees, wailing just as loudly as everyone else. Before I can stop her, she begins clawing at the earth, coating herself in mud and filth. I reach for her, but then she flings herself backward, screaming.

Because there's a face in the dirt. A man.

One with open, unseeing eyes.

As Mance collapses, clutching the dirt and sobbing, I realize that I know him. He was one of the faces I passed every day. Someone who sometimes slipped me a piece of bread that I knew he couldn't spare when I really looked like I needed it. And now he's . . .

I fall to my knees, but as soon as I do, I almost leap back up. It suddenly occurs to me that I have no idea how many bodies I might be kneeling on.

How many people I know, who I lived among, might lay dead in the earth beneath me.

"What happened?" I rasp. "Who could do all this?"

Mance looks at me with tearstained cheeks that match the ones Heart had when I last saw her, and I can see Heart's stark vulnerability in her eyes. "I don't know," she whispers. But then her gaze hardens, and it's Asset who takes control, cold and calculating. "But you'd better believe that I'm going to find out."

5
Livid

The animals that respond to my summons are the predators. Bobcat. Wolf. Cougar. Grizzly. Jaguar.

They are mine and I am theirs.

For the last few months, they've been my only company. We prowl this cell together. We claw at the walls, we hurl ourselves against the magic that binds us, heedless of the sick, slick feel of the blood that Mara used to weave it. We tear apart every pretty bit of furniture Mance sends down to make our imprisonment more *comfortable*. And when we are finished reducing each bit to splinters and bolts and ripped fabric, we display them. A testament to the fact that an armchair will not make us forget her abandonment. A polished end table will not erase her betrayal.

At first, she would only send more.

But at this point, with the cell crammed to bursting with the aftermath of our destruction, she has stopped.

Which means that now we are fully deserted, fully forsaken. For all I know, fully forgotten. And still we prowl, pacing in the dark. Trapped in a cage of broken things.

Tonight, we are particularly on edge, because something is happening above us. As usual, we have no idea what it might be. I hear the frantic stomping of many boots. I hear muffled shouting. There's an unease that taints the air.

I pick up a piece of shredded chair and lob it at the ceiling with a scream, then listen for any reaction, any indication at all that someone has heard me. The stomping and the yelling don't falter, but the growls of my companions rise, echoing off the bare, rock walls and nearly drowning them out.

I'm so focused on straining to discern what's going on above my head that I don't even realize someone is standing right in front of me.

Until he speaks.

"So. She has even locked up a part of herself."

My head whips to the speaker, along with the head of every animal prowling around me. In my current mood, I feel ready to attack anyone in range, even a friend, though I don't think I have any of those.

But the person standing in front of my cage is no friend.

It's my father.

My reaction is immediate. A white-hot flare of shock, followed by burning, choking rage.

He's walking free. Standing casually before me, arms folded leisurely across his chest, like he has all the time in the world to regard me.

My creatures leap for the bars, snarling at him and snapping their teeth, and I join them without hesitation, my fingers clawing at the invisible, bloody shield.

He only laughs, unharmed, as our efforts glance off Mara's barrier.

"I think I like this side of you," he muses.

My lips curl back in a sneer, and I claw more ferociously, imagining the squelching blood is his flesh beneath my fingers. Longing to shred him as easily as we shredded the furniture. Wanting him to hurt, to suffer, to *burn*.

If he truly likes this side of me, then he's never understood me at all. Yes, he has always wanted my power, wanted to use it, but only if he could control it. And I would never, *ever* submit to him.

I would die first.

In a flash, I remember the last time I saw this man, when I had beads pulled taut against his throat. The moment when he stopped gloating and felt true fear for the first time. When all the violent strength he taught me was unleashed back on him. I was so close. So close to ending him, so close to taking everything. Not only his title, but also his life, and all of his power. It would have been mine.

If only Mance hadn't stopped me.

There's movement behind him, and it snaps me out of the memory, because it's not until then that I realize my father isn't alone. A figure stands behind him, hooded and half in shadow.

"I'm confused," the stranger hisses, and I don't recognize the voice. "Isn't that . . . ?"

"Just part of her," my father says dismissively, and I bristle at the casual sharing of our secrets.

The stranger looks over his shoulder. "All right . . . You can fill me in on the particulars later. We have to go."

Go?

"What is this?" I demand. "You're breaking out?" My voice is a near growl, and it's not just because I want this monster to stay locked up forever.

I'm jealous.

I'm nearly choking with raw fury at the idea that he might get to feel the sun on his face while I'm forced to cower in the shadows.

But my father seems to have lost interest in me already. Instead of answering my question, he nods to his companion and starts to move past me. The mysterious man falls into step behind him, trailing like a shadow, ready to leave me to my fate.

I panic.

My throat closes with desperation and a cold sweat breaks out across my back.

Am I really about to watch him walk out? *Stroll* out, like he hasn't a care in the world? Am I really going to stay behind?

I dig my fingernails into the palms of my hands.

No.

Never.

I *have* to convince him to break me out, too.

But how?

My eyes latch on to his retreating back, and my thoughts race as my predators stir around me.

What I know about my father is that he's practical. Viciously so. I need to persuade him that getting me out is in his best interest. Which, of course, it isn't.

But unlike other forms of Mance, I'm not above a lie.

"Even if you could get out of your cell, you won't be able to leave the dungeons!" I call after them.

My father stops walking. Then he looks back over his shoulder at me.

"Don't listen to her," his companion urges. "We need to go."

"The door is magically warded," I say. "It only opens for authorized guards. You can get in, but you can't get out. And any attempt to open it will notify all the people who *are* authorized, and they'll come running."

"No one has magic like that," the mysterious person retorts.

"It's from the Grasslands," I bluff. "Remember how Sangua forced a whole pile of her servants into the Broken Citadel to see what magic they came out with? Well, Azele has kept many of those powers secret, but she shares them with those in her alliances. This magic was a gift from her. And it was specifically meant to help keep *you* contained."

They're both hesitating now, looking at each other. It's working.

I swallow my excitement and hold up a hand, wiggling my fingers.

"But I have Mance's hands. I'm authorized. I could open the door."

My father takes a step back toward me, scrutinizing my expression.

"And why would you help free me? You hate me. Even if your creatures didn't make that clear, I can see it in your eyes."

"Of course I hate you," I spit. "But I hate confinement more. Let me out of this cage, and I'll free us both. After that, we'll call it even for tonight and we'll go our separate ways. Deal?"

He starts to shake his head. "You'll merge with Mancella, and then she'll know how I escaped. Who I was with."

This last statement surprises me, because I'm sure I don't know the man. But Mance must if he's worried about her identifying him. I glance at the stranger, only to find him already looking at me.

And when our eyes collide, for a second I think maybe I *do* know him. There's a spark of recognition in my chest that makes the animals behind me stir.

But, no. His features are all unfamiliar.

It's just the anger lurking behind his stare that I know all too well.

I turn away from him and press my advantage.

"I won't," I assure my father. "I won't go to her at all. Why would I? She'd only lock me up again. You think I want to be here?"

He considers me carefully.

"Put your animals away," he says finally.

I do, my heart hammering. And the air feels vast and empty without their breath at my back.

Then Father steps forward and unhitches the cord Mara wrapped around the front of my cage. I bite my lip, not trusting myself to speak.

"Can I borrow your lockpick?" he asks the stranger.

The man shifts from one foot to the other, still eyeing me. I wonder if he saw something familiar in my own stare, something that might make him second-guess opening my cage.

But before he can answer, the footsteps above us go thunderous, like a rainfall turning into a torrent. Whatever is happening up there has just gotten worse.

And the man seems to know why.

With a frustrated sound in the back of his throat, he unlocks my cell door and swings it wide.

I don't wait a second more. I dash forward and past him, sprinting down the hallway.

"You said you'd let us out, too!" my father yells at my back.

And then they're both barreling after me, no longer concerned with keeping quiet.

There's no magical lock on the door, but that doesn't mean I want them to get out. I loose all my predators again, sending them snarling down the hallway behind me.

The stranger pulls a sword from somewhere in his cloak, and my father withdraws a splintering stake from his pant leg, one that looks suspiciously like it used to be the leg of a table. I curse Mance and her ridiculous gestures.

When I make it to the door, I barrel into it, shoving it open, but somehow they're right behind me. My father slams his stake into the side of the jaguar's head, whipping her snout away long enough for the stranger to slit her throat and then arc around to plunge his sword into the heart of my wolf as well, with brutal, awful efficiency. I feel both creatures return to me and it seems harsher than usual. Like they brought the aftershock of those injuries with them. Probably because I'm sickened by what I just witnessed.

But I don't have time for that. Blinking back angry tears at the cruelty of it, I wince and send them out again. At the same time, I duck through the door and slam it shut behind me, groping around for the lock. I want to trap them with all of my creatures, with all of my rage. I want to give my jaguar *immediate* revenge.

But just as I find the latch and move to engage it, the door swings outward again, and my father thrusts his arm through the crack. I abandon the latch in favor of bracing both hands against the wood and wrestle with him for a moment, my animals clawing at his back, even as the stranger continues his attack against them.

My father holds firm through the onslaught. And behind me, the booted footsteps are getting closer.

I grit my teeth, straining hard. But in terms of brute strength my father has always been my superior. Despite my struggle, the door starts to inch toward me. And then the stranger starts pushing, too, and my stomach sinks.

I can't do it.

I can't stop them from getting out.

The realization slams through me, bitter as poison.

If I stay much longer, we'll *all* be caught. And I am *not* going back in that cage.

With a frustrated scream, I let the door go and run for the windows that line the hallway. Without looking back, I wrench one open, crouch in the window frame, and then fling myself onto the lawn.

I flinch as I feel my grizzly return to me, meaning that they've finally managed to end her. Again, strangely, I feel the slashes as though I took them myself. As the minutes tick by, the bobcat, jaguar, cougar, and wolf slam into me, too, making me feel wrung out and ripped apart. It makes me sick how ruthlessly they cut them down. I hope it was the guards who did it. I hope they caught my father and the stranger and marched them right back into the dungeons.

But I have no way of knowing.

And my hopes aren't high.

I duck into the hedge maze and make a couple swift turns, taking cover in the heart of the leaves, and trusting that if anyone pursued me, I would know how to navigate my way out faster than they would.

My heart pounds in my ears and my breath comes in short gasps.

But I don't hear anything else.

The night is silent.

Which means no one is coming after me.

I huddle against the bushes, trying to catch my breath. Trying to think about what I need to do next as my predators pace beneath my skin.

I'll have to figure out a way out of the grounds. That's first.

Most people don't know that Mance can split, but if I run into someone who does, then I'll have to pretend to be a part of her they won't be threatened by.

I look down at my outfit. It's crumpled and dirty, so I can't impersonate Poise. And I don't have anything to put my hair up with, so that cancels out Mance and Asset.

I'll have to be Heart.

I comb my fingers through my hair and force a smile.

It doesn't feel right.

Maybe I'll just keep my head down.

With a groan, I lean back into the leaves, looking up at the moon I haven't seen in so long. Then I inhale the heavy night air. I devour the scent of flowers. I relish the breeze on my skin.

No, I can smile.

I can smile, because I am finally free.

With my head held high, I walk out of the hedge maze and straight through the front gates.

No one stops me. There are a couple of confused glances, likely from people who know Mance to be in another location, but when I make eye contact the puzzlement resolves into respectful nods of acknowledgment. Mere confusion isn't a strong enough basis to question a Prime.

And that's what I am out here.

A *Prime*.

My smile deepens as I disappear into the night.

6
Silver

This isn't the first time I've stood in the wreckage of my own home. The sinking feeling in my stomach, the sights of carnage and ruin, it's all familiar to me.

"Kinda feels like we just rebuilt this, doesn't it?" Rooftop asks, echoing my thoughts.

I look over at him.

He hasn't lived in this house with me for months, and it's jarring to realize that he looks out of place here now. His clothes are clean and pressed, made of nice materials. They match, like the outfit wasn't cobbled together from multiple sources. His boots shine. But more than that, his eyes aren't hollow and he no longer looks like it's been weeks since he got a proper meal. He's a regular townsperson now, working a regular job in the palace kitchens. Living a normal life.

I'm glad.

Glad that he got what he wanted, glad that it fits him so well, and also glad that he's not too wrapped up in it to come back down here to be with me in my wreckage.

Again.

Because he's right, we *did* only just rebuild this place, after a magical explosion from Mance's cousin ripped it apart.

At least that time it was somewhat my fault. I was working for the guy, after all. He wouldn't have been anywhere near my house if I weren't helping him betray the girl I was falling for.

This time, though, I feel powerless. I don't even know who to blame. Mance described a white-haired girl, but I'm acquainted with pretty much everyone in this neighborhood and she doesn't sound familiar.

Mance also told me about the scroll, which she said was covered in names, but by the time we found it and dug it up, it was blank. More magic. More tragedy. More death.

It feels a little *too* familiar.

And just when this place was starting to take a breath of new life. To be more than it was.

Like me.

There's a soft, misting rain on the wind, and it makes me nostalgic for the nights when Rooftop, Vie, and I huddled together through Outskirts storms, barely shielded by our rickety shelter, wondering if this was the time our home would be destroyed for good.

Through the downpour, we would share a blanket and the food we managed to steal or gather that day, and we'd light a candle. And somehow, as long as the candle kept burning, it felt like we would all make it through. Even in this broken place.

My friends didn't stay after the explosion, and I can't blame them. I know they both sleep better now that they don't need to keep one eye open for threats.

Meanwhile, for the last few months I've still been here, not sure I could fit anywhere else.

Now, though...

Now I *know* there's somewhere else I need to be.

Because yesterday when I held Mance in my arms and I couldn't find a pulse, the sense of helplessness that gripped me was the deepest I've ever felt. It dawned on me that *she* has become my anchor, my softly glowing flame in the middle of the storm. Her midnight eyes my candlelight. And now, as I stand in the remains of my broken house, there's a certainty that settles over me. There's something that I need to do.

"I don't like it when your face gets that way," Rooftop says, studying me through springy locks of hair that are always falling in his eyes. "It usually leads to you doing something reckless."

I cough out a wry laugh. "Yeah. Probably."

"What are you thinking?"

"I'm thinking that I'm going to tell Mance I love her," I say.

The realization rocks through me even as I voice it, but it feels right. I've known my feelings for a while. It's just been hard to express them out loud. I mean, she's a Prime and I'm a nothing. Unlike Rooftop, I *belong* here in the glass and the dirt. But now I know that I also belong with her. By her side.

For the past few months, she's been trying to juggle her many duties as Prime on her own, rather than leaning on me. I need to show her that she's not alone, that we're in this together. That I'll always lift her up.

I don't know if now is the right time to say the words. She was pretty broken when we said goodbye. But I can be with her, can *show* her that I love her, until the time is right to say it. And when it is... I'll know.

Rooftop quirks a smile at me. "Now that's the kind of

recklessness I can actually support. What are you waiting for? Go be with her, then."

And it really is that simple. I don't have to have everything else figured out, don't have to know what I want to do with my entire life right now. I know one place that I fit, and it's by her side.

Because with everything Mance and I have been through already... what could *possibly* come between us now?

7
Poise

P rime Reltas is coming to propose today.

In the chaos of everything, we nearly forgot. Since getting back from the Outskirts, Mance has been holed up in her room, and she's not inclined to leave it now. So she's sending *me* out to handle things.

I coalesce across from her and she blinks at me from the bed, her hair a chaotically unkempt mane framing sallow skin and bleary, bloodshot eyes. *Well, that's going to take a minute to fix*, I think dryly. Without saying a word, I turn my back on her, pull the vanity toward me, and get to work as she once again buries herself in blankets.

By the time I bustle out of the room an hour later, I am sporting an elegant chignon, a flattering silk dress, and several layers of makeup to cover the under-eye bags that Mance earned for me by tossing and turning through the night.

I smooth down a wrinkle on the hem of my bodice, my movements unusually stiff.

Most of the time, I'm proud that I'm the face of our strange little team. After all, it's not easy to make things look easy. I am a master at striking the right tone, at reading and reflecting the right expressions, and all without a hair out of place. It isn't vanity;

it's survival. It's the art of making others believe that I have it all together and that they can trust me, rely on me, ally with me.

Today, though, I'm struggling to find that pride.

I wasn't with Mance when Heart died. I was speaking to some dignitaries from the Coast Realm. But Mance made sure to merge with me before sending me on this assignment so that I would know everything that happened. So that I would have context. I believe she thought she was being considerate.

And yet . . . what she put me through doesn't feel like context. It doesn't feel like a helpful packet of information.

It feels like someone forced horrifying, traumatizing memories into my mind and then told me to get out there and smile.

Well, I am smiling. As I approach the throne room, my expression is smooth and picture-perfect. My gait is airy. My hair is even more intricately styled than usual, and if there's turmoil happening behind the mask I wear—if I wish I was the one back in that bed—well, no one will ever know. We all have different skills, and one of mine, to a large degree, is pretending.

So pretend I shall.

I swing the doors to the throne room wide, walking through them like I'm strolling through a garden, not a care in the world, skirts rustling smoothly around my legs.

When my father ruled, he had an ornate, gargantuan throne that looked like it was made of twisting glass brambles. You had to keep your back ramrod straight when you sat in it or you'd be skewered.

My throne is simpler, made of stone and carved with flowers. The glossed engravings won't impale me if I lean back on them.

But my back is ramrod straight anyway.

Within me, my animals—the birds—are going wild, their wings flapping a frantic rhythm behind my rib cage.

Because I never got to tell Silver this was happening. And we never really came up with a plan for it, either. And both of those facts make me feel a little sick.

But it's not until I'm seated, hands folded delicately in my lap and skirts arranged in an artful pool of fabric around my feet, that I allow myself to take a couple deep breaths in the quiet of my throne room, readying myself for what's to come.

I can do this. I have to.

All too soon the doors swing open, and a servant announces Prime Reltas of the Forest Realm, arriving at last. I remain seated, as is customary, and watch him approach, wariness prickling my scalp as I study the man who wants to spend his life with me.

Quite frankly, he's . . . not what I was expecting.

I remember Prime Gore, the last Prime of the Forest Realm, as stocky, bearded, and gruff. In contrast, the teenager striding toward my throne is wiry and clean-shaven. Instead of tawny brown hair, his is raven black. And instead of the cowed stare of a man who has been beaten, this boy's gaze is oddly intense.

He appraises me openly, as though I am the one who needs to be puzzled out. I feel him taking stock of my choice of attire, my posture, my expression.

So I do the same, although more subtly. I observe the shadowy green color of his fitted doublet, the tension in his gait, the frankness of his countenance. It strikes me that he looks vaguely familiar, although I can't place why. I must have seen him at some banquet or another. It doesn't matter.

When he reaches the space in front of my throne, he bows, the gesture fluid and rehearsed. I incline my head to him. "Welcome," I say.

He straightens, eyes quickly finding mine again. "Am I?"

Although his question came out friendly, the stiffness in his shoulders remains, and I wonder suddenly if he's nervous. He is proposing *marriage*, after all. He must have contemplated it, wondered what a life with a stranger would be like, as I have.

I soften my smile toward him. "Of course," I say carefully. "Although I don't intend to commit either way on our first meeting, I am eager to hear your full proposal and how you feel it may benefit both our realms. And regardless of the result, I am certainly honored by your offer."

I expected the statement to put him more on guard, but to my surprise, he relaxes, as though deciding that whatever he was bracing against is no longer a threat, after all. Perhaps he's no more eager to finalize this than I am, and my putting it off is a relief. Tension leaks from my own posture as well, and the birds within me settle, cooing softly to one another. This is going well.

Reltas adjusts his sleeve, seeming more confident now. "Actually," he says. "There is nothing to discuss. You *will* be my bride."

It takes a couple seconds for his words to sink in, and when they do, my expression stiffens, and I feel the birds pecking at my insides as I try to keep my tone polite. "You flatter me," I start, "but aren't there a few conversations we'll need to have, a couple of formal commitments we'd need to mutually assent to, before I've earned that title?"

"No," he says matter-of-factly. "There are not."

I dig my fingertips into the arms of my chair, careful not to make the action noticeable. "Under the Treaty," I point out, and I'm proud that I still sound cordial, "you are at least required to get my seal on an official contract of engagement, are you not?"

But he's barely looking at me now, as though he's already moved on in his mind. "Yours?" he says. "No. It would be Merod's signature, if we're being technical. You may outrank him now, but under the same Treaty you just cited, there is still one tiny but crucial bit of control that he retains over you, and that . . ." He holds up a ring. ". . . is the ability to dictate your marriage."

His words are like a slap, and the birds within me begin to thrash, a barrage of beating wings climbing up my throat, as I barely restrain myself from rearing back in shock. For a moment, I can't speak through the feathers. I allow a small moment of silence to pass while I gather myself, contemplating the absolute *gall* it took for him to say that to my face.

What he's referencing is a small and infrequently invoked section of the Treaty, which was probably grandfathered in from an older version. It states that anyone of a royal bloodline who has entered the Citadel has the right to dictate the marriage of their offspring, and it was designed to add legitimacy to promised political matches. No one wanted their alliance to depend on some wayward teen who might run off and marry a stable hand in secret. They wanted to know that a son or daughter promised would be a son or daughter delivered. Usually, all it means is that the reigning Prime and their immediate heirs have the authority to arrange matches for their children.

But *usually*, a Prime would not have any living Citadel-touched parents of their own or they wouldn't have become Prime in the first place.

So, yes, he's got me on a technicality. But if he thinks he can come into *my* throne room and sneeringly ask to go over my head, then he's got another thing coming.

"You're saying you'd like to speak to my *father*?" I ask. He opens his mouth to respond, but I talk over him, firmly and clearly, though still maintaining a polite formality. "Regrettably, he is unavailable to see you—and will continue to be unavailable indefinitely. You see, he is currently imprisoned in my dungeons, at my command. So I suggest that you speak directly to *me* about any—"

Reltas laughs.

He *laughs*, and I break off speaking in the middle of my sentence, stunned, my birds fluttering in confused circles in the pit of my stomach.

"In the dungeons, huh?" he asks with a smirk. "When's the last time you checked?"

Before I can even begin to parse what that means, he takes a document out of his coat and unfurls it for me.

And it's . . .

A codified engagement agreement.

With my father's signature at the bottom.

Now the birds burst into a frenzy, and my ears are filled with their caws and shrieks, but outwardly I go very still. I cannot tear my eyes from the document, as though if I stare at it long enough it will somehow start to make sense.

How could this have happened? *When* did this happen?

Reltas seems to enjoy my inability to respond, his smirk widening, and his tone turning decidedly condescending. "It was an easy trade for him," he tells me, spinning the ring between his fingers.

"Freedom in exchange for the daughter who dethroned him? Barely even a loss. Anyway." When the ring spins over his last finger, he flicks it with his thumb into my lap, and I stare at it as though he's tossed a handful of mud onto my skirts. "So sorry I couldn't take the time to woo you properly, my dear, but we have the rest of our lives to get to know each other. I'll let you know when the wedding details are finalized."

And without any further discussion he, bafflingly, turns to go.

I stand quickly, the ring clattering to the ground at my feet as I scramble to put all this together. "The brutal attack in the Outskirts," I blurt. "Was that you? Your magic? Was it all just a distraction so you could *break into my prisons and free my prisoner?*" The idea of it makes my insides feel hollow.

Reltas snaps his fingers and turns back around, like he'd forgotten about that part. "Oh, yes. It was. Did you like it?"

Amid the wings, I now feel talons. Scraping at the deepest parts of me. Behind my painted lips, I grit my teeth. "You killed dozens of my people. Do you know that? Forty-seven, to be specific. And all as a *distraction?*"

For a moment something passes over his eyes, but it's gone before I can parse it. His gaze hardens as he takes a step back toward me. "Forty-seven, you say? A good start, I suppose. But nowhere near even." His words are casual, but there's a sudden coldness in his voice that gives me chills.

"What does that mean?"

He approaches the throne again slowly, his expression shuttering.

"Do you know how my magic works?" he asks, though he doesn't seem to expect an answer. "The limbs I raise can only come from real people. People who died within a set range of the place where the scroll is buried." He leans toward me, one lip curling in a sneer, his face now uncomfortably close to mine. "I wrote two hundred and twenty-six names on the scroll that was buried in what you call the Outskirts. Two hundred and twenty-six names of citizens from *my* realm who died in that field, at *your* father's command. And even that number is a fraction of what we lost. One field of many. You're worried about forty-seven? We lost thousands. And I know *all* their names. I can't stop knowing them. Once I learn another, it burrows into my mind, just waiting to be called upon. Waiting to surge up in vengeance for my cause."

My stomach lurches, but I don't have Heart with me right now, so I can't fully access the sorrow that I'm sure she'll feel later. Instead it feels like bumping up against a void. A boundary I can't quite cross.

I swallow and open my mouth to express condolences anyway. To diplomatically remind him that my father's actions are not my own, and to express how much despair that war has caused me as well. To delicately suggest that we might start a new era together, one in which we can resolve disputes away from the battlefield.

But when his hard, hateful eyes lock on mine, I let my sympathies die on my lips.

"Why free him, then?" I ask, holding his gaze so I can study his response. "And why force me into a marriage? It's obvious you despise us both, that you have no regard for anyone in my realm. This isn't an alliance, so what is it?"

He pulls at the collar of his doublet, disinterested again, already turning away. The anger that made him lash out has either burned up or been buried. "It's no use worrying about that. What does it matter to you what this marriage means to me? All you need to know is that you can't get out of it. Your father's word is binding. If you break it, it's tantamount to breaking the entire Treaty. You would incite war. Not just with my realm, but with all of them, per the terms we each signed. And if you need any extra incentive than that, I'm happy to provide it." He glances back over his shoulder at me, his expression cool now. "Do you remember the book your father had in his possession when I released him? Some volume from your Census?"

I nod hesitantly, dread creeping down the back of my neck.

He gives me a humorless smile. "I've been meaning to thank you for that. A very helpful and well-organized tome. If you recall, it includes an index of deaths, right down to location of demise."

I feel the blood leech from my face as I realize what he's saying.

He makes it clear anyway. "I've been studying. Getting to know your dead as intimately as I know my own. And now, should I so choose, I could lay waste to your entire realm." He flicks one more glance at me before turning away. "I would love it if you gave me a reason to."

He retreats, heading back toward the main doors. Done with me.

And I feel my composure cracking.

I can't just let him leave. I'm not clever like Asset, I can't reach him emotionally like Heart could, but I know I can't let the conversation end with me so completely cornered.

If I want to avoid inciting a war, prevent my entire citizenry from suffering the same fate that the Outskirts did, then I need to start by stripping away the legal backing for his actions. I need to find my father and get him to take his promise back. Renegotiate. *Something.*

"Where is my father now?" I demand.

Reltas spins lazily but continues to walk backward, a disinterested smirk on his lips. "My future father-in-law?" he asks. "He's cozied up at my place, of course."

I fold my hands in front of me and swallow, glad that my father is at least in a known location. I would not have enjoyed tracking him down. "In that case," I say, my tone reflexively yet robustly formal again, "I think it would be prudent for me to visit my future home *before* the wedding day, don't you? Would it suit you to receive me . . . tomorrow?"

Reltas spreads his arms wide, uncaring. "Of course," he says. "As my fiancée, you'd be welcome anytime." I release a small breath of air, but then he continues, one brow arched. "*Are* you my fiancée, though? Because if so, I'd like to hear you say it."

My skin prickles at the pleasure in his tone. How much he enjoys seeing me made small.

I don't have a choice, though. I *have* to get to my father, and the only way to do that is to play along. For now.

Even so, the word is painful in my throat, and it takes me a minute to work it up to my lips. "Yes," I say finally, and it comes out like a hiss between my teeth.

His smile turns dark at my assent and he crosses his arms over his chest. "Then put on the ring," he says.

I take a breath.

He's stopped walking now. He just stands, rooted and waiting. Wanting to watch me do it. And it chafes to give in, but I have to.

I have to.

Slowly, without breaking eye contact, I kneel.

I pick up the ring.

74 poise

And I slide it onto my finger.

The cold metal makes me shiver. It feels like tightening handcuffs. Like one of Mara's bracelets trapping all my magic inside me where it coils and snarls and waits, just beneath my skin. It makes me feel sick, beaten, defeated. Afraid.

But you'd never know it from my persistent, practiced expression. Calm as the surface of a lake.

The only thing that causes it to slip is when Reltas makes it to the other end of the throne room and swings the door wide.

To reveal Silver's stricken face.

8
Silver

I picked her flowers.

I wanted starsprouts, because I know how much they mean to her, but the colder winter months have forced them into slumber, making the nights darker than we'd all grown accustomed to. So I did the next best thing—a collection of wildflowers in the bold hues of a sunrise. Her favorite time of day. I had to hunt the forest for warm, sheltered patches of grass where bits of fall foliage still survived. It took almost an hour for me to gather enough to fill my hands.

But when I hear a male voice ask Mance if she is his fiancée, when I hear Mance say *yes*, the flowers fall from my hands, splaying across the marble at my feet.

And then, before I even have a moment to think, the door swings open, bringing me face-to-face with the man who spoke. And my head is spinning for a completely different reason.

"*You?*"

Staring down at me like I'm a bug beneath his feet is the guy who fought so viciously in the fighting rings. The guy I tried to get a job for so he could have a better life. Ruin. I had thought the name self-deprecating, but now it feels like a threat.

How could Mance's fiancé *possibly* be him?

"Silver," he greets me, smiling unkindly. "So nice to see you." Then he turns back to Mance and tosses a parting comment over his shoulder. "If you're wondering how I got into the palace and close enough to free your father, by the way, you can thank this man right here. He was *embarrassingly* easy to trick into it."

He shoulders past me, and I let him, stunned.

What does he mean that he freed her father? What does he mean it's *my fault*?

And then he gives me a parting comment, too, one that pushes all the other thoughts out. "Hands off her from now on, by the way. She's spoken for."

I feel a surge of incredulous anger, dark and all-consuming. And for a rare moment I am speechless. Ruin's footsteps echo down the hall, each one like a hammer to my head, and yet I do nothing to stop him, nothing to stake my own claim. I don't even punch him in the face, although if I'm being honest, the prospect is appealing.

Finally, I raise my head and look at Mance.

Or rather at Poise. I realize it immediately, because only Poise can look this specific brand of stunning. All the parts of Mance are gorgeous, of course, but Poise's beauty is the most deliberate, the most intentional. She can wield her beauty like a weapon, and right now it's spearing me in the heart. My breath catches in my throat, and it hurts.

Did she get all dressed up like this for *him*?

"I feel like I've missed a couple things," I say bitterly, crushing the flowers beneath my boots as I step into the room. The grand double doors click shut and I lean against them, arms folded across my chest. "Would you care to fill me in?"

Poise rises, slowly, studying me like she's trying to figure out what tactic will make this conversation go smoothly. "I can understand why you might be agitated, given the upsetting nature of whatever you heard—"

"Don't do that with me, Mance," I snap. "Don't speak formally, don't cater to my feelings, don't be delicate. Tell me what is going *on*. You're engaged to Ruin?!"

She sighs. "That man's name is Reltas, actually, and he's the Prime of the Forest Realm."

What?! I flash back to the way Ruin—Reltas, whatever—had another kid's face ground into the floor as he punched him until he vomited. That guy has control of an entire *realm*? That's ... alarming. But also quite definitely not the main issue here. "His name wasn't actually the thing I was hoping you'd deny," I scowl.

Poise's eyes flick down to the frankly enormous jewel on her finger and my stomach curdles as my own gaze is drawn to it, too. It's gaudy. Garish. More than I could ever afford. "Unfortunately," Poise starts, "due to circumstances that—"

"Just *say* it," I lash out.

Her mask slips, and for a moment she looks heartbroken. "Yes," she says softly. "Yes, all right? I am engaged. But not by *choice*, Silver!"

I stalk toward her. "How could it not be by choice? You're a *Prime* now. No one can make you do anything."

She launches into some kind of legalese explanation of the situation that I couldn't care less about, but I cut her off. "What happened to the girl who *took* the throne instead of waiting for it? You're really going to let some old piece of paper tell you that you *have* to marry a sociopath whether you want to or not?"

"Just because I'm a Prime doesn't mean that I'm above the law!

If I refuse to acknowledge the engagement, then I am breaking the Treaty, which gives every single realm the right to declare war on me. When I took the throne, I didn't do it by ignoring the statutes; I just found a way to use them to my advantage."

"Then do that here!"

"I'm going to, Silver! I mean, I'm going to *try*. This only just happened!"

"Really? The Prime of the Forest Realm just waltzed into your throne room to tell you you're engaged with no preamble at all?"

She shifts uncomfortably. "Well... he did send a letter in advance, but—"

I grit my teeth. "When?"

"A week ago?"

"And you didn't *tell* me?"

"Mance did try. Remember? She—"

"She tried *yesterday*. What about all the days before that?"

Poise winces. "We couldn't agree on how to handle it. And we didn't want you to worry about it until we knew the full situation. We didn't think it would be *this* bad, but—"

"So this is what you've been dealing with, all by yourself? I asked you *multiple* times what was going on, and yet you—"

"Don't yell at me! I told you I was trying to handle it. And maybe I would have been able to if *you* hadn't let him into the palace!"

I must look stricken, because she shakes her head quickly, putting one delicate hand on my shoulder. "I didn't mean that. I'm sorry. I don't blame you for this."

But it's too late to take the words back. They sink into me, like the wreckage of my home sank into the mud of the Outskirts.

Because she's right.

This *is* my fault.

"Silver—" she says, but I pull away from her, and her hand drops into the yawning space between us.

Because it's not just the fact that I let him in. Yes, I did that, and everything that happened afterward is entirely on me. I'll own that. I'm used to that.

But the fact that she never talked to me about this hurts. She tried to, maybe, at the very last minute, but more because she didn't want me to feel left out than because she actually wanted to lean on me. It fully hits me that she hasn't leaned on me in months, shouldering everything about being a Prime all on her own. Like she said, *she* wanted to be the one to handle this.

And I don't even blame her. It's not like I have any power in this situation. *Reltas* is a Prime. He may be scum, but he knows who he is and what he's worth. He and Mance are on the same level, playing the same game. If they did get married, no one would blink. People would look at them and think that they make sense.

Who am I? What am I even doing here? I was going to declare my *love* for her? It's pathetic. Like a gnat claiming to love the stars.

What is my handful of flowers compared to the giant rock on her finger? What is my heart compared to an alliance with another realm?

"I need a minute," I say.

Her eyes flick down, which is Poise's version of flinching. "I leave for the Forest Realm tomorrow. Can we talk more when I get back?"

I scoff, unable to stop myself.

When she gets back. She's not even inviting me to come with. And why would she? I clearly add nothing. Standing in the Outskirts, I was so certain that my place was by her side, no matter what else was going on.

But I guess she doesn't feel the same way.

I turn on my heel and stalk into the hallway without even deigning to respond.

And she doesn't call after me, either.

The only thing that splits the silence is the sound of the giant double doors slamming shut behind me.

9
Asset

Hours later, I stand in Livid's empty cell, surrounded by nothing but broken, clawed-up furniture and silence.

Another problem I'll have to solve, when I already have too many.

Fix it, the other parts told me.

Because that's what I do.

But what am I supposed to fix? Our engagement to the man who slaughtered our people? The consequences of breaking the Treaty if we don't follow through with it? The reality that we broke Silver's heart and have been replaying and agonizing over it every second since he stormed off? Or the fact that *somehow* when Reltas stole into my prisons he managed to free not only my father, the man responsible for all the most difficult parts of my childhood, but also the girl who represents the worst, most volatile parts of me?

The pounding of a stallion's hooves reverberates within me.

I know the answer: all of it. I am supposed to fix all of it. Myself.

And I will. I just need some time to *think*.

I stalk out of the dungeons and into my father's old war room, ripping maps off the wall and putting up blank parchments that I quickly fill with frenzied notes.

I notice right away when my sister, Mara, leans against the doorframe, her long hair pushed back from her face as she studies me with her one good eye, but I don't address her until I've finished my thought. Then I bark out a terse "What is it?"

She doesn't seem put off by my tone. Instead, she holds up a letter in two fingers. "This arrived for you," she says. "It looked important."

Finally, I glance up, only to scowl at the torn edge of the envelope in her hand. "You opened it."

"I said it looked important!" she protests. I roll my eyes. What she means is that it looked like a secret, which Mara likes to know.

I snatch the letter out of her grip, shaking out its contents, even as I mentally grouse that I don't have time for this.

But my thoughts grind to a halt as an ornate, pearl-crusted piece of stationery falls into my hands.

It's an invitation.

To my *own wedding*.

In . . . one week's time.

I almost laugh. It's a bold move. Reltas must have sent it before he even came here, just counting on the fact that I wouldn't be able to find a way out of his trap.

But if he thinks setting the date so soon will prevent me from thwarting his plans, then he is vastly underestimating me. I can still do this. I'll just have to cut corners. I'll be smart, efficient, committed.

I tear all the papers off the walls again and start over, scribbling even faster now, ink blots flying.

Mara doesn't leave. She watches my frantic scrawling with a hooded gaze.

"So, you're . . . engaged?" Mara asks. "Since when?"

"A couple hours ago. And I'm working on it."

She nods, but her silence is heavy, as though she wants to say more. She doesn't, though. She just keeps standing there.

"Can I help you with something else?" I finally snap, impatient to have the room and my thoughts to myself again.

"I was actually . . . going to ask if I could help *you*," she admits.

"How?" I ask. Although it comes out as more of a demand.

"I . . ." She seems perplexed by the question. "I don't . . . know?"

"Then probably not. At least not right now. I'll let you know if I think of something."

Mara looks down, pursing her lips. "All right," she says softly. And then she finally leaves the room.

It's not until several minutes later that my hand freezes and I finally recognize what Mara was trying to do.

A few months ago, on the roof of this castle, she and I talked about how she wanted to be there for me more. How she spent our childhood protecting herself, sometimes at the cost of, well, me. And it's true. Mara is good at cropping up in the aftermath, but usually absent in the middle of things, when it's most dire. Like now.

She was trying to be there for me.

And I completely brushed her off.

My horse nickers and I glance back at the empty doorway, wondering if I should go after her. At least to let her know that I appreciate the attempt.

But no. I'm not the part of Mance who should be having that conversation. Maybe Heart can catch up with her later. Right now,

I need to focus on the thing that I'm good at: plotting and planning. Getting us out of this mess.

I step back to review my handiwork, taking in the map of the Continent that I've just covered in arrows and times as I review it all in my head.

Tomorrow we go to the Forest Realm. Mance—the core Mance, I mean—will have to be stationed there, trying to talk to our father and persuade him to cancel the whole arrangement. But he's notoriously stubborn and we haven't done much recently to gain his goodwill, so we'll need backup plans, too. While Mance commits herself to hounding Merod day and night, other parts of us will sneak off to the different realms to make discreet but diplomatic visits.

We need to know if any of them would back us, should we break the Treaty by breaching this accord. We are not helpless, after all. We have other alliances. And just because the law states that any realm *can* declare war in these circumstances, it doesn't mean they *must*. Perhaps if we can mitigate the damage before the breach, then if Reltas declares war we will have allies to help end the conflict quickly and without too much bloodshed. It's a solid plan to fall back on in case it gets that far.

With travel time, though—journeying to each realm and back—while still keeping our ability to split a secret, meaning that we can't appear in more than one realm at a time (not counting the Forest Realm, which we'll just have to try to contain) then the only way we'll fit it all in is if—

I put down the quill.

If I go to the first realm myself *now*—and fill the rest of Mance in on the plan when I catch up with her in the Forest Realm tomorrow. She's holding a meeting right now, trying to set up a system for her absence, and I can't exactly go interrupt it or everyone will see me.

When we merge again she'll understand. I'll just have to trust that she'll be all right without me until then.

I jot out a note for her at the bottom of my gibberish so she'll know generally where I went, jabbing a pin into the invitation so it dangles below my message.

Then I head for the tower, picking at the corner of my mind that holds Alect's memories as I walk.

It can be discomforting, plumbing the recollections of a dead man. Especially when that man was my own cousin, and his memories were only conferred to me because he died at my hand. I can feel the presence of his experiences like an open wound in the corner of my mind, one that never scabs over. One that I need to prod at until it bleeds insights into my thoughts, because, unsettling as it may be, Alect's life is a valuable resource.

His memories are not as clear and crisp as they would be if I'd lived them myself, but when I focus, I can feel his past emotions, channel his impressions of things, and, most valuably, learn from his discoveries and sometimes even adopt his skills. There's a sort of muscle memory I can tap into if I let my mind go blank and allow my—his—instincts to lead.

Right now, what I need is his knowledge of his own magic. Alect invested a significant amount of time testing it, pushing it to its limits, and one of the things he came up with was a method to travel vast distances very quickly. It's how he was able to go back and forth between the Grasslands and the Cliff Realm so often, and it's also how he was able to do such a tremendous amount of travel in the eight years he was away from our realm.

The ability is . . . fairly unpleasant.

But it's also extremely practical, which in my mind makes it worth it.

I reach the top of the steps, a chill winter wind whipping my hair about my face. Surrounding me are the frost-covered cliffs, stretching into the distance, with buildings and streets crisscrossing along their ridges and slopes. Far below, at the base of the city, I can just make out the foggy forest. But it's too distant for my purposes, so I pick a rooftop in the town instead.

We can summon a copy of ourselves into any space we can see, so, according to Alect's discoveries, the key to fast travel is a good vantage point.

Steadying myself on the edge of the parapet, I mentally isolate a sliver of my soul, the smallest piece I can manage, and project it into the distance, ignoring the awful, splitting pain of doing so. After a beat, I can just barely make out my own pale figure and black hair crouching on the roof I picked.

At least I think that's me. Maybe it's a shadow. Or a cat.

Nervousness prickles my skin and my sheep bleats within me as I worry that I aimed too far. But there's only one way to find out.

Before that piece of me gets any ideas and moves out of my viewpoint, I grit my teeth and *thrust* myself into it.

For a moment, as always, I reel, trying to fit two simultaneous sets of memories into one mind. My foot slips in the midst of the muddle and I start to slide down the tiles toward the hard ground below. But we were only apart for a handful of seconds, so it doesn't take too long to settle, and I catch myself just as I reach the edge of the rain gutters, my heart hammering in my chest.

I should probably try to project myself onto solid ground next time.

Still, though. That worked. And it's taken me only seconds to traverse halfway through my city.

I clear my throat and brush myself off. Then I hoist myself up onto the chimney and do it again, this time aiming for a clearing in the forest.

And when that works, I keep going. I do it again and again and again and again.

By the time I have the Jungle Realm in sight, there are miles of distance between me and the rest of Mance, and yet not even an hour has passed.

But I've never split myself and merged back together so many times in such quick succession, and for a moment I need to crouch down in the vines, waiting for the last of the vertigo to settle, breathing in the humid jungle air as I fervently hope that all the lurching stops soon.

Unlike the stark cliffs I just came from, the Jungle Realm is lush, even in winter. Plants in vibrant colors explode all around me, twining into one another to create an enormous tapestry of life, with each part vying for dominance. Instead of short grasses and hearty shrubs, here there are Sumaumeira trees, their roots splayed aboveground in sweeping arcs to avoid floodwaters during the wet season. They're imposing, but some have a lattice of Strangler Figs growing in the cracks of their bark. I know the species. It slowly leeches nutrients, eventually withering the host completely and making a home in its corpse. Then it stands tall, still holding the outline of the trunk and branches, but with nothing left inside it, the original tree having wasted away within its throttling mesh.

But even amid such savage vegetation, the city manages to look imposing. It rises above the canopies, built in the shape of a massive pyramid. As our realm uses glass to honor the first magic we brought back from the Citadel, so the Jungle Realm honors their first magic as well. Prime Vega could manipulate clouds, which meant she could both summon and dispel them, but she could also make them do things that were unnatural.

The entire pyramid is one giant rain cloud, somehow solid enough to step on and yet constantly spitting water and flashing with lightning. It is an ever-present storm, raging in the middle of the jungle.

I rise, straightening my clothing to the best of my ability. I'll need to get this over with if I have any hope of getting back before Mance starts to worry.

Carefully, I compose and review a speech in my head, detailing our longstanding alliance and the reasons that backing me makes sense. It's not perfect, but it will have to do.

And then I set off, a crack of thunder echoing around me, as the jungle welcomes me in.

10
Silver

|6 DAYS UNTIL THE WEDDING|

I never thought I'd need that soldier's uniform again, the one Mance stole for me all those months ago. I'm not even sure where it is. But as I watch Asset disappear from the tower without even realizing I had come up behind her, I make a decision.

I'm not a real "wait around until you get back" kinda guy. And I'm not one to abandon someone I love when they need me, either. Even when I've seemingly been spurned. So rather than twiddling my thumbs here or trying to force Mance to talk to me while she's clearly in problem-solving mode, I will be going to the Forest Realm, too.

Whether Mance wants me there or not.

It takes some digging (as in literal digging; my house is still half-submerged in dirt), but I find the uniform. Stealing a horse from the royal stables is trickier, especially since I don't *technically* know how to ride. The entire sum of my experience is the times I have clung to Mance's waist as she rushes us away from—or occasionally toward—danger. But the lock is not hard to pick and Rooftop gets me some carrots from the kitchens to use as a bribe. So I manage it. And it turns out that riding a calm, walking horse is significantly easier than riding one in acute emotional distress as it thunders forward in a panicked gallop. So I manage that, too.

And soon I'm falling into ranks as one of Mance's soldiers, delving deeper into the forest than I ever have before.

At first I'm tense, trying to act the part of a soldier. I watch my posture; I mentally review commands I learned at the Academy. But after a few miles, when it's clear no one is really questioning my presence, I relax. Enough to turn my attention to Mance, simultaneously hoping she won't see me and also wishing that she would.

Her expression shifts through multiple emotions as we ride. Not blatantly. I can tell she has Poise with her, because she keeps up a careful facade. But I quickly become addicted to watching the slightly downturned lips and subtly furrowed brow that belie internal turmoil. What is she thinking about?

Him?

. . . Me?

I wish I could read her mind.

I wish she would *talk* to me.

My gut clenches, and I rip my gaze away, opting instead to take in our surroundings. Because for the first several miles, the wreckage was as familiar to me as the back of my hand. But now . . . it's starting to change.

Like the Outskirts, this land tells a story. Mance's father and grandfather came at the Forest Realm brutally, viciously, and Prime Gore defended his people with ferocity as well. We ride through trees—both glass and organic—that have exploded, leaving gaping holes in the pulp of their trunks. The dirt is so thick with shards that the horses' hooves have been armored to endure it, and the clang and clink of metal on glass drifts eerily through the air. We pass several hollowed-out bunkers and hastily constructed shelters where soldiers on both sides took their stands.

Every now and then there are bones sticking out of them.

None of that is new.

What I haven't seen before, though, are the cities, and as soon as they rise out of the mists in front of us, I begin to understand why some believe them to be haunted.

They must have been beautiful once. The homes were built between the trees, incorporating the branches and trunks into the artistry of their architecture until it's hard to tell what was constructed and what was natural. There are soaring cathedral-like buildings with roofs made of branches and windows of twigs arranged to look like the patterns of stained glass. Everything is made from wood, either raw or polished, and it's clear that carving was a popular profession, because every wall, balcony, porch, and rooftop is covered with designs and statues. Lifelike wooden creatures and intricately designed flowers. I can see how the city would have once felt bursting with life and joy.

It now stands completely ransacked. As the tide of the war began to turn, our realm's armies made raids into the city, pushing civilians back into the trees. It's easy to see where homes were abandoned on short notice, doors hanging open, and even easier to tell where conflicts erupted during the flight, with broken porches and shattered windows. All the houses have a chilling, macabre feel, as quiet and lifeless as the six dead realms. And the carvings feel sinister, like the statues stand in judgment of us as we walk by.

I sneak another glance at Mance, who has let some of the sorrow she clearly feels at our surroundings leak into her eyes. It makes me feel guilty for not having the same reaction. I wonder what it's like for Mance, *always* having more compassion to give.

Forcing my eyes away from her, I try to see our surroundings the way Mance must. I imagine the people who fled the city trying to hold this ground. I imagine them failing, their homes eaten up by soldiers and war and death. By trees they couldn't carve into something beautiful.

I know that if any part of her is considering marrying Reltas, it's to keep more destruction like this from happening, and I wish I could understand that kind of selflessness. But I'm not selfless, and even just envisioning them standing together at an altar brings an awful, gnawing pain to my chest.

When we finally arrive at the new Forest Realm, the one constructed in the last ten years on what little land was left after the borders of the Cliff Realm's victory were drawn, it's a shock. Compared to the soaring buildings of the original city, it's small and ramshackle at best. Not trusting the ground, all the structures have been moved into the heights of the towering trees, largely hidden from sight, except for the rope bridges strung between them.

The only point of beauty is the castle, an enormous wooden structure built around several lofty hickory trees. Though, in the last stages of winter, the branches are stark and bare, revealing a castle in disrepair. Even falling apart in some places.

Still, there is a dignity to the edifice. It stands tall, daring anyone to judge it for its state.

And Prime Reltas stands in front of it, with a similar angry pride.

My lip curls at the sight of him, and I clench the reins hard in my fists, which seems to irritate my horse, because she tosses her head and nickers at me in a "do you mind" sort of way.

As we approach, there's a large crowd already gathered. They're dressed like they're preparing for a battle, with earth-colored paints on their faces and swords strapped to their sides. I don't know if the intimidating attire is just for Mance's arrival, or if this is how they dress all the time. If fighting has become such a part of their culture that they never put their weapons down.

Reltas moves through the crowd, and they part for him, clearly respectful toward their leader. Mance straightens her shoulders and slides off her horse to meet him. And when they stand face-to-face, both in full realm regalia, my heart clenches.

They look good together. *Right.*

As soon as I have the thought, something dark sears through my stomach, and I wish I could unthink it. But it's there. Suddenly, I'm overly conscious of the dirt under my nails, the way my hair never stays flat. The fact that these two people each have dozens standing behind them pledging loyalty, and meanwhile I'm just some guy.

Out of deference to my horse, I don't pull on the reins again. But I do bite the inside of my cheek until it throbs.

"Welcome," Reltas says, spreading his arms wide. "To the Forest Realm. Or what's left of it, anyway. I trust your journey was pleasant?" There's a cruel slant to his lips that tells me he *wanted* Mance to see the horrors in the space between their realms. To atone for the sins of her family.

She notices it, too. But instead of viewing it as manipulation, as I do, her gaze softens. Like she's *glad* she got to see his hurt.

I have to look away for a minute.

"It was illuminating," Mance says quietly. "But I'm sure my people are wearied. Can you have someone show them to their quarters, please? Meanwhile, I would like to see my father as soon as possible."

Reltas doesn't respond right away, and I turn back in time to see the tail end of a smirk and some kind of coded gesture to the guards, who then disappear from behind him into the castle. "Of course. He'll be out in just a moment," he says.

I don't like the way he says it, all smug and self-assured.

So it doesn't surprise me when, instead of strolling out the front doors, Merod instead appears at an upper window of the castle, well out of reach. He props his chin on one hand, looking infuriatingly nonchalant, and I can't stop a sneer from curling across my face.

There are plenty around me with worse reactions. The crowd at large hisses, even boos, many clutching the weapons at their sides as though barely restraining themselves from flinging their blades at their enemy's face. In the middle of the mob, Mance's back visibly straightens.

Reltas, on the other hand, remains cheerful. "There you go. You've seen him. Happy?"

I could strangle this guy.

Mance, infinitely more patient than I am, purses her lips. "I was hoping to *speak* to him, actually. Preferably in private."

Reltas makes a face of exaggerated regret, but whatever he was about to reply is cut off when Merod says, "I have no interest in speaking with you, Mancella. You wanted to be Prime? Then act like one. Handle your *own* messes. I told you the world was hard, and you thought you could hug and smile your way through it anyway. Well, now you'll learn. Now you'll see what power *really* is. I hope you don't regret taking it."

Mance doesn't react obviously, but she does draw in a breath and hunch her shoulders ever so slightly. Meanwhile, I'm trying to glare a hole into the side of Merod's head.

Wait.

For a second, as Merod turns away, his eyes snag my attention. There's something... *off* about them.

As soon as I realize it, he's already gone, and I question whether it was anything, after all. I can't even put a finger on what it was that gave me pause. I just know that when I looked at his eyes, they felt... wrong.

Mance is already back in conversation with Reltas, asking tersely whether she could schedule a meeting with her father in the morning.

"Doesn't seem like he wants you to," Reltas taunts. "I wish I could help, but I don't control the man."

There's a brief spark of something in Mance's expression, but she shields it quickly. "Fine," she says, her tone becoming curt. "Then let's talk about something you *do* control." She brandishes a pretty-looking piece of stationery in a manner that seems completely at odds with its delicate lace and pearls. "You set the date of our wedding for *six days* from now?"

My leg jerks, accidentally prompting my horse to surge forward and I have to duck my head while I get it under control in case either of the arguing Primes glances over. The mare gives me a look like she is absolutely over my nonsense, but this time I'm not paying attention.

Because...

Six days?

The words are a gut punch, one that momentarily takes the

wind out of me. I don't think any one sentence has ever caused me so much physical pain.

Until Reltas's response.

"I think we should discuss that in private. Shall we go up to our chambers?"

My head snaps up, in time to see shock on Mance's face as well.

"*Our*—?!" She seems to choke on the word, but it's nothing compared to how I'm feeling.

Which is *rage*.

My mind goes blank. I can't even hear the rest of their conversation, because the blood rushing in my ears is too loud, too overwhelming.

All I can see is his hand on her arm, gripping way too tight, pulling her toward the privacy of the palace.

And she's frowning, her jaw clenched hard, looking like she wants to rip her arm back.

But she doesn't.

She looks around, at the surrounding crowds, their watching eyes and waiting weapons. She wipes her expression blank.

And then she goes with him, disappearing into the crumbling castle by his side.

I, on the other hand, am frozen in place, stomach churning and my fists so tightly clenched that my nails are biting into my skin.

Is this . . . a joke? It *must* be a joke.

I think about the first time I shared a room with Mance, on an ivy-covered boat in the woods. I think about the way I devoured the sight of her, the way I held myself back out of a desperate attempt to hurt her as little as possible, to care for her as best I could in the awful circumstances we were in. I remember how much it *meant* to me, even though I was still fighting it, to feel her beside me in the night. To have her warmth curled around me, a shield against the chilly air. My candle in the storm.

That night felt sacred.

And now Reltas—murdering, rage-filled *Reltas*—thinks he can have that place beside her? Thinks he can *demand* his way into her bed?

I *am* going to stop this from happening.

Even if I have to burn the whole palace down to do it.

11
Mance, Without Asset, Without Livid

|6 DAYS UNTIL THE WEDDING|

R eltas shoves me into the room and I stumble backward, colliding with a settee.

"We should discuss this," I say hastily. "As we are not yet wed, surely it's not appropriate for us to . . . to—"

He raises an eyebrow, smirking. "To what?"

I scowl at him. "You *know* what," I say through gritted teeth.

He laughs, shrugging out of his overcoat and tossing it onto a chair. "Relax," he says, "I have as little interest in sharing a bed as you do. There are separate suites."

With a flick of his wrist, he indicates two doors on either side of the room, one painted blue with green carvings like vines, and the other orange, with yellow carvings shaped like flowers. My creatures squirm under my skin, not sure if he's being serious or still toying with me.

He's fully turned away from me, though. He isn't watching me the way he would if he were only trying to get a response. I finally decide he's being sincere and release a breath in relief. "At least I have a week, then."

I don't realize that I spoke aloud until he scoffs, his vivid green eyes cutting over to me in cruel amusement. "Not interested means not interested," he says bluntly. "I want you for political reasons, not for your body. You can go ahead and sleep alone until we die."

I bristle at his tone. Not that I *want* to lay with him, of course. The idea of it makes my creatures restless and unsettled, pacing the length of my insides.

I just don't believe that Reltas is telling the truth.

"The marriage isn't binding until it's . . . consummated," I point out carefully.

He doesn't seem concerned, doesn't even look up. "As long as the vows are public, the union won't be questioned. It's not like anyone is going to come into our chambers to double-check that we followed through."

Fastidiously, I weigh his tone, watch his movements. He doesn't *seem* to be lying. And if he were tricking me, wouldn't his words be kinder? The fact that he's being so caustic is oddly reassuring. I sit down, deciding to accept the sentiment at face value. "Well . . . thank you," I say.

He rolls his eyes. "It's not a kindness. I just don't want you."

"I got that," I reply testily. "Even so."

He takes a cloak off a hook on the wall, less decorated than the overcoat he was wearing before, and wraps it around himself, making for the door.

"You're leaving?" I ask.

"Do you care?" he shoots back. "It's not like you'll miss me."

"I thought we were supposed to be discussing the wedding date."

"Later," he says. Then he slips into the hallway without looking back, leaving me alone in my—our—new chambers, the silence dusty and still.

I wrap my arms around my knees, taking in the room around me.

It truly does look like a couples' suite, although it feels aggressively clean and suspiciously new. I realize he must have only moved into it recently, when his father passed. Perhaps he had it redecorated then.

I try the blue door, but it's locked, so I enter the room behind the door painted yellow.

It's been stripped, like Reltas took everything remotely meaningful out of it before he let me in. I can see outlines on the walls where pictures must have been. His mother's, I assume. And I run my fingers along their edges, wondering what they used to contain.

It's disorienting to be alone in this foreign place. I feel a bit like the walls, shucked of everything familiar. Incomplete. Exposed.

And I miss Silver already. I wish we didn't leave things on such a hard note. I looked for him before I left to try to make up but couldn't find him anywhere, and there was so little time.

I hope he doesn't hate me.

Though, how could he not?

The very thought makes my chest feel heavy with creatures collapsing in dismay.

I hope I'll be able to figure this out *soon* and get back to him.

Twisting the chain at my neck, I draw a small leather pouch out of the top of my dress, fiddling with the strings that bind it.

Inside, there is a collection of flowers. Squashed, bruised ones from the pile I found splayed in the hallway after our fight.

It doesn't matter that they're broken. They're still beautiful to me. They're still the colors of a sunrise.

I tuck the pouch away again and start to pace.

What I need is a plan. Because this cannot really be my future. I refuse to be bound to a man who despises me and then stuffed away in an undecorated room like a broom in a closet. That will not be my life.

The problem is that with Asset away on her hastily arranged mission, it's difficult for me to formulate a plan on my own. When I try, it's like my mind won't hold still long enough to think things through logically. All I'm left with are wild impulses, powerful feelings, and a pretty mask to make it *look* like I still have it all together.

I don't, though.

What am I going to do?

Something flashes by my window and I stiffen.

There are many shadows in the forest, of course. Many things moving in the brush. But my rooms are on the third story, so I didn't expect any movement up here. And it almost looked like . . . a face.

I approach the window cautiously, peering out into the night. Wondering which of my animals might defend me best from a threat, given that the predators are gone. A large bird? A . . . raccoon?

At first, I see nothing but the outlines of trees and the deepening gloom.

Then the face appears again, right in front of me, and a frantic pair of amber eyes locks on mine.

My mouth falls open. "Silver?!"

Without waiting a moment, he wrenches open the window

and pushes his way in, landing on all fours like a cat. "Where is he?" he asks, voice dark.

My mind is struggling to catch up. "Who—Reltas? I don't know; he went somewhere."

"Good. Let's barricade the door before he gets back. Does this armoire move?"

I start to respond before realizing that I don't actually know. I don't know whether the armoire is movable, I don't know how Silver got to the Forest Realm, and I certainly don't know how he managed to find and access my window. I really only know one thing.

I am *so* glad to see him.

"Silver—"

He braces against the armoire with one shoulder, only to discover that it is, in fact, bolted to the floor. "Okay, the bed maybe? Or I could just take you through the window with me. We could run."

"*Silver—*"

"No," he says, wheeling on me. "Don't try to talk me out of it. I'm *not* letting him force you into bed with him, Mance. It's not happening. I don't care if it affects inter-realm relations or whatever; there are some lines you shouldn't have to cross. It's not *right*. He can't—"

I cut him off by throwing my arms around him and pressing my lips to his.

Silver takes a second to catch up to the situation, but when he does, he responds with a fierceness that startles me, burying his hands in my hair and kissing me like he may never get the chance again.

Something flickers in the back of my mind, trying to remind me that this may not be the best of times for this, but the warning is fuzzy, and it flits away before I can fully examine it. My voice of reason isn't in right now. So I return his fervor eagerly, leaning in so far that he falls backward onto the bed and I end up on top of him, our lips never parting. In this place of dangerous, unfamiliar things, his hands on my body feel like home. They feel like warmth and safety, and I curl into him, craving more. Soaking in the feeling of his fingers digging into my hips, his chest beneath my palms, his tongue brushing mine.

"I'm so happy you're here," I gasp, in one short break for air.

Before I know what's happening, he flips me, pinning me to the bed, his eyes blazing. "Really?" he bites out. "Then why didn't you tell me to come with you in the first place?"

I blink up at him, my mind irritated to have to compose an answer to his question when all I want to do is touch and taste and *feel*.

But when I arch up and try to claim his lips again, he stops me with a hand on my collarbone. "*Why*, Mance?" he asks again.

I sigh, falling back onto the bed and trying to clear my brain enough to think it through.

Because why *didn't* I? I want him here, after all. Clearly.

It just didn't occur to me. I'm not used to having the option. In the past when I've asked people to show up, it only led to disappointment.

"I . . ." I swallow, trying to be honest. "I should have. I'm sorry. I don't really know . . . how."

Silver's eyes are still molten, but they soften a little. He cups my face, his touch gentle. "I know you've been burned in the past," he says. "But I'm not your history, Mance. When have I ever let you down?"

"Well, there was that one time."

He rolls his eyes. "I mean *since* then."

I smile. "Never."

"Exactly. And I'm not going to let you down now. I'm here, and I'm ready to build a barricade or stage a kidnapping. I even contemplated burning down the whole palace if that's something you'd be interested in. There's plenty of flammable stuff around."

He gestures vaguely at the forest, and I laugh. "I appreciate that, but it doesn't sound like it will be necessary. We'll be sharing quarters, but not beds. He has his own. Somewhere thataway." I point toward the door.

Silver follows my finger with his eyes, then blows out a long breath and sags on top of me, making our bodies press even closer together. I feel heat rise to my cheeks, and when he raises his head he sees it. And he smirks. His eyes re-caramelize, but there's a spark of playfulness in them. "So you're saying your bed has . . . a vacancy?"

I pull his face down again, and this time he responds immediately, his lips meeting mine and his hand trailing up my leg. I get lost in the sensations, so happy to have him here that I give in to his kiss completely, melting beneath him, languishing in the way it feels for us to touch like this, despite all the things threatening to stand between us. In this perfect moment, we feel inevitable.

Until a pointedly cleared throat makes us leap apart, breathing hard.

I sniff, annoyed. Exactly how many people are going to sneak into my room tonight? Who could possibly—

Oh, it's me. Or, rather, Asset, crouching in the windowsill and looking us over with dry amusement. "As much as I'm sure I'll enjoy the memories of all that in a minute, might I suggest that this is perhaps not the time or place, and our focus should be on strategizing a way through this, rather than throwing all caution to the wind?"

I pout. Asset is such a buzzkill. "Well, that was supposed to be your job," I remind her. "Where have you even *been*? I haven't seen you since yesterday afternoon."

Her eyes are steely. "Find out."

Unable to help myself, I give Silver one final, messy peck, and he grins at me, his mouth lopsided and his hair disheveled. His dimples on full display.

Then I pull Asset back in, expecting it to feel the way it's always felt before. A quick merge, slightly painful and disorienting, but over quickly.

Only that isn't how it goes at all.

I gasp, clawing at the sheets. Because pulling her back into me is like pulling a knife into my own chest.

"Whoa," Silver says, reaching for me. "What's going on? Are you okay?"

I'm not. I'm dizzy. I feel ill, and yet I can't respond to him. My body doesn't feel like my own.

We've never been apart for this long before. We've never had such incredibly different experiences in the same day. It's too *much*. Instead of our memories bumping into each other and melding, they collide. They *war*.

I see the thundering pyramid in the jungle, covered in guards with iridescent, skintight armor like mine. Prime Tibits's throne room, with heat rocks embedded into the walls to make an audience with him stifling and uncomfortable. I feel sweat running down my neck as I hear Asset's—my—arguments and his replies. The words, "The alliance I made was with your father. *Not* with you." And I feel the sick sensation of failure in Asset's stomach as she leaves in defeat. All this interspersed with the ride to the Forest Realm, the shock of these quarters, the kiss that I can still feel blazing through me.

It's overwhelming.

And it *hurts*.

Eventually, I come to cradled against Silver's chest, his arms gripping me tightly. His whole body is tense with concern, and I wonder how long I was out of it.

"You good?" he asks, and the rasp in his tone makes me think it may have been a very long time.

Gently, I push out of his embrace and get up, pacing the room unsteadily as it spins and lurches around me.

"What happened?" Silver asks, voice low.

"We have a plan," I say, processing out loud. "She's trying to convince other realms to back us if we break the Treaty. But the first one didn't go so well. Prime Tibits. He has *always* been our ally, so we thought it would be an easy place to start. But . . . he thinks me weak. He doesn't believe I have what it takes to achieve the military might my father offered him, so he won't back me. And he's . . . not even wrong on that point. We don't want war. We were planning to reallocate those resources elsewhere."

"Others will support you," Silver assures me. "Come back. Lie down. You've done enough for tonight. We'll figure everything else out tomorrow when you're better rested."

I look at the bed—at him—with longing, but slowly shake my head. Unfortunately, my reason has returned and my mind has cleared.

So even though it pains me to say it, I say it anyway. "You can't stay in this room, Silver."

He stiffens, as though bracing for an attack. "Why not?"

I make my tone as gentle as I can. "Because this is a delicate situation and I'm not sure how Reltas will react."

"I don't care how Reltas reacts," he shoots back through gritted teeth.

"You should. If I'm going to find a way out of this, then I need to get on his good side. And that means playing nice. With him and... with my father. Because they're the only two with the power to break this agreement legally, and so far we don't have a fallback. We're working on it. But for the moment... let's not do anything risky. Okay?"

He looks like he wants to argue, but after a tense beat he bites back whatever he was planning to say and hangs his head. "If that's... what you want."

"It's not," I tell him. "What I want is you as close to me as possible. I swear. But, at least for right now... it's what I need."

He nods, his jaw flexing. "I get it. I do. I'll leave your room. But I'm *not* going far."

I cast a glance out the window. We're three stories up, and there are no other buildings near. "Where are you going, then?"

Silver juts his chin at the shadowy boughs of the trees that surround us. "It wouldn't be my first time sleeping in a bed of branches."

I nod, accepting. Slightly relieved, even, although I try not to let that show.

He gets up and clasps my forearms, grip firm. "If anything happens, I can be here in seconds."

I nod again, smiling sadly. "I'm glad."

His grip loosens, and he sighs, pressing his forehead into mine. I can feel his breath across my lips. One small tilt and we'd be kissing again, pressed into each other and tangled together.

Instead, he drops my arms and steps back, and I resist the urge to stop him. With a final, regretful grimace, he ducks back through the window, leaping onto a branch and running along its length until he reaches the trunk. I fold my arms on the sill and watch him look for a halfway-comfortable spot against the bark. When he finds one, he hunkers down, taking off his coat to use as a blanket. Then his eyes return to mine.

Something warm unfurls in my chest watching him prepare for an extremely uncomfortable night just so he can be near me. It's a painful kind of happiness to know that he would do something like that for me.

I blow him a kiss. Then I take the time to rearrange my pillows so I can lie down directly in his line of sight. I think I see one side of his mouth lift in the darkness at the gesture.

After changing quickly in another corner of the room, I settle down, facing him, trying to find his eyes in the shadows. He leans back against the trunk, his whole body angled toward me, and I can feel him looking back. The night is still and quiet, but knowing that Silver is there, watching, feels intimate. At first, I wonder how I'll ever sleep.

Eventually, though, the stress of the day—both mine and Asset's—weighs me down, and my eyes flutter shut.

And even though my sleep is restless and unsettled, I don't have nightmares.

Because I swear I can feel Silver's watchful gaze even in my dreams.

12
Silver

|5 DAYS UNTIL THE WEDDING|

I wake up with a knife to my throat.

I can't say it's the first time, but it's not exactly something a person becomes accustomed to, so it takes me a minute to get my bearings.

I seem to be in a tree.

The girl on the other end of the knife has long white hair pulled back in a ponytail. Her face is wreathed in vines and her expression is murderous.

"Good morning," I say politely. "Who are you?"

"Kiar, and you?"

"Silver."

"A pleasure."

"Is it?" I ask, pressing back against the bark in an effort to put some distance between my neck and her blade. "I'm not sure I can say the same. Not to be rude, but may I ask why you picked this particular method of awakening me?"

She only presses the blade closer, cutting off my attempts at escape. "You're camped outside the Prime's quarters," she hisses.

I scan the windows across from us to see that Mance's room is empty. In the next window over, I spot her sharing breakfast with Reltas, the two of them making what looks like stilted and awkward conversation over a spread of eggs and an assortment of fried root vegetables. My lip curls. "Technically, I suppose."

"And you're dressed as a Cliff Realm soldier. Are you planning an assassination?"

"Not unless he gives me a reason to," I answer without thinking.

Kiar's eyes widen, and she looks toward the window, then back at me, now sporting a feline smile. "Oh, I see."

My attention snaps to her, and I'm irritated with myself for being so transparent. "Great," I say. "You see. Care to remove the knife, then?"

She laughs unkindly. "Not likely. You're in *love* with her. And love makes people do unwise things. Like try to kill Reltas in a fit of jealous rage, for example. Which means that for the foreseeable future you have earned yourself a watchdog. Namely, me. Because I *promise* you. You're not touching him, and you're not going to mess up this arrangement."

"Seems a little extreme," I grumble. "Surely, you have better things to do with your time?"

"You're right. It would be much simpler to just kill you now, to be safe, and free up the rest of my schedule."

My lips pull back in a sneer and I'm about to retort, but then Mance laughs at something Reltas says, loudly enough for the sound to carry through the glass, and I glance over, annoyed. What could that violent, straggly-haired scumbag possibly have said that was so funny?

Remembering myself, I quickly return my attention to Kiar and the whole life-or-death situation that I should probably be concentrating on.

Only to catch her breaking off her own heated glare to focus back on me.

Well, now, that's interesting.

I raise an eyebrow, my sneer settling into a smirk. "You know, it occurs to me that you are *also* squatting in a tree to watch other people eat breakfast. And you seem really eager to promise death to anyone who might harm your Prime."

"Of course I am," she bites back. "I am loyal to the Forest Realm, and Reltas is its head."

"Is that why you keep using his name without his title?"

Her face turns severe, her mouth pinched and her cheekbones jutting outward as she sucks in her cheeks. But as quickly as it appears, the expression passes, and she tosses her leaf-threaded hair over her shoulder with an exaggeratedly unaffected shrug. "Whatever," she says. "It's not exactly a secret that I care about him. It doesn't change anything about the situation, and *your* feelings don't either."

I raise my eyebrows. "So you're saying you *want* them to get married?"

"Obviously. I want what he wants. And I'll make it happen, too. No matter who I have to kill to do it. Happy to add you to the list if needed."

She's making a show of puffing out her chest in a misguided attempt to intimidate me, but I've stopped listening, my gaze fixing on her hair and its odd color, its strange ornamentation. A part of Mance's story triggers in my mind.

"You were the one who buried the scroll in the Outskirts, weren't you?" I ask.

Again, she flits through several expressions in rapid

succession. From what I can guess, she doesn't like that I've guessed two things about her correctly, but she doesn't mind taking credit for the deaths, so her features ultimately resolve into a terse smile.

"That was *my* neighborhood," I snap at her. "Those were *my* friends and neighbors you slaughtered."

"You slaughtered mine first."

"Actually, most of the people in the Outskirts were actively trying *not* to get involved with any wars."

"You think I care? They were still camping out in the bones of our city's corpse. Yes, I set the hands on them. And I don't regret it, either. That's just *one* example of the kinds of things I'm willing to do. So unless you have the stomach to meet me on that same level, I would advise you not to meddle in this engagement."

I shift, still scowling. "And if I do have the stomach for it?"

Her smile widens. "Then game on, lover boy. I've got a lot of pent-up aggression lately and I've been looking for a new outlet. Tormenting you will do nicely."

"*Kiar.*" Reltas cranes his head out the window, glaring at us.

Actually, mostly at me. Unease slices down my spine as I wonder if I've just messed up Mance's plans to get on his good side. The cold rage on his face right now matches the expression he wore in the fighting rings, and I'm getting more and more certain that it was never a front at all.

Kiar, meanwhile, seems unaffected. She sticks her tongue out at him, although she does sheathe her knife and skip backward along the branch, launching herself off the end of it without even looking. After landing smoothly in the next tree over, she quickly fades into its shadows, but not before holding up two fingers and flicking them between her eyes and me to let me know she'll be watching.

By the time I turn back to the Prime's chambers, Mance is looking at me with wide eyes, but Reltas is watching Kiar's retreat. The way his stare lingers leads me to believe the girl's interest might not be entirely one-sided. And when his gaze cuts to me with a palpable menace, I'm even more certain.

Well, it's too late for me to hide. I have to play the cards I've been dealt.

So instead of fleeing in the opposite direction, I smile back at him, slow and dark.

Because maybe, just maybe . . .

I've found a weakness I can use.

13
Mance, Without Asset, Without Livid

|4 DAYS UNTIL THE WEDDING|

My first couple days in the Forest Realm have been tense. Chaotic.

My father refuses to speak to me, despite repeated requests. I haven't so much as seen him since my arrival, not even for meals. My fiancé treats me with nothing but contempt, despite my attempts to be aggressively amicable. And every time Silver gets close to me and I think I'll get a moment's break from planning a wedding I'd do almost anything to forestall, that white-haired girl shows up to start trouble.

I do not like her.

Meanwhile, Asset left for the Swamp Realm to make a second attempt at securing an alliance, one it appears increasingly likely we'll need, since *I'm* clearly not getting anywhere. But without her logic to ground me, my emotions are overwhelming, my animals squirming and twisting beneath my skin so intensely that I feel like I might burst.

Especially because she's *late*.

She was supposed to meet me in this creepy, shadowy forest clearing an hour ago, and yet I am the only one here. What's keeping her?

What if this all falls apart?

Somewhere, a wolf howls, cutting through the stillness of the night, and my heart rate ratchets up as my thoughts completely derail.

That wasn't . . . *my* wolf, was it?

Staring into the darkness, I struggle to remember whether wolves are common to this area. I keep quiet, hoping to hear the answering calls of a pack, anything to let me know that the call I just heard was random, completely unrelated to me.

Not from the throat of the creature who responds to Livid's summons.

But the forest is silent again, almost as though it is waiting, and I shiver.

Is she here?

Is she watching me?

Suddenly, the shadows seem closer. Darker. *Inhabited.*

I'm just on the edge of a full panic when a girl with my face suddenly appears in front of me, her expression dark.

I shriek and scramble backward, only to belatedly register the utilitarian bun and practical, pocket-covered pants. The swamp muck she's covered in from head to toe.

Embarrassed, I swallow, casting one final, frantic look around before closing the distance between us and grabbing her arm.

"You're late," I huff. "And look at you! What happened?" But then I shake my head. "Never mind, I'll find out in a minute." And she'll find out what I just heard. She'll know what to do. I reach for my magic, ready to pull her back into my body, when—

"Wait!" Asset cries.

I pause, surprised by the show of emotion. Asset is usually so controlled. "What is it?"

She runs a hand through her slick, muddied hair, and I notice for the first time that she's breathing hard. She looks exhausted.

"Just . . . brace yourself," she says softly.

Apprehension prickles down my spine as I realize how badly shaken she is. My animals squirm again, causing goose bumps to break out across my arms. "For what?" I ask. "Are you all right?"

She shakes her head once, and my unease only grows. It feels like the whole forest is watching, breathing down the back of my neck.

Finally, I decide that not knowing what happened is too much. I pull her back quickly, thinking that the waiting is worse than the finding out.

I am wrong.

I see the Swamp Realm, stinking and fetid, with stringy moss and slippery mud beneath my feet. The whole realm is protected by an enormous dome of woven, magical ropes created by Prime Artro. They're a marvel, artful in their arrangement, and in the way that they create patterns in the shadows.

But I've never tried to pass through them unannounced before.

I didn't know that they had orders to attack intruders.

Until they attack me.

I—Asset—*I try to yank my arm free, but it only makes the rope coil more tightly around me. Tendrils snake out from the rest of the wall and stretch for my body, twisting tight bands around my skin faster than I can fight them off.*

Then they wrap around my throat.

I summon a copy of myself on the other side of the wall and she takes off running toward the castle, but it's no use. A rope over my head lashes out and wraps around her ankle, tripping her, then dragging and binding her, too. I hear her scream.

Frantic, and starting to see spots from the lack of air, I do the only thing I can think of and summon as many copies as I can handle, in rapid succession. I thrust them through the boundary of my skin, hoping one of them will be able to evade the Prime's magic long enough to get help.

But the ropes are seemingly omnipresent, striking and capturing and entwining until dozens and dozens of versions of me are struggling against the binding, awful power of rough hemp and magic.

And I, Mance, live every single one. I suffer scores of strangulation experiences simultaneously, one layered on top of another until I am feeling my own fear from every single angle, my own imminent death from dozens of perspectives. I feel rope burn on every inch of my body, and I can't stop myself from gasping against cords that are no longer there. I fall to my knees in the dirt of the forest, begging for it all to stop.

It does, eventually, and I live through the rest of it. Prime Artro called off the ropes, but for all that suffering, we didn't even convince him to support us. As if his dome weren't enough to get the message across, he made it very clear that he and his people want nothing more than to be left alone. He refused to back us, and when Asset pressed, he had his ropes throw her back out of his realm for good.

Not only did we not get his support today, but we may have damaged our relations with him in the future. The whole thing was a complete and utter failure.

And Asset knows it.

I feel the burn of her shame, the bitter taste of defeat in the back of my throat. I've visited two realms now and I have nothing to show for it. This is not going well at *all*.

Asset was supposed to go to the Coast Realm next, but she decided long before we merged that we should send a different part. Perhaps her blunt plans and practicality aren't what's needed here.

Following her train of thought, I send Poise out instead, and she appears in front of me, blinking in the starlight.

She must be just as exhausted, just as beaten down as I am, but when she stands across from me in the clearing, there is a dignity to her raised chin, an elegance to the curve of her spine. Her face is carefully impassive as she looks at me through the gloom, absently twisting her hair into something presentable as she thinks.

"Will you be all right here without me?" she asks delicately.

"I'll be fine," I snap. "I don't *need* you." The words are brusque and blunt without Poise in me to soften them, but she's too polite to point it out.

"Good luck, then," she says, pinning the last stray hair in place. "I'll be back as soon as I can."

She turns to the east, moonlight illuminating her profile. Her eyes go distant as she fixates on something far-off. Then she disappears, leaving me alone in the dark.

After a minute, I tear my gaze away. I need to focus on what I'm doing here, and that starts with getting back to the palace as soon as possible, before anyone realizes I'm missing.

There's no point trying to find that wolf. It was probably just a random one. They *are* native to the area; now that my head is clear I can remember that. Besides, if Livid were really here, she would have attacked while I was on my knees in the mud, helpless under the onslaught of memories.

So, doing my best to shake it off, I hoist myself up into the branches of a nearby pine, climbing upward to get a better vantage point, heedless of the scratch of twigs and the sticky feeling of sap beneath my fingers.

It's been two days, and I have nothing to show for it. Only dress fittings, napkin selections, and endless consultations on music and color schemes. Which is especially irritating because I strongly suspect Reltas is only giving me all this busywork to keep me out of the way.

Since our first, tense breakfast together, he has had absolutely no interest in talking to or being around me. Clearly, he has no need or desire for me at all beyond my hand in marriage and whatever that gains him, a subject he continues to be tight-lipped about whenever I corner him long enough to press him.

Remembering his attack on the Outskirts, the anger always seething within him, I fear the answer.

And in the meantime, I feel like an animal in a cage.

Like Livid must have felt, I suppose.

The thought startles me as soon as I have it, and I push it down, striving harder until my head finally breaks through the foliage and I can look around, searching for a clearing in the direction of the castle to transport myself into.

Only it's darker than it was when I came here, and I can't see as far. Clouds moved to cover the moon while I was climbing. Everything around me is just . . . black. And unfamiliar. I'm not even sure which way the palace *is*.

A creeping panic begins to overwhelm me as I contemplate the possibility of getting completely lost in these shadows. My creatures wriggle in the pit of my stomach as I strain to make out any kind of landmark.

Then, suddenly, I see a single light bobbing in the distance. There and gone again in a blink.

I peer at the place I saw it, hoping it appears again.

It does, and thankfully it stops in an opening between the trees, glowing brightly enough for me to see the outline of a shadowy figure holding the light aloft.

I don't recognize the person; I'm much too far away.

But I do recognize the cloak.

It's the one Reltas puts on every night before he leaves our chambers, always evasive about where he's going and when he'll be back.

Something like hope makes my animals skitter up my spine. After the day I've had, I could really use a win, and perhaps I've finally found one.

It's time to see exactly what Reltas has been hiding.

He sets the lantern down and steps away from it, facing the other direction, and I take my chance.

As soon as I see my body appear in the ring of light, dusky and distant, I throw myself back into her. Then I retreat quickly into the shadows, crouching down as I blink through the memories and the pain.

I don't think he saw me.

Holding my breath while my mind settles, I take a moment to look around. I realize this isn't a clearing at all, but rather a part of the former city that's been flattened by an explosion. Reltas is standing in the middle of a ramshackle home, its walls destroyed and its furniture collapsed, and I have inadvertently fled into one of the dilapidated bedrooms.

Suddenly, I am uneasy. This isn't the situation I was expecting.

The murky, yellow illumination of the lamp reveals small markers of a shattered life. A corner of embroidery on a frayed quilt. A box of abandoned toys. A splintered post sticking up from the ground with notches on it for height, names carved into the wood beside them.

I glance back at Reltas, but he isn't doing much. Just digging around for something in the bare dirt between the floorboards. I crane my neck to see what it is, but when he rises his hands are empty, and my shoulders slump.

Then he just stands there, staring at his shoes, and it seems increasingly unlikely that I'm about to discover anything at all.

I shift, wondering if I should speak. If I should *make* him tell me what I'm doing here. Not just here in this broken house, but *here* in the Forest Realm, preparing to become his wife. Perhaps in these woods, in the quiet of the night, he would be more forthcoming.

But just as I take a hesitant step forward, the ground shudders, like the first gasp of an earthquake, and I freeze.

Because I recognize that tremor.

I act fast this time, scrambling on top of a half-broken chest of drawers, while Reltas perches on the high back of a torn sofa across from me, looking decidedly unsurprised at the unnatural quaking.

Between us, in a patch of bare earth that lays exposed in the midst of the planked flooring, two sets of hands break the surface, sending the dirt flying.

I rip a dangling piece of splintered wood off the side of the dresser and brace for the rest of the onslaught, trying to get as much height atop the battered wooden structure as I can. There's a fluttering of fear behind my rib cage, as well as a profound exhaustion. Haven't I been through *enough* today?

But nothing else comes.

He only summoned two sets of hands. Here, in this abandoned wreck surrounded by miles of nothing.

I pinch my eyebrows together, confused, trying to figure out any possible purpose for such a thing.

And I'm not about to ask him *now*, so I start by studying the arms themselves for clues.

They're unremarkable. One set is slender and feminine, and the other is muscled and male, but they have no distinctive markings, no rings or bracelets.

Interestingly, neither one of them heads for me, not even for a second. They scramble to claw at the dirt under Reltas, ripping the fabric of the sofa beneath their dirty nails in their effort to reach him, fingers contorting in their haste.

And I note that the couch's fabric is already completely shredded in that spot, a mess of ribboned, threadbare cloth.

Slowly, I raise my eyes to his hardened face, realizing that he has summoned here before. Many, many times.

I wonder who they are. Someone he knows, surely. His . . . parents? Remembering the broad, brawny figure of Prime Gore and matching it to the male pair of limbs, I'm sure that's right.

And I feel a wash of conflicting, churning emotion at the realization. It leaves me a little sick, wishing I hadn't followed Reltas after all. Whatever he's doing here, with the reaching arms of his dead parents, it's not part of his schemes for me. It's personal, *private*, and I don't want to be here any more than he would want me to be. I do still have Heart, after all.

So I go quiet, hoping to do him the kindness of never revealing that I saw this. Willing to wait until he leaves and then climb a tree and beat him home so he never even suspects. I hold as still as I can, in tense, awful silence, for several slow, stiff minutes. The only sounds are the quiet hum of the forest and the scratch of nail on cloth, the subtle tumble of shifting dirt.

His parents must've died here. I can't believe I've intruded in such a hallowed place. I keep my eyes down and occupy myself by counting the scars on my fingers, remembering the battles that brought them, as my creatures crawl along my scalp. It's not until I hear Reltas inhale sharply that I glance up, and my eyes widen.

He's sweating, gripping the back of the couch with white-knuckled hands. His gaze is intensely focused on the arms and he's leaning toward them, dangerously close. He looks like he's a breath away from falling.

The hands become more frantic in response to his proximity. They swipe at the air just in front of his face like they want to grab him and pull him down with them. Like they want to bury him, too.

That's exactly what they want, I realize.

And judging by the way that Reltas strains to keep himself away, there's a part of him that wants to let them.

My stomach turns over. Is this the dark side of his magic? Would all his hands act like this toward him if he were near, or is it only because he had an emotional tie to these hands in particular? I remember that it was Kiar who buried the scroll in the Outskirts and Reltas was nowhere near. He was busy with other things, of course, but it's also possible that he *couldn't* have been near or he would have been swarmed.

Or, based on his behavior now, he might have walked right into the middle of the onslaught and let them take him.

"Don't," I say softly.

In the quiet of the night, my words may as well have been an explosion.

His eyes snap to mine, finding me in the shadows, and he snarls, his features completely overtaken by fury. "What are you *doing* here?" he thunders.

But the hold that the arms have over him seems to lessen when he's not staring at them so intently. So I keep his gaze, hardly even thinking about why, as I climb down from the dresser and step into the halo of light. "Not like this," I say.

There's nothing but hatred in his expression as he regards me, like he's caught me reading his journal or going through his things. And yet he doesn't look away. Slowly, under the weight of my stare, his breaths even out and he leans back again, farther out of reach. The sound of nails on wood and ripping fabric pierces the silence, but our eyes stay locked on each other, neither one of us looking down. His expression is grim, but the scratching eventually slows down.

Then, finally, after what seems like a small eternity, there is a strange slithering sound and he relaxes, breaking our eye contact quickly, angrily, clearly upset that he held it for so long. That he needed to.

And then there is nothing left between us but silence, and a patch of empty dirt, freshly overturned.

A beat goes by, the stillness weighted.

Then he surges off the couch, closing the space between us in two strides, lantern light exaggerating the contours of his glower.

"How *dare* you—"

"Do you really do this every night?" I interrupt. "Alone?" Reltas is not exactly my favorite person, but even so, the thought makes me ache.

"It's *none* of your—"

"Whose home was this?" Without Poise, I'm not so worried about talking over him or whether my questions are rude. After all, I've already intruded and he's already upset. I may as well ask what I want to.

"It was my mother's, if you must know," he scowls. "Until *your* father brought the war to her doorstep."

"Didn't she live in the palace by then?"

"Of course she did. But that particular day she was hiding *me*. It never occurred to her that your father would attack civilians." He spits the last word, and it's clear he's only answering this particular line of inquiry because it's another barb he can throw at me, another action of my father's to heap on my shoulders.

But I heard the quaver in his voice when he said "me." And I can put the pieces together, figure out that she must have died saving him that day. Because he's standing here in front of me, and she's reduced to a pair of hands in a broken house.

"I'm so sorry," I breathe.

It only makes him angrier. "I don't want your pity."

"I know."

"In fact, it's pathetic."

"Okay."

"At least what I'm hiding is my weakness. You actually hide your *strength*. You refuse to use it at all. You'd rather *mope*."

My mouth opens to say something else placating, but when

his words register, the breath evaporates from my lungs. "How . . . How do you know about—"

He smirks, obviously pleased to have found something I'll react to, something to finally turn the conversation away from him. "I met her, remember?"

I hadn't remembered. Or, rather, I hadn't thought about what it meant. The fact that he saw that part of me. That piece of my soul I hardly want to look at myself, that I haven't even shown to *Silver*.

My creatures skitter around my body, not knowing where to settle. I feel the void where her predators used to prowl, and for a second I swear I hear a wolf again, in the distance. But most of my creatures are too consumed with the urge to hide, desperately burrowing deeper inside me, covering their snouts with their paws.

"What did she do?" I ask, afraid of the answer.

He snorts. "She almost killed me, to be frank with you." He rolls up his sleeves and stretches out his collar to show me scabbed-over gashes on his skin, disappearing beneath the fabric. I remember how much he kept adjusting his shirt when he stood in my throne room the next day. I didn't realize it was because he was hiding open wounds.

"I'm s—"

"*Stop* it," he snaps. "This is what I'm talking about. Do you know she actually made me nervous for a minute? Like maybe forcing you into my plan wouldn't be as easy as I thought? I could even respect her. But when I met *you* it was clear she didn't go back to you. You had nothing of her fire. Everything went as smoothly as I'd hoped. And now she's gone, and you'll *never* have the strength to stop me. I don't know why you did it, Mancella Cliff, but you cut out all your own power. So don't you dare judge *me*."

He keeps trying to hurt me, but without Livid's fury I don't feel the need to scream back. I feel exposed, raw, even a little afraid. But I also feel sad.

For *him*.

I let the pause stretch long before I say, "Power. Yes. You seemed *very* powerful tonight. It must have felt wonderful."

He grits his teeth, glancing back at the overturned dirt behind him, before returning his glare to me.

But for once he has nothing further to say.

And it dawns on me that for all our stark differences, there are many things about us that are the same. We have both experienced terrible traumas. We are both possessed by dark magic we can't always control. We both have secrets to hide, parts of ourselves that we're ashamed of. We were both suddenly stripped of any guidance and thrust into rule. And we are both . . . doing our best to live up to that responsibility. Albeit in very different ways.

I don't realize how hard I'm returning his stare until his changes, recalibrating into something less confrontational. Something that on anyone else I would call . . . searching.

It feels significant, this moment. Like we're seeing each other for the first time, here in the ruins of a war that changed us each. I find that I can't look away.

He doesn't either.

And so we keep our eyes locked, both of us ripped open and speechless, as the night continues to darken around us.

14
Silver

|4 DAYS UNTIL THE WEDDING|

Kiar will not leave me alone.

Which, honestly, is fair enough. I've spent most of my time breaking into various places around the castle in an effort to figure out where Merod is hiding, which is the kind of behavior that I would want supervised, too.

But so far I've turned up nothing. A surprising amount of doors in the palace are unlocked, which betrays either a high level of trust, a high level of naivete, or a high level of confidence.

I've found a *few* locked doors, though, and I'm making a point of breaking into every single one of them. Disappointingly, so far all the ones I've gotten open have been letdowns. No self-important Primes waited within, and no clues to Reltas's plans.

But there are two specific doors that always prompt Kiar to intervene. One is on the top floor, and the other is tucked away in the basement. When I get close to them, she tends to create a distraction. Usually in the form of a fight. So, clearly, these two doors are my best bet.

I'm working on the top one today.

Dust swirls in the candlelight as I close in on the end of the hall. A shadow flits through an adjacent room, letting me know that Kiar is watching. The other guards who roam the castle move in predictable patterns, easy to evade, and there aren't that many of them. With the Forest Realm's depleted numbers, palace security wasn't high on the priorities list, I guess. Which is probably why Kiar feels the need to pick up so much of the slack, and she's proven significantly harder to shake than the rest of them.

This time, though, I'm ready for her. Yesterday when she drew me away from the door in the basement, I was able to linger long enough to determine that the lock on *that* door is too difficult to pick. It's not like the other locks in the palace; it's something more complicated and ornate. Which means I'll probably need a key.

Fortunately, I happen to know Kiar has a key ring. One she carries on her person at all times. Which is exactly why I'm going to draw her toward me now.

I reach the end of the hallway, somewhat surprised to find that Kiar's let me get this far, and kneel in front of the door. When she still doesn't show, I stick my picks into the lock, making a show of jingling them around.

But when I do that for several seconds and she *still* doesn't show, I rock back on my heels and look around, confused.

Was I wrong about the shadow? The hall is quiet, my own breath loud in my ears. But I know she was there. I even spotted her on the way up here. Why would she not stop me this time, when she did all the others? Has she trapped the door or something?

I eye the lock, looking for tampering, but find none. Deciding it's worth the risk, I redouble my attempts to open it until the lock springs with a satisfying click.

And still, no one approaches.

Does that mean this door is worthless, too? Or maybe

something was here before, but now they've moved it?

I shove the door open, only to be greeted with Reltas's personal office. It looks... very lived-in. There are papers strewn everywhere, many written in his own hand, and the coat he was wearing yesterday is draped across the back of the chair.

I rise back to my feet, puzzled. This seems worth guarding to me, especially considering how particular Kiar is about protecting her Prime's personal safety. After all, I could be slipping a snake into his desk drawer or setting up some kind of ambush, and yet she's not following me. She's not here at all.

Maybe it's just a lucky break. The logical thing to do is to take advantage of the opportunity and start rifling through cabinets and correspondences just to see what I can find.

But I don't move. Because her absence bothers me. If she's not here, then she's been distracted by something more important. And what would she consider more important than this?

Out of the corner of my eye, I see movement in the window at the end of the hallway.

It's Kiar, sprinting away from the castle and into the woods. For a moment, I get a flash of her expression, just before she disappears into the trees.

She looks... terrified.

Without considering it further, I slam the door to Reltas's office shut and give chase. If I can break into this room once, then I can break into it again, but whatever's got Kiar so spooked is only happening right now. So I rush to the end of the hall, fling open the window, and throw myself into the branches below.

And then the chase is on.

She leads me through the war-torn outer city, winding

between collapsed buildings and shattered glass trees. She's running with a desperation that negates stealth, so it's not difficult to follow. I'm sure she must hear me behind her, but she doesn't turn.

Then, suddenly, she comes up short in front of a house with no walls.

Panting, my throat burning, I stumble to a stop behind her.

And there's ... Reltas and Mance, standing in the glow of a lantern and staring at each other in weirdly intense silence, as though absolutely unaware of anything around them.

In front of me, Kiar is shaking.

"You brought her *here*?" she demands. Her voice is harsh and piercing, and both Mance and Reltas flinch as it cuts through the stillness of the moment. Almost like they've been caught doing something they weren't supposed to.

I narrow my eyes. What *did* we interrupt?

Reltas's head whips toward us, and his expression flies through surprise, guilt, and anger before hardening into something impassive. "I did not *bring* her here," he says through gritted teeth.

But Kiar presses on as though he didn't speak. "You don't even let *me* come here. In fact, you don't even tell me when *you* come here, even though any time you do this could be the time that you give in. I only knew tonight because I paid some kid to tell me whenever you went into the woods just so I could try to get here fast enough—"

"I never asked you to do that."

"—only to find *her* standing cozily across from you, *staring into your eyes*, right next to a pile of freshly overturned dirt. *Her.*"

She jabs a finger in Mance's direction and I don't like the

aggressiveness with which she does it, so I slip a knife out of its holster, just in case.

You okay? I mouth to Mance. She moves her head in a jerky motion that is neither a yes or a no and then lifts one shoulder in a shrug. Which is not especially clear.

"I did not invite her," Reltas repeats. "I didn't ask her to be here at all. Although, it's . . ." He swallows like the next part is difficult for him to say. ". . . probably good that she was."

I tense, my whole body snapping to attention. Partly because, if I'm honest, I don't really like the intimacy of whatever we've stumbled on here any more than Kiar does. But mostly because Reltas is badly misreading the source of Kiar's anger. She wants him to be safe, yes. That's why she ran here with such desperation.

But she very specifically wants him to be safe with *her*.

Kiar makes a noise in the back of her throat. It starts as an incredulous sound of protest but quickly morphs into something harsh and frustrated. She lashes out, and I'm moving before the dagger even leaves her hand, striking it aside with my own thrown blade and then flinging myself into the space between Kiar and Mance, roughly where the front door of this broken home used to stand, another knife at the ready.

"Hey," I snap. "You're not mad at *her*, so don't take it out on her."

"Are you volunteering instead?" she snarls. Before I can answer, she charges me, all swinging limbs and flashing metal.

I let her, taking the brunt of the attack in my abdomen, only just twisting away from her slashing blade. We grapple for a minute, with her making sharp, angry movements and me mostly dodging. But her assault was fueled by emotion, so she's not as precise as she normally would be. She's not really trying to win, just trying to hit something. I manage to disarm her and trip her in one motion and she sprawls into the dirt, wincing as she clutches her stomach, which she must have landed on wrong. Reltas takes a step forward, only to be pinned in place by the look on her face.

For a moment she just lies there, breathing hard and glaring at the three of us. Then she flips back onto her feet and takes off running into the woods, like a beaten animal retreating to nurse its wounds.

Reltas levels a stare at me that I really don't think he has the right to deliver before taking off after her. But just as he gets to the tree line, he casts one more look back at Mance. Their gazes latch on to each other for a heartbeat and something passes between them that makes me stiffen. Then he's gone, leaving Mance and me alone in the empty ruins.

I open my hand, looking at the keys I just lifted from Kiar's pocket, expecting to feel victorious.

But the way that Mance and Reltas looked at each other plays on a loop in my mind, spoiling any sense of triumph.

Slowly, I put the keys in my boot without mentioning them. Then I take my time retrieving and sheathing my blades before turning to Mance fully, only to feel a pang when I realize that she's not even looking at me. Instead, her gaze is focused on the patch of woods Reltas disappeared into, her mind clearly running after him. I don't even know if she registers that I'm still here.

Self-consciously, I stuff my hands in my pockets. "What exactly did we walk in on here, Mance?" I ask in a low voice.

It takes a full second for her to tear her eyes away from the trees and focus on me, and even when she does she's not fully with me. "I don't . . . really know," she says. "I'm not sure I want to talk about it."

I clench a fist. "So you two have secrets now?"

She flinches. "Not . . . *secrets*, just—"

But I cut her off. "Do you know, I've spent so much time trying to understand your different parts that not only can I tell which part of you I'm talking to, I can even tell, when you have multiple parts in you at one time, which one is leading?"

Her lips press together as though she's trying to figure out my point.

I wish I didn't have to say it out loud.

"The way you were looking at him just now, Mance? That was all Heart." The name comes out with a bitter edge to it that I can't hold back.

Her eyes flare, and I finally have her attention. "You think I have *feelings* for him?"

"I don't know what to think."

She shakes her head, not even bothering to yell back. She only mutters, under her breath, "I don't believe this."

"Don't," I lash out. "Don't act like I'm making things up. Something *shifted* between you two; I saw it!"

"Yes," she concedes. "Something did."

And as soon as she says it, it becomes clear that I wasn't expecting her to, because I didn't brace for it at all.

The breath evaporates from my lungs and pain rips through me. Immediately, I wish I could take this whole conversation back.

That I could undo the last several minutes and decide to go into Reltas's office instead. Then I could be there right now, rummaging through his things and merrily unraveling all his sinister plots. Instead of here, in the forest, getting my heart ripped out.

Slowly, Mance turns and approaches me. I fight the urge to run, like Kiar did. If I'm honest, I think the only thing that stops me is that I'm afraid she would let me. That she wouldn't chase after.

When she reaches me, she puts one hand on my cheek and I wince, certain she's about to let me down gently.

"What shifted is that I understand him better now," she says, "in a way that I wasn't expecting."

Stop it, I think. *This is torture. I should have run, after all.*

"But what I can't believe," she presses on, "is that you think there's room for anyone in *that* part of my heart but you. Do you really not know how I feel about you?"

I'm so focused on tensing for the blow that I don't immediately realize what she's saying. And when I do, I'm not ready to believe it. There's a tightness in my chest that won't ease. "What do you mean?" I ask, voice taut.

She takes a necklace out of her shirt and holds it up between us. A small leather pouch on a metal chain. "Do you know why I've been wearing this ever since we left the cliffs?" she asks.

Seems like a trick question. "No?"

She takes it off, then puts the pouch into my hand. It's soft against my palm. "Open it."

I pull on the drawstrings and find a pile of bruised, pathetic-looking petals inside. At first I don't understand.

And then I do.

These are the flowers I gathered for her, the ones I left splayed on the marble after storming out on our argument.

"You noticed them," I breathe. She noticed *me*. Even while we were fighting.

In fact, not only did she notice, but she took the time to pick the flowers up. To turn them into a treasure, one she could carry with her. My heart stutters, and the band around my chest eases, just a little.

But then I look at the browning petals, the bent stems and wilted leaves, and I feel ashamed. "They're so . . . withered."

"I don't care," she says stubbornly. "You gave them to me."

I shake my head. "You deserve better. I should pick you new ones."

"You do that," she answers, with unexpected force. "Pick me new ones every day. I'll take them all. But even when you do, I'm not getting rid of these. Because I want *everything* you're willing to give me, Silver. No matter how broken. As long as it's from you."

An incredulous laugh escapes my lips, and the fist in my pocket unclenches as warmth washes over me. The tightness in my chest cracks, before finally releasing completely, and I'm left feeling lightheaded.

This . . . this is why she's my candle in the storm.

Almost in awe, I pull the drawstring shut again, then hook the chain back around her neck where it belongs, realizing for the first time that it's probably made of silver.

And suddenly, whatever I saw pass between her and Reltas doesn't bother me.

As the metal settles against her skin, she peers up at me

through lowered lashes, and the glow that I love to see is burning softly in her eyes. I cup her face in both hands, letting it light me up from within. "Thank you," I say. "For wanting them. For wanting me."

I don't quite realize how else the sentence might be taken until her gaze lowers to my lips.

But when it does, I still completely, a new kind of tension building.

No version of Mance has kissed me since that first night, when Asset decided it wasn't wise. And I can see Asset in her eyes now, calculating.

I also see Heart, though. Longing.

So I wait. Not wanting to pressure her. Hardly even daring to breathe.

The forest seems to quiet, and the darkness is a wall around us, shutting out the rest of the world. Like this moment is really only us. Only ours.

And then she leans up and glides her lips softly over mine.

I exhale, thrilled and eager, bringing one hand up to run through her hair as my eyes flutter shut. It's clear that Heart is still leading, because this kiss is tender. Slow. Sweet. There are breaths and there are caressing fingers, but they're never frantic. They're affirming, grounding. Kind. Warmth spreads across my skin, even in the chill of the woods, and I sink into it, reveling in the emotion I can taste in the corners of her mouth.

When we pull apart, we don't separate completely. Our foreheads stay pressed together, and when I open my eyes, hers are still closed, as though she wants to linger in the moment as much as I do. Our breaths mist and mingle together in the cold bite of the evening as I stroke the corner of her jaw with one thumb.

"I—" she starts. But then she stops, seeming to wrestle with herself. After a minute, she swallows, looks pained, and tries again. "You *have* to know that I—"

And in a shocking burst of insight, I suddenly *do* know what she's trying to say.

That she ... loves me.

A joy so deep it's almost painful explodes through my entire body. I think I see stars. And after the initial burst of stunned elation wears off, it turns into something deeper. The knowledge wraps itself around me like a blanket. No, like armor, because I feel like I can take on anything as long as I can be certain of this one single fact. That *this girl* loves me.

It's dizzying to feel so sure. Because, normally, without the certainty of words, I know I would doubt. I would question. But right now, Poise isn't here to hide what Mance is feeling behind carefully composed expressions. The mask has been ripped off and her midnight eyes are *blazing* with emotion. With the things that she feels about *me*.

She loves me. She really, really does. Just like I love her.

Mance opens her mouth again, in another attempt to give voice to the sentiment, Heart and Asset probably warring in her mind, but I silence her with a second kiss. And this one is more profound, more intense. New, even as it is achingly familiar. I pour my own feelings into it, trying to echo the same kind of certainty that she just gave me. Trying to convey, through touch alone, that I belong to her. That I *always* will.

"It's okay," I say when I finally pull back, a little breathless. "I don't need the words right now. We'll say them when all of this is over. When there aren't any reasons left to hold back." It will mean the most then, and it's not something I would ever want to force. For a gift like that, I can wait.

She seems surprised, even a little embarrassed. But then her face sets and she nods, looking both pained and relieved at once.

And for now it's enough.

We're enough.

In fact, we're everything.

15
Mance, Without Poise, Without Livid

|3 DAYS UNTIL THE WEDDING|

I can't remember the last time I woke up smiling.

It's not an easy smile. The emotional weight of everything that happened yesterday is heavy in my chest, difficult to parse. And yet, somehow, I feel lighter than I have since I took the throne. I glance at the tree outside, but Silver must have already gotten up because the branches are empty. So I stumble into the living area of our chambers, groping around for the tray of hot tea and pastries that is usually left for me, hoping for a moment to myself before I start my day.

Only to come up short when I realize that there's a full breakfast set up by the window.

With Reltas waiting for me beside it.

I swallow, unsure how to react, but it's not until he looks me up and down with one raised eyebrow that I realize I'm still wearing my nightgown and I haven't done a thing with my hair or makeup since I came back from traipsing around in the woods in the middle of the night. I must look a mess. Poise would never have let this happen, but she's not back yet. Ergo, I merely lift my chin and wait for Reltas's response.

He doesn't say anything, though. He merely pushes a plate of breakfast crepes toward me in clear invitation and nods to the chair across from him. So instead of going back into my room to change, I take a seat and help myself.

We eat in silence for a moment, and it's awkward. Both of us are stealing glances, regarding each other anew in the light of day, overly conscious of the heavy emotions of last night and unsure about how we should act now. Every clink of silverware on dishes seems inordinately loud.

"Can we just . . . pretend it never happened?" Reltas says finally. The question is gruff, as though hard to get out.

And, of course, I understand why.

I slice my crepe into smaller pieces, considering it.

Poise would say yes. She would make it easy for him and then smoothly change the subject, returning our relationship to the distant and barely cordial one Reltas would clearly prefer.

But she's not here. And the words that come to my mind are not smooth.

"I don't think I can," I say.

"You could *try*," he snaps testily.

"I don't want to."

"Why not?"

For better or worse, I give him an honest answer. "Because it's the first time I saw something in you that I can actually understand."

It's the wrong thing to say. His lip curls in an immediate snarl, and his eyes shutter. "You will never understand me."

He thinks that because I don't have Livid in me now. But we have so much more in common than just rage.

I pick up the tea and take a sip. Then, instead of replying, I summon all my animals into the room in one blink, filling it with their presence.

I don't have every single one, of course. Livid has the predators, Poise has the birds, and I can no longer summon the bugs. I shudder at the memory of Mara's necklace stealing away my magic, erasing some of my creatures, before quickly dismissing it from my mind.

Even so, I have enough to make the space feel uncomfortably crowded.

Reltas jolts, ripping his eyes from mine to take them all in.

When I summoned them, I meant to explain. To tell him that I killed each of these with my bare hands, that I was forced, that carrying them with me is both a reminder of what I've been through and also, somehow, an integral part of who I am, one that I don't want to get rid of even if it *is* painful.

But it turns out I don't have to say any of that.

Because in the same way that I understood more corners of his pain than he actually put into words last night, Reltas understands me now. I can tell by the way that he collapses back in his chair, like a puppet whose strings have been cut, wordlessly surrendering the argument to me as he studies the memories I'm willing to show him.

For a moment, it's almost nice. To share this, to see each other this way. For him to recognize pain and history in the power that I have. To be known, even by an enemy.

But then . . . something happens.

Something that hasn't ever happened before.

My creatures have always reacted to my emotions, but instead of relaxing into the moment the way I am, they all suddenly and simultaneously tense up.

Out of nowhere, wounds erupt on their bodies. Familiar ones, exactly as they were on the days that they died. Each one even replays their final pose, their final sounds, all at once, be it yowl or snarl or gasping breath.

Instead of living, breathing creatures, we are suddenly surrounded by zombies.

I panic, surging to my feet and sending my chair toppling, as I am brought right back to that place. I feel like nothing more than a child, forced to hurt, not knowing how to make it stop. In a desperate attempt to cut off the display, I call them all back. But that only transfers their battles to my mind.

When I kill, I am barraged with memories and impressions of the animal's life, but those usually settle down quickly. They blend into the rest of me, never to be relived.

Only now they're rising up again. All the death that I brought, all the lives that I stole, all assaulting me in an overlapping cacophony.

And Reltas just sits there, studying me, watching the turmoil play out on my face. Probably thinking that I meant to show him this. "Enough," he says coolly. "I get it. Maybe you do understand."

I make a noise, though I'm not sure if it really came from me or from one of my creatures, because the sound isn't entirely human. I back up, tripping on the fallen chair behind me and crashing into a heap on the floor.

"Hey," Reltas says, eyebrows drawing together. "Are you—"

But I don't hear the rest of his question, because I've put my hands over my ears, futilely trying to shut out the babel of discordant death rattles that I can still hear. It's too much. Too overwhelming. I can't—

Suddenly, there are fingers under my chin, forcing my gaze up. And then all I can see is his acid green eyes.

They're not kind. They're not gentle. But they won't let me go, and that's all I need right now. I latch on to him like an anchor until the turmoil within me eases, quiets, and then finally, mercifully, subsides.

Then a beat passes, and I swallow against his fingers.

If I thought the silence was heavy before, now it is screaming. Because he watched every change in my expression, observed each moment of pain as it crossed my face. And his own eyes have shifted as well, into something I don't understand.

I can tell that he realizes he could let me go. For that matter, I could break away. But just like last night, neither of us moves, as though doing so would be admitting surrender. Unlike last night, though, our stares are not so intense, not so angry. It's harder to hide anything in the stark light of day than it was in the shadows of the forest, and there's an openness to him now that wasn't there before. As though seeing me struggle made him realize that I'm human, too. Just as messy and complicated as he is.

"So," I say finally, my voice raspy. "Do you think you could forget what *you* just saw?"

His eyes flick between mine, as though he might find the answer there. "No," he admits after a pause. "Probably not."

"What if we just didn't, then?" I press, leaning closer. "What if you stopped trying to hate me and admit that we have more in common than you'd like to think? We could be . . . friends. If you're willing."

At the word, something hard flashes across his face, and I know I've said the wrong thing again. He drops his fingers from my chin as though I've burned him and backs up rapidly.

"No," he grinds out. "That's impossible."

"Why?" I don't ask the question in an accusatory way. I genuinely want to know. "Because of my father? I know he caused you incredible suffering, but he wasn't exactly kind to me, either." I gesture around the room even though my animals are no longer there. "If we could just talk, I truly believe we might come to some sort of . . . understanding."

He scoffs, shooting me a glare. But when I refuse to return the sentiment, the glare turns pained. The silence stretches again, as I stubbornly refuse to fill it, waiting on him to speak. Instead, after several tense minutes, Reltas turns on his heel, stalks into the hallway, and slams the door shut behind him. I pull my knees up and let my head thunk onto them as I listen to the thud of his heavy footsteps retreating down the front steps.

Impossible, he said.

But I know he's wrong. Suddenly, I can picture it, unfolding in front of me. There could be a way to make a marriage between us something more than political. I could earn his respect, over time. He could win my affection, by degrees. It would take an incredible amount of work and dedication, probably over the course of *years*. But . . . it could happen.

And even considering that feels like a betrayal.

My creatures, only just settled, begin to riot again, and I feel completely unmoored. Restless and anguished. I want to throw my chair out the window, cast the table into the fire.

Clutching my stomach as though trying to hold the rampaging animals inside, I return to my room, only to find Poise waiting for me. Her lips are pursed, either because of my appearance or whatever she overheard, but I don't bother defending myself as I call her back.

Only to be shocked once again by the vicious pain of it.

I double over the bed, gasping. Why does it *hurt* so much? I thought I was getting used to the discomfort of being apart for so long, but somehow it feels like it's getting worse every time. Did Alect feel like this when he would split for weeks at once? Strangely, his memories are getting fuzzier, like the open wound in my mind is finally closing. I feel a spike of grief at the thought of him fading away. Perhaps soon I won't be able to access his memories at all, and then he truly will be ... gone.

What is going *on* with my magic?

Poise's memories aren't traumatic, but they are still concerning. I see myself arriving at a sparkling castle in a cove, covered in sea glass and surrounded by magical water displays like fireworks in the air. My mother is there, looking every bit the Coast Realm royal in a flowing, beachy dress and windblown hair.

But she wasn't happy to see me.

Nor was my aunt, the Prime.

Prime Apea runs her realm with *aggressive* perfection. Which is where my mother got her habits in the first place. Where I got them. My aunt's magic takes the form of music, always playing around her, and able to coax—even control—those in her vicinity. She is meticulous in keeping everything and everyone harmonious and idealized, not a hair or a note out of place. Instead of changing Apea's mind, Poise ended up falling into *her* rhythm, moving, even *breathing*, in accordance with the song she set. Until it began to hurt not to.

"Marry him," my aunt says. "And never speak of these doubts again."

Her command is harsh, and I open my mouth to protest, only for my protests to dry up in my throat as my aunt finishes the sentence.

"...Just like your mother did."

I feel a final wave of aching at the words, as Poise's memories finally settle, mixing with mine. It makes me sick, seeing the way my mother has been reduced to a shadow. Seeing *myself* act that way. And now that Poise is back, I am also horrified by how I've acted in the Forest Realm since she left.

It all mingles into a potent cocktail of despair, garnished with the deep, awful sting of having failed yet again.

I sit down on the bed, my head in my hands.

Clearly, neither Asset's practicality nor Poise's honeyed words are enough to get people on our side. Not even our own family.

And we only have one realm left to try. The Grasslands, with Prime Azele. We established a truce a few months ago but haven't seen much of each other since. I want to believe that she'll support me, but with the alliance so new, it's hard to know.

I decide to send Heart this time.

After our moment in the woods with Silver, she's brimming with confidence. And she's also the only one of us who hasn't tried yet. Maybe she'll succeed where the others failed.

I summon Heart in front of me and immediately I miss the joy. But I'm surprised to find that there's a comfort to her absence as well. The last few days I've just been feeling so *much*. It will be nice to get a break from it. I can think clearly for the first time since all this started happening.

She smiles at me with affection, despite the handprint-shaped bruises that still linger on her skin, and I feel an odd pulse where the reciprocal feelings should be. It's hollower and emptier than usual. Almost like I cut out more of myself than I typically do. Under my skin, my animals are unnaturally still.

But before I know it, she's gone.

In the wake of her absence, I feel sort of... fuzzy. Listless. I want to fall back on my bed in exhaustion. Unfortunately, Asset's practicality and Poise's dignity push me to get dressed and fix my hair instead.

With my emotions dampened, my mind turns back to planning while my fingers work through tangles. There is so much I need to do, and time is running out fast. This morning I made a plea to Reltas from the heart, and that didn't work. But perhaps he will respond to reason. I have to try, anyway. Our strategy with the other realms is failing. I need to focus back on my main strategy here.

And if that ultimately fails, too... it's time to come up with a Plan C. Hope and want can only get me so far. I need to be practical about the situation. I need to prepare for all possibilities.

No matter how difficult they may be.

I head to the library, hoping the environment will help me think.

But I've only just started pulling books from shelves when I am startled by a soft kiss on the side of my neck, right where the chain of my necklace lays against my skin.

"Silver!" I say, quickly looking over his shoulder to see if anyone happened to be passing by. "What are you doing here?"

"Looking for you." He gives me one of his full-dimpled smiles, clearly in a good mood after the kisses we shared. He even ducks to give me a peck on the lips in greeting, but I sidestep the attempt, glancing quickly around the hallway.

"Don't."

His smile wilts, and my heart throbs with that strange absence of emotion at the sight of it. "So it's back to that, then?" he asks.

"We are in a library," I remind him gently.

"An empty library."

"An empty library in my *fiancé's* castle."

Silver's expression folds into a glower. "Do you have to call him that?"

I slide the book back on the shelf.

Actually, this is good, too. Silver and I need to talk. He needs to understand the situation as well as I do. If he can see it rationally, too, then it will hurt him less in the end.

"I think . . . ," I say delicately. "It may be time for us to acknowledge that that's what he is."

Silver stiffens. His amber eyes rake my face, testing my expression. "What are you saying? You think I don't know? You think I *ever* stop thinking about it?"

I cast another glance into the hallway and then pull Silver deeper into the stacks of books, drawing him behind a lofty set of oak shelves where we won't be immediately visible to anyone walking by. "What I mean," I tell him, "is that none of the other realms are supporting us. Heart is in the Grasslands right now, but even if she manages to convince Prime Azele, we still have to contend with the fact that Reltas has the names of thousands of dead in our city. He could wipe us off the map completely. Two realms' worth of protection may not be enough to keep him from unleashing a large-scale attack."

"So what are you *saying*?" he asks, more forcefully this time.

"I'm saying that you and I have to talk about the possibility that I will need to go through with this."

There's a pause, then Silver's shoulders square. "No."

"No, I won't have to go through with it, or no, you don't want to talk about it?"

"Either. Both."

"You're being irrational."

"And you're being *too* rational! Mance, I don't understand. Yesterday, you said—I mean, you *almost* said—"

Again, the void within me seems to throb. I put a hand on his arm. "Yesterday was real. What we shared was . . . I *want* that." Even without Heart in me that's true. My love for Silver transcends the form I'm in. We may each feel that love a little differently—Asset as a fierce fondness and respect for a partner, and Poise as a source of comfort, one strong enough to coax her to lower the mask—but we all feel it. "But feelings are not everything. What I, as an individual, want is not more important than the lives of all my citizens. Surely you understand that?"

He scoffs. "Yeah, I understand it. Just like I understand that scaling a cliff to break into a tyrant's castle is extremely ill-advised. Just like I understand that taking the throne while your father still lives isn't how it's supposed to work. But you and I, Mance, we do impossible things!"

"I'm not saying I'm giving up. I *am* still trying. But the wedding is in three days, and I just think we need to be realistic. About all the feasible outcomes. Just because it's worked out in the past doesn't mean it always will. You can't live your life thinking that if you want something hard enough it will just happen."

"Of course not. You *make* it happen."

"Fine, but sometimes making it happen will take sacrifice. We need to come to terms with the fact that this is one that I may have to make."

"*No!*" Silver says more forcefully.

I purse my lips. "I am just trying to prepare you. But if even thinking about the possibility is this difficult for you, then you don't have to be here."

I regret the words as soon as they leave my lips. I meant that he didn't have to stay for my planning session. That if the stark realities were too painful for him, then I could work through them on my own. I am used to that.

But Silver seems to take my statement differently, as me telling him that I don't want him in the realm or by my side at all. A stunned hurt flashes across his face.

And without giving me the chance to clarify, he actually does it.

He spins on his heel and walks out.

So quickly that now *I* am the one who is stunned.

Because I believe this is the first time he's walked out on me . . . ever. Even when I came to this realm without him, he was there when I arrived. He's *always* there.

Surely, he's only walking out on the argument. Maybe he interpreted my statement correctly, after all, and is simply giving me space to think things through.

And yet I can't shake the feeling that the way he just left was something bigger. That it won't be a mere couple of hours before I see him again.

Inside me, the void of Heart's absence is aching. I keep bumping up against it, only to find nothing there. I know, logically, that I should be feeling so much more than I am right now.

But throughout the whole argument, my creatures did not stir once.

They are not even stirring now.

So, after a beat, I turn away from the empty doorway and get back to my books.

16
Silver

|3 DAYS UNTIL THE WEDDING|

L eave, she says. As if I'd *ever* do that.

Within minutes, I am setting off a small explosion on the first floor. Not a big one, totally manageable. Just enough to keep Kiar occupied while I break into that door in the basement.

Because if Mance is this close to giving up, then it's time to kick my own plans up a notch. *I'm* not quitting. Not even if she does.

In spite of myself, I flinch at my own thought.

Obviously, I know Mance is only trying to be rational about a hard situation. But that doesn't mean her dismissal doesn't hurt. Heart isn't with her, that was clear, but it's almost as though there was something else missing, too. Why isn't she *fighting* like she used to? It worries me.

What I need to do is get her out of this marriage *now*, so that we can go home and get back to our regular lives. I'm sick of her sharing chambers with another guy, sick of her wearing his ring, sick of the secretive glances and private moments, sick of *all of it*.

So I'm breaking into this final door, because I *know* that Merod has holed himself up behind it like a coward, and one way or another I *am* going to make him release her from this agreement.

My hands are shaking so hard with emotion that it takes a few tries to find the right key. But when I slide an oversized brass one into the lock and turn it, there's a loud click, and then a groan, like I've unlocked more than just one bolt. I take a breath to steady myself, listening for footsteps in case the noise alerts anyone to my presence, but fortunately there's only dusty silence. Everyone must still be preoccupied with the chaos I created above.

I push the door open, expecting to enter a room, but instead there is only a narrow, sloping tunnel that quickly descends into murky shadow. A thrill goes through me at the discovery. No wonder Merod hasn't come out; there could be a whole living space down here. I step inside, eager. But the second my hand leaves the heavy door, it shuts behind me with a bang.

And I am immediately plunged into darkness as the lock clicks shut behind me.

Alarmed, I spin and rattle the knob, trying to shove it back open with my shoulder, but it won't budge now.

I swallow, flexing my fingers.

Forward it is.

Heart hammering, I turn back to the tunnel and take a couple steps, feeling my way carefully. After a few seconds, something ahead flickers brightly and then goes out. I still, pressing against the side of the tunnel until it flashes again. When it does, I realize that it's one of those solidified storm clouds from the Jungle Realm. A tiny globe of thundering gray surrounded by a ring of metal to render its lightning harmless.

Which . . . seems like an unnecessarily ornate way to light a random tunnel.

Especially because, unlike the rest of the castle, these halls don't give the impression of old, half-rotted grandeur. They seem new.

So new that there isn't even flooring or constructed walls, just carved-out earth.

But I've come this far and there's nothing to do but push on, so I do, warily.

As I continue through, it gets even clearer that this passage is a recent construction. Newly exposed roots poke through the ceiling and wind around the walls, sometimes forcing the tunnels to change direction suddenly in order to navigate around them. I must be underneath the forest itself now. How far do these tunnels extend?

There are more solidified clouds strung up every few feet, which means the lighting is inconsistent. Darkness, darkness, then a flash of illumination. It makes it easy to hide but difficult to figure out where I'm going. As I walk, I skim my fingers along the earthen walls, feeling for the seam of a door or the empty space of another opening.

It's quiet down here, the sound of my footsteps lost in the soft dirt. And it smells like a fresh grave.

Finally, my fingers skim over wood and in a flash of light, I see a door.

I nudge at its edges, pushing it gently open, then steal inside.

It takes me a minute to process what I find there.

At first glance it's fairly innocuous. Just a storage room for magical items. There are more solidified clouds, their bolts lighting up the space in a more frenzied way because of how many there are. A whole wall is lined with Prime Gore's trademark bottled explosions, which is expected. This was his realm. There are heat rocks, although they're sitting on a wooden table, so it seems unlikely they're hot enough to melt anything. None of that takes me aback.

But when I look further, there are so many things that shouldn't be here. So many things that shouldn't *exist*. I know there were days when magic was unregulated, so surely one or two artifacts from that dangerous period must have survived, but this room seems like it contains every scrap of magic that has ever taken form.

There are things that ooze and things that fester. Things that wilt and things that stir. Things that whisper and things that feel like they are staring at me, even if they don't have eyes. There are rocks and statues and items of clothing . . .

And there are weapons. There are so, so many weapons.

With an arsenal like this, Reltas could wipe out every other realm. Why would he need so much power? And where did he *get* it all?

I'm afraid to touch anything, because I don't know what any of it does.

No, wait, I know what the explosive jars do. I grab a few of them.

And, like, *one* sword made of ice, because I'm only human.

The blade is cold to the touch, but not unpleasantly so, and the heat of my skin doesn't melt it. I wait a second to see if I spontaneously combust or turn into a clock or something, but nothing else happens.

So I hurry back into the hallway and shut the door firmly behind me, relishing the renewed darkness of the tunnels.

Troubled, I continue forward, but in the next flash of light I find that there's a second door, not far from the first. And this one has a necklace bolted around it, one that looks suspiciously like one of Mara's. Probably the one she put on her father's jail cell, which Reltas must have pried free after disengaging it.

Promising.

Still reeling but determined to see this through, I unhitch the latch and ease open the door, holding my breath. In the wake of what I just saw, the silence feels suddenly heavier. Weighted.

I brace myself and slip inside.

This room is completely unlit, so I can't make out anything at first. He must be sleeping.

I don't want to announce myself in case there's a guard inside, so I shrink behind some boxes I feel by the door and wait for the next flare of light.

Shouldn't I hear someone moving around, though? Breathing, at least?

There's a weird smell, but I can't quite place it. I strain my ears, but I don't hear a thing, and the lightning feels like it's taking forever to flash again.

Then, suddenly, it does.

And Merod is there, lying on his side in a bed.

I found my prey.

The lightning winks out as quickly as it came.

I creep closer, ready to pounce. Ready to demand he annul the engagement, not even caring about the threat of his magic. It shouldn't be too hard to keep out of his reach.

But then, when I'm only few steps away from his bedside, the lightning flashes again and I jerk away, noisily toppling several boxes in my haste.

Because this time I got a much better look.

And Merod's face is mottled with bruises and cuts, like some kind of morbid painting. There are long red lines that imply he's been whipped, some with flecks of skin peeling off. Blood cakes his skin in different shades, from crusty brown to dark, slick burgundy, which leads me to believe that he was tortured more than once.

His head is lolling to the side at an unnatural angle.

His eyes stare sightlessly, straight at me.

And his neck has been brutally slashed, the jagged edges of flesh curling away from the wound, slathered with old, dried-up gore.

In short, he is unmistakably, unequivocally . . .

Dead.

As the light flickers out again, I stumble back into the hallway, shocked.

My mind races to make sense of what I just saw. I can't say that I'm exactly . . . sad about it. No tears spring to my eyes. I don't fall to my knees in despair. That man was a monster, and some part of me thinks that what happened to him was justice. He was responsible for so much suffering. If those actions caught up with him, then it's hard to say he didn't deserve it.

But the smell—which I now realize is *blood*—pours out of the darkened doorway, and the image of his tortured body is burned inside my eyelids. I feel bile at the back of my throat.

Is justice really the right word for this?

I shake my head, trying to get it together. Trying to figure out what this means. How long has he been dead? And when were they planning to tell us?

Of course. They *weren't* planning to tell us. Because if Merod is dead, then *Mance* is the one who has the power to dictate her betrothal. A rush of elation washes over me, because this means that it *is* over. Finally. I only have to run upstairs and tell her and then we can . . . leave. Be together. Have control again. We can—

In the darkness, I suddenly feel a blade at my throat, and I freeze, my thoughts completely derailed.

"He deserved what he got," says a voice. "And worse."

When the lightning flashes, I am unsurprised to see Kiar on the other end of the knife, her pale hair catching the light.

"Fancy meeting you here," I mutter.

She walks in front of me, tracing the metal along my throat. "I told you to leave it alone," she says in mock regret. "Now I'm going to have to do something about you."

"Oh, yeah?" I ask. "The same thing you did about him?" The light flashes again, and my eyes are drawn to Merod's beaten corpse, slumped against the wall in full view.

"It'll be quicker, that's for sure," she assures me with a sneer. "We don't have as much pent-up anger to work out on you. But the end result will be similar, yes."

"We?"

The light flashes on her bared teeth. "Yes, we. There were quite a lot of citizens who came down here to work out their personal grudges over the last several days." Even in the dark, I can feel her smile widening. "Some even took trophies." In the next flash, I notice for the first time that Merod is missing several fingers. And an ear. His hair is chopped in uneven slashes. I even see a large red stain around his left kneecap that I'd rather not think about.

"Because he conquered you?"

"Because of *all* of it," she spits. "Every blow was for a friend or family member whose death was on that man's head. For our Prime, Reltas's father, who was left alive but broken, a man too shattered to lead an empire in shambles. For those of us who survived and were forced to live in the shell of our former grandeur, ghosts haunting our own city. We *deserved* to give him that pain. And he deserved his death, too. Even if it wasn't exactly part of the plan. Can't blame people for getting carried away when we've waited so long for this."

I recognize the vehemence in her voice. I've heard it in my own, ranting to Vie about the injustices the same man had heaped on our heads as well. The lightning doesn't flash again, but I feel like I can still see him there, pale and bruised, his wounds gaping and gruesome. Ripped apart by the ones he trampled under his feet.

"Did it work?" I ask sincerely. "Do you feel better now?"

She presses the metal harder into my neck, pricking my skin until blood beads beneath it. "Not yet."

I swallow, feeling the cold of the sword against my side. Does she know I have it? Can I use it to get out of her grip? "What's next, then?" I ask, just to keep her talking.

The tunnel we're in is narrow, and she definitely knows it better than I do. That makes escape difficult, but I need to figure something out. Because there's a deadly intent in her voice. The next time it all goes dark, I move my hand to the hilt of my new blade, suppressing a shiver at its chill.

"Why would I tell you?" she sneers.

"Why not? You're clearly going to kill me anyway."

She laughs unkindly. "I suppose that's true. But it's your own fault. Can't have you telling your vapid girlfriend that she has a way out of her betrothal, now can I?"

I shift away from the knife but don't make a move to run yet.

Instead, I weigh my words, wanting to make the most of this opportunity. "Right, so, since we both agree I'm dying anyway, tell me: Why does your Prime *really* want a marriage with Mance? If it was just about an alliance, she would have gladly agreed to one without all the legal assurances. She *still* would, even after all this. I mean, she won't be happy about the murder of her father, but she can forgive it. She'll understand your pain more than you realize. It isn't too late for peace." Despite my words, when the light flickers away again, I ease the sword out of its sheath.

Kiar scoffs derisively. "There is no trust between our realms. There can never be."

"Between you and Merod? No. But Mance is not her father. She's not a warmonger."

"And Reltas is not his father, either. He's not a coward."

I flip the blade in my hand, testing its weight in the shadows. "But if what you really want is vengeance, then a straight-on attack makes much more sense," I push back. "I already know that you have the magic to make large-scale damage. So, again, why marriage?"

"If we conquer you, we'll have to kill a lot of people. And we don't want to do that."

I raise an eyebrow. "So you *do* have a heart. I'm touched!"

She sneers in the flickering light. "You misunderstand. We don't want to save them. We want to use them."

I let the sword settle in my hand, gripping its hilt tightly. "Use them for . . . ?"

She smirks. "Let's just say the Cliff Realm isn't the only one he has his eye on. He plans to take over all of them, one way or another. Because Merod may have been the one holding the noose, but the other realms didn't help us escape it. They *all* looked away as we swung. So they deserve what's coming just as much. The Cliff Realm is only our first stop."

My gut clenches as I think about the amount of magical ammunition just down the hall. When I saw it, I thought it would be enough to take out the whole Continent, but I didn't think that was Reltas's *actual* plan.

"Where did you get it all?" I ask, tilting my head back toward the room, certain that she knows what it contains.

"The Broken Citadel."

"Obviously," I shoot back. "All magic comes from the Broken Citadel, but how did you gather so much?"

She grins, unnervingly at ease. "Everything in there has been brought out by one of our own citizens. Mostly brave volunteers, although some needed to be . . . compelled. They've been going in for weeks and coming out with all kinds of fun things."

My stomach lurches, partially at her words and partially at the way she's being so candid. She was holding back when this conversation started, and now she seems to have no problem spilling everything. Which means she must be really certain I'm not making it out of this tunnel alive.

My sword is ready, but I don't strike. If I can get the full plan out of her and *then* escape, I'll be able to tell Mance everything. She might not be willing to start a war just to get out of a marriage, but she definitely would to avoid her citizens becoming fodder for a continental takeover. I try to keep focused on the conversation, probing to get as much information as possible, even as my mind races. "But you can't do that," I say. "Only members of the royal line can enter the Broken Citadel. It's in the . . . uh, one of those stuffy agreements everyone cares about.

Mance would know the one. Anyway, it's not allowed."

"Sangua did it. And they let her fake heir, Azele, rule anyway. Besides, the rules only matter if you plan to continue the system as it is. But if you want to overthrow the whole thing, then they don't really matter much after all, do they?"

I consider this carefully. "So . . . to be clear, your plan is to make an army out of Mance's people, equip them with magical weapons your citizens create, and take control of the entire Continent from there? You *have* to see that doing that would immediately backfire. You can't enslave people and then give them fantastical ammunition. They'll rebel immediately. They'll destroy *you*."

She shrugs dismissively. "I'm not too worried about that. If they fought for Merod, then they'll fight for us. Besides, once Reltas is Mancella's husband, he can use her seal to make any decree he wants. And when the people see their beloved Prime at his side, supporting him, they'll fall in line."

I start to shake my head, but then remember the knife against my throat and still. "Mance would never do that. No matter what you threaten her with. Not for my life, not for her sister's life, not for torture, not for anything."

"I'm not too worried about that, either."

Alarm blares in my ears. This is the information I'm missing. The crucial piece. "Why not?" I demand.

"Because I was one of the first to go in, and I came out with something pretty useful. But I'm tired of this conversation now. You've been a diverting opponent for the last few days, but our contest has reached its end."

She makes a move to slash across my throat, but I've been expecting it and I'm faster, falling sideways and swinging upward with my sword at the same time, hoping to either disarm or wound her.

To my surprise, though, ice shoots out from the tip of the blade, leaving a sheet of frost suspended in the air in front of me. Kiar's eyes widen, but before she can recover, I slice through the air a couple more times, making a full ice wall between us, then I take off at a run.

Unfortunately, running in a root-filled tunnel is not the wisest choice. I trip and go sprawling, the lightning flashing only long enough for me to watch my sword go flying from my hand as the dirt rises to meet me, sharp ice arcing in every direction.

With a scream of frustration, Kiar plunges her knife into the wall behind me, but the ice only freezes over it, and she barely withdraws her hand in time to avoid it fusing to the ice as well. Then she goes quiet, looking for an opening, her form blurry through the frost. I wrench my foot from the root, wincing as it throbs, and go quiet, too, waiting this time for the lightning to show me the path forward. Because there aren't just roots anymore; there are new, haphazard walls of ice, too. And I don't want to accidentally bump into one and end up with my foot frozen to the floor.

"Clever," Kiar says dryly in the darkness, and I take that to mean she didn't find a weakness in my fortification. I exhale, only to tense again when I hear a rustling sound. It seems like she's rifling through her bag. Why isn't the lightning flashing anymore? I get to my feet, wondering if I should risk trying to run again anyway.

"Only magic can affect other magic, right?" Kiar asks behind me. And my heart sinks. She must have some other magical weapon in her satchel. Maybe even something that will kill me on the spot.

I feel in front of me with my toe, only to hit something cold and fast-spreading. I withdraw quickly, cursing. Did I accidentally make myself a cage? Where's the *light*?

The rustling stops. She seems to have found whatever she was looking for. "Not the command I would have preferred to use right now, but it will probably do," she mutters to herself. Then she raises her voice, clearly speaking to me now. "I told you I came out with something fun, didn't I? Hopefully you will, too."

The light finally flashes in time for me to see her make a sudden move with her hand behind the ice. And then something small and round, like a seed, bursts through the wall and hits me square in the forehead.

I falter in confusion, and through the hole in the ice, I catch the edge of her smile, just as the object hits my skin.

And continues right through it, cutting through skin, flesh, and bone as easily as it cut through the ice.

I reel back, expecting pain. Afraid that my head will burst open like the wall did.

But that's not how it feels at all. It feels . . . almost like my head is full of dirt, and the seed she threw is digging down into it and implanting itself. Growing. I feel my mind being split by its roots, and my thoughts distorting around them. I claw at my forehead in terror, but the skin there is already smooth, even as I feel the roots sprout and spread, invading my very mind.

"What is this?" I demand.

When the lightning blazes again, I see my eyes in the polished surface of her suspended knife, and the veins in the whites of my eyes have turned green.

They're vines, stretching toward my irises.

I have a second to realize that *this* is what was wrong with Merod's eyes when I first saw him.

Then suddenly I am possessed with one thought and one thought only, a command that has burrowed itself into my brain.

ENTER THE BROKEN CITADEL.

And immediately that's all my body wants to do. Even as I rage against the idea, I am singularly focused on getting to the Desert Realm, where the Broken Citadel lies. Here, underground, there's no way to determine which way is north, but the magic seems to know. Against my will, I take a first step in that direction. And then another.

"So . . . you can control bodies," I process aloud. "You can make them fight even if they don't want to. That's how you plan to get Mance's people to go to battle for you. How you plan to get Mance to command them."

I strain against my own muscles, trying to get myself to stop, but my legs keep moving and my hands even uncork a bottled explosion to take down the wall blocking my way. Without my consent, they throw it, and the inky magic hovers in the air for a moment before bursting into fire. Kiar cackles as the wall comes down, crumpling in the face of the hovering black flames. And my traitorous body just walks right through them, in the direction of the Citadel, forcing me to duck and weave to avoid getting burned.

"That's right," Kiar says, picking my pockets as I walk,

reclaiming the rest of the bottled explosions that I stole. "Killing you would have been nice, but there's a certain tragic poetry in making you a recruit in our new army. Plus, as a bonus, this will tear Mancella apart. And I find myself very interested in doing that right now."

Ignoring her words, I strain as hard as I can, veins popping in my neck, but my legs continue to amble forward. I can move my arms a little, but when I try to grab onto a root to hold myself back, they lock up and won't let me. I can only use them if I'm not hindering the overall goal planted in my mind.

My only consolation in all this is that it will take me forever to walk to the Broken Citadel. Weeks, easily. Maybe I can get deliberately lost. If I do it right, I can delay this long enough for someone to catch up and restrain me. And that will give us time to find some kind of magical cure.

As if reading my mind, Kiar smiles. "Don't worry," she says. "I can get you a ride. You'll be at the Citadel by morning."

17

Mance, Without Livid

|2 DAYS UNTIL THE WEDDING|

❃

When Heart comes back, the merge is the most painful one I've experienced so far.

Not because of her memories, but because of mine. With Heart's emotion back in my chest, I am *devastated* by the way that I treated Silver. And even more devastated by the fact that he actually *left*. I thought for sure, especially after that suspicious explosion by the entrance, that he would show up at my window last night to yell at me.

But he didn't. He's . . . gone.

An old fear takes root in my chest, that the ones I love will always abandon me. That it's foolish to think otherwise. I've been fighting that fear lately, pushing it down, trying not to let it mess up what I have with Silver. But now that I am staring at the empty branches where Silver used to sleep, it blossoms once again.

This is why I have to do everything alone. Because everyone leaves me eventually. It was only a matter of time until he did, too.

So now here I am, back to being alone in a foreign realm where everyone despises me, where my own father refuses to even see me, and where my fiancé can barely stand my presence. With a wedding planned for the day after tomorrow, and no support from any of the realms. Not a single one.

Azele was sympathetic, and she told me that if we needed an individual or two she would gladly pledge herself or Rift to the cause, but she couldn't find a way to justify giving her entire realm's backing in a war just to help me get out of an engagement I don't want, not when it would mean her own citizens dying.

I'm an idealist, too, she'd said. *I wish you weren't in the position you are. I wish we lived in a world where hard choices like that don't exist. But in the world we do live in, idealism needs to be tempered with practicality. With priority. My people can't fight every battle; they have battles of their own. I have battles of my own as well. I'm sorry.*

And I understand. She told me a little about the battles she has to wage. Like how her magic has been developing beyond her control lately, but she doesn't know why. How she accidentally turned a rabbit to ash a few days ago, and has been afraid to touch another person since. Rift stood behind her, anguish in his eyes.

So of course I don't blame her.

But it doesn't make it any easier to stomach the fact that I'm on my own again.

Restless in my chamber, I decide to head for the woods, hoping their sun-dappled beauty will soothe me.

But instead I run into Reltas, stepping out of a shadowy clump of trees and looking haggard.

We both pull up short when we see each other. His features twist into a sour look, like he's stepped in something rotten, but I ignore that, focusing instead on the weariness in his eyes and the slump of his shoulders. Then my eyes drift to the woods behind him. And I know what lies in that direction.

"Again?" I ask softly. Despite everything, I feel a rush of sadness that he chose to go through it alone this time. Knowing that there are people who would have gladly been there by his side, it's hard to think that he opted to fight that darkness by himself. Especially when I don't get that same choice.

I expected him to get defensive, but his guard seems oddly lowered. Perhaps because there's no point in hiding where he's been anymore. He only raises one bony shoulder, hair in his eyes, and says, "It can be hard to fight."

I nod. "I get it."

He nods back, leaning against a tree, his hands buried in the pockets of his cloak.

And I'm surprised to find that the atmosphere between us is more comfortable now. That we can actually have a conversation like this without animosity.

Then Kiar bursts through the trees and doubles over, panting.

The concern that transforms Reltas's face is instant and palpable. His features become softer at first, in the vulnerability of his care for her, and then turn much, much harder. Like he's ready to go to war as soon as she directs him. "What's happened?" he demands, shoving off the tree and taking Kiar's shoulders in his hands. "Where have you been all night?"

She's about to answer when she realizes that I'm there, too, and her eyes narrow to find us, once again, alone together in the woods.

Awkwardly, I look down, occupying myself with shaking dirt off the tips of my skirts.

Kiar continues to glare at me, even as she leans into Reltas and whispers something in his ear. His hand is on her hip and he arches protectively over her, but as she speaks his expression darkens.

Then his eyes cut to me.

"Change of plans," he says. "The wedding is moved up."

Kiar's eyes fly wide and my mind reels. "Moved up?" I ask. "It's the day after tomorrow. How much sooner can we possibly make it?"

"Meet me in the square in an hour," he says, nudging Kiar toward me. "She'll help you get ready."

Kiar's expression is fierce and heart-wrenching, but she quickly schools it, turning to me with grim determination. I have a moment of pity for her being asked to dress the bride of the person she so clearly cares for. But then I cast the thought aside and take a step backward, shaking my head.

I can't get married now. I haven't come up with a plan yet. And the last thing I said to Silver was . . .

"What about my father?" I ask desperately. "Surely you can't expect me to get married without *ever* having met with him?"

"I'll be sure to extend your invitation to him," Reltas says, with a cold smile I don't understand.

Silver

I've tried to fling myself out of this carriage multiple times, but just by looking at me you wouldn't know it. Not a single muscle has so much as twitched, except that my arms keep flailing hopelessly around and then locking up the second before they might actually do something useful.

When Kiar was with me, I spent a good amount of time cursing her out, since the magic doesn't seem to have a hold on my mouth.

But she only came with me far enough to meet someone coming from the other direction, convey the plan to him, pass him a seed, and then disappear into a weird rift she carved in the ground, presumably headed back to the Forest Realm.

My gut twists as I think about why:

Mance's wedding is in two days.

And if Mance doesn't go through with it willingly, then she'll be subjected to the exact same magic that binds me now. Kiar will be standing by, ready to implant her with the order.

I picture her walking down the aisle with forced steps, going through the rituals of matrimony even as her mind is screaming at her not to, the way mine is screaming now. I imagine her binding herself to another man against her will.

I have to get *back*.

Mance, Without Livid

A mere hour later, I am wearing white and walking down an aisle.

Kiar left me with four very forceful women, all of whom worked together to muscle me into the gown I'm wearing now. I haven't had a second to think, or breathe. And the dress isn't making it overly easy to breathe now, either. It's beautiful, with glass beads that look like dewdrops embroidered in patterns that spread like delicate explosions, a lovely—although somewhat violent—blending of the original magic of our two realms. I can't help but appreciate the artistry, especially considering how quickly it had to have been completed. But a pretty dress doesn't mean much compared to the fate that awaits me at the end of the aisle.

Around me, the square is beautiful, with gently glowing lanterns strung between the trees, and delicate, sweet-smelling flower petals strewn on the ground. People are huddled quietly in their balconies, dressed in their finest and clutching candles between their fingers. There's a soft, lilting tune in the air, though I can't see any musicians. And in the center of the square waits Reltas, one hand extended down the aisle toward me.

Meanwhile, my creatures are in an uproar beneath my skin. My heart feels like it's going to beat straight out of my chest. None of this feels real, and certainly not *right*.

The eyes of the realm burn through me, and I take a tentative step forward, if only to appease them, but I need to gather myself before I take another.

Where are all the people I care about? Why, on my wedding day, am I surrounded by complete strangers? Why isn't anyone *ever* there for me?

Silver left. My family isn't here. Clearly, my father chose to ignore my invitation *again*. And beyond that, not a single Prime in any of the realms has my back.

Swathed in intricate lace and gauzy veils, I have never felt so alone in the world.

What do I do? What options are left to me?

Do I start a war, right here and now?

I take another step.

Do I break Silver's heart along with my own? Do I commit to a life with the man who once murdered a part of me?

Although... our recent interactions have shown me that there is at least some humanity in him. A suffering that matches mine. Over the course of a lifetime, there is a chance we could grow closer. Build something that doesn't hurt.

It hurts now. Silver's absence feels like a shard of glass wedged in my side, and I wish I could talk to him about all of this before it's final. I wish I had been vulnerable in our last conversation instead of hard.

I realize with a jolt that I might never see him again. Because once he hears about *this*, why would he come back to me?

I should have kissed him goodbye.

Silver

The final minutes of the journey are agony. We've been traveling through the night, but I haven't slept. I'm torn between imagining Mance walking down the aisle toward Reltas, never knowing about her father's death and its implications, and dwelling on the very real possibility that I may never come out of the Citadel at all.

Many don't.

And those who do are often broken by it. Will I be, too? Will I not be strong enough?

I experience a glimmer of hope when we approach the border of what used to be the Desert Realm. I've never been this far north, but I've heard stories. And aren't there guards posted around the perimeter, specifically to prevent unauthorized people from gaining access to the Citadel? I know each realm is obligated to send some troops to serve in the role, and the vows they undertake are severe. Surely they'll stop my carriage. After all, I don't have a single drop of royal blood.

A great wall rises on the horizon before us, and my heart leaps.

But then the gate creaks open, without a scrap of interrogation or fanfare. The guards stand in formation on either side, seemingly completely unconcerned with our entrance.

"Hey!" I scream out the window as we approach. "They're breaking the Treaty! We shouldn't be here! You guys have *one job!*"

Not a single one so much as looks my way. They just continue standing stiffly at attention, facing forward.

It's not until I get close enough that I see why:

Their eyes are filled with vines.

Just like mine.

The driver snickers at me and the carriage rattles on.

Mance, Without Livid

My train and veil drag through the dirt, catching petals and grime alike. The flowers that line the aisle are in shades of deep burgundy and ash gray, nothing like the vibrant sunset hues in the pouch tucked into my bodice.

And then all too soon I am there. At the altar, standing across from Reltas. Nothing and no one to save me.

I bite my lip.

Saying no means starting a war, and how could I be so selfish? How could I put my people through that, *again*, after vowing to them that my reign would be peaceful?

I remember Petrice telling me that I needed to decide which sacrifices I was willing to make, and when it's my own comfort pitted against the very lives of my people . . .

There's no choice at all.

Even if I wish there were.

A lump forms in my throat and tears prick at my eyes when I come to the decision. It doesn't seem like Reltas is waiting on me anyway, though.

Without preamble, he takes out a knife, drags it across his hand, and holds it over the altar, letting his blood drip onto the stones.

My creatures writhe.

For Primes, a wedding is serious. Irrevocable. It's more than the tying together of individuals, it's the binding of realms. Which is why instead of stated vows, we ceremonially mix our blood together on an altar, to symbolize the joining of bloodlines and the alliance of our peoples. This altar was built from wood and stone, another symbol of our two realms joining, and it's lovely, even with the speckles of scarlet that now mar its face.

Reltas wipes the knife off on a white handkerchief, staining it with dark streaks. Then he passes the knife to me.

Silver

༺✶༻

The ground beneath us turns from solid stone to soft sand, and the going gets slower as the wheels stutter and sink. Dragging out the inevitable. If I'm going to be forced into a mass of twisted, dark magic no matter what I do, then I'd rather get it over with. The abandoned city around us reflects my own crumbling hopes. Buildings half toppled and streets disintegrated beneath our wheels. Ruins in every direction.

Until there aren't. As we draw farther into the city, parts of the ruins have been fixed up, with temporary wooden structures constructed on top of incomplete sandstone walls. Tents have been erected in alleyways. And there are *people* in them. Scores of them, presumably all of whom are either waiting for a chance to enter the Citadel or have already gone in and come back out.

Reltas has a whole base camp out here. An entire operation. This is where the hoard of magical items came from; they are literally farming people into magical resources. And even weirder, the people don't seem to mind.

To my right, the ground is shaking and a woman is toppling buildings into rubble. To my left, there's a void in the side of a wall that temporarily blinds me when I look at it. I see one man grow enormous vulture wings and take flight, circling above me, only his feathers are spears. I see another making a slash in the sand and opening it like a door, with a strange, shadowy pit below.

The carriage crunches to a halt, and my body jolts up as soon as it does, my legs unfolding and my arms unlatching the door before we're even fully stopped.

A few people look at me in alarm, clearly recognizing me as an outsider, but as soon as they see my eyes, they relax and return to whatever they were doing. I walk easily around them, their faces blending together as my attention is pulled forward.

Because there it is.

The Broken Citadel.

And somehow, in the middle of everything else, it still has the power to stagger me.

Mance, Without Livid

The lace of the dress feels tight around my neck, and I pull at it with my fingers. It reminds me of the ropes that bound Asset in the Swamp Realm. Of the suffocating dirt Heart inhaled in the Outskirts. I can't breathe. I can't *breathe*.

But I wrap my fingers around the knife, my hand touching Reltas's for a brief moment, before he draws back. I try not to flinch at his haste.

The blade now clutched in my fist, I draw in a ragged breath.

Now's the part where I'm supposed to cut my hand, too, and yet I'm frozen.

I will myself to make the wound, but my arm doesn't move at all.

It's irreversible if I do this. It's forever.

But I *have* to.

I have to.

Silver

✼

I've seen the Citadel's light on the horizon all my life. But I never thought I'd be standing in front of it. I never thought the colors would be so vivid, the pull so enticing, the tang of magic in the air so strong.

I lean my head back and look at the acidic green lights arcing through the sky as my feet drag me closer and closer. They are the color of poison, but I didn't know that the magic closer to the core of the Citadel was darker, more like a shadowy pit or the depths of an ocean. It stands like a blot against the clear blue sky.

Is this it?

Will this be my last glimpse of the sun?

And even if I do manage to come out . . . will I still be me? Or will I be changed so irrevocably that I don't even recognize myself?

Will Mance recognize me?

Will she still want me after this?

Will it even matter, or will she be a married woman by the time I see her next?

Questions race through my mind as my stomach clenches in panic.

And my feet just keep plodding forward, uncaring.

Mance, Without Livid

For a moment, Silver's face sears itself into my mind, and it's like I've taken the knife to my stomach instead of my hand.

Why did I suddenly get such a bad feeling?

Who am I kidding; nothing about this feels good. I've had foreboding premonitions ever since I stepped into the square.

But this one feels different. Suddenly, the creatures beneath my skin are *rioting*. Something's wrong. Something bigger than I know.

"I, um . . ." I swallow, looking around. Taking in all the eyes still latched onto me. "I—" I cast around for something, anything to stall the proceedings long enough for me to at least catch my breath.

"You're taking too long," says an exasperated voice behind me.

I whip around, grateful for any distraction or delay, even a condemning one. Kiar stands there, her mouth dour and her eyes angry. Her white hair has been done up in a nest of hasty braids interspersed with leaves and flowers, even more of them than usual. And in her hand, there is something small and oblong.

It looks like a seed.

"Hold still," she says, darting toward me.

Silver

For all my struggle, it's only moments before I pass through the door of the Citadel, plunging into its powerful depths.

And the very second I do, Kiar's magic wears off.

There's a tingling on the inside of my skull and a burning in my eyes as the plant that sprouted withers and dies. Bits of dried vine flake away as I blink and the muscles of my legs unlock.

I spin on my heel and lunge back toward the door, arms outstretched, but it disappears before I can reach it. The last thing I see is the Forest Realm citizens jeering from the midst of the ruins.

And then blackness.

I knew there would be blackness. I've heard Mance talk about this experience in terse generalities. So I expected to be plunged into a place without light.

But I didn't know the blackness would . . . see me. I didn't know that it wasn't empty.

And I've *never* been seen like this. Since the day Prime Merod took my parents, my life has been a series of facades, and I don't know that I've really shown my full self to anyone. Only parts of me, different masks.

Like Mance has, I suppose.

But this darkness sees it all.

Every part, every memory, every thought.

I want to hide, but there isn't anywhere to take cover. I want to run, but there is no escape.

I don't want to be scared, but as I feel the magic probe me, I am terrified. This magic is so much more powerful than I am. And so much darker than I know. Literally. Figuratively. In every way.

The waiting is agony.

Then all at once, the magic rushes in.

And it turns out the waiting wasn't so bad, after all.

Mance, Without Livid

Then—just before Kiar reaches me—a familiar dagger flies through the air, slicing her fingers, and blood sprays across my face. She cries out, shaking her hand and spattering even more crimson spots onto my pristine white dress.

"Get away from her," a voice screams from above me. "Or I will burn this whole city to the ground."

My stomach flips and my eyes search the trees for the speaker, but even before I find her, I already know.

Livid.

There she is, crouching in the branches like a wild creature, her hair hanging in her face and her glare piercing. Predators appearing around her, growling deep in their throats.

My stomach flips and then plummets.

Our eyes meet.

And hers look *furious*.

18
Livid

|THE DAY OF THE WEDDING|

I am offended by the shock on Mance's face. Did she forget about me entirely?

Well, I'm still here.

I kick over a lantern and it careens to the ground, shattering on impact and igniting the dry forest floor. People cry out and run into their houses, coming back out with water or blankets to use to suffocate the blaze.

But I'm not nearly done yet.

I leap from the trees, the wolf and my larger cats springing after me, fangs bared. I summon the grizzly into the middle of the square and watch it roar.

Meanwhile, from my hips I draw two bottled explosions.

"Don't!" Mance cries, but I'm all done listening to her.

I uncork them both simultaneously with my thumbs and chuck them at each side of the clearing, the coal-black substance hanging in the air for a moment, suspended just before the point of destruction.

Now the onlookers scatter, climbing, swinging, jumping, running away from what I've just dropped in front of them.

And then it all explodes.

I'm not afraid of death. I've been watching, and it sounds like if I die I'll just go back into Mance anyway. And then she'd have to understand what she's put me through the last few months. There are worse outcomes.

So I throw myself down into the square with reckless abandon, getting burned by hot orange flames and cold black ones alike. I don't care about the pain. I barely even feel it.

Reltas is hauling Mance and the white-haired girl to the back of the square, but I drop in front of them.

"I *said* let her go."

To my surprise, he gives me a smirk, his poison-green eyes flashing. "Nice to see you again."

"Wish I could say the same," I sneer, making a swipe at him with my knife.

"Don't touch him!" Kiar cries. She lashes out with her own knife. I dodge, but a bright red slash blooms on my cheek where Kiar caught me with the edge of her blade. I bare my teeth at her in a grin, even as I feel the blood soak my lips.

"Stop it, both of you!" Mance cries.

"No. We're doing this *my* way now." I press my last bottled explosion to Reltas's forehead, thumb on the cork, ready to flick it away, and everyone in our little circle freezes. Around us, the citizens are still scattering, and the black and orange flames continue to rage, but their eyes are only on me.

Finally.

"If you uncork that bottle, you'll kill yourself, too," Reltas says calmly.

I only shrug and dig my nail deeper into the cork, easing it out.

"No, *please.*" Something vulnerable flashes across Kiar's face. Something that changes it completely.

Good.

My glare turns to her. "Tell me where you sent Silver in that wagon and I'll let you both leave."

Her face flushes, but Reltas and—infuriatingly—Mance only look confused.

"Silver left because he couldn't bear to see me marry someone else," Mance says, in the tone of a person trying to calm a wild animal. "Kiar had nothing to do with it."

I curl my lip at her. "As usual, you don't seem to have any idea what's really going on."

"Kiar?" Reltas asks.

Her expression hardens. "He knew too much. I took care of him."

I press the glass into Reltas's forehead. "What does that *mean*?"

Her eyes are defensive, but her voice is steely. "I sent him into the Citadel."

"What?!" Mance looks horrified by this news. Sick.

But it is nothing compared to how I feel.

With a scream, I fling the explosion at Kiar instead, and it shatters on her forehead. Inky magic blooms around her face as her expression resolves into one of dawning horror.

Then many things happen at once.

In the seconds before the magic ignites, Reltas cries out, throwing himself at Kiar to push her backward and out of the range of the blast.

Mance grabs me, yanking me away and hissing in my ear. "This—*this*—is exactly why I locked you up. You're a *monster!*"

Then the second blast goes off and we are flung backward, Reltas and Kiar on the other side of the explosion.

We slam into a tree, but somehow Mance maintains a death

grip on my arm. I rip it away savagely, snarling at her. "I'm a monster? You haven't seen *anything* yet."

She coughs, dirt on her face and ash on her dress. She puts her head in her hands, her nails digging into her own face. "What do I have to do to make you stop all of this?" she moans.

"Try *listening*," I snap.

She whips her hands aside and fixes me with a glare I'm almost proud of. "There's nothing you have to say that's worth listening to! You're just thoughtless rage!"

A burning branch falls between us, crashing to the ground and sending sparks flying. Some of them singe me. I've lost count of how many parts of me hurt.

I look at her through the crackling flames and decide it's time for me to take my leave. The wedding is off, like I wanted. I got my answers about Silver, and now I need to find him. To fight for him the way Mance will not.

But I can't help making one more comment before I go.

"You know," I say. "Father never listened to me either. You're a lot more like him than you realize."

I have just enough time to take in her stricken expression before I kick the branch toward her and run, blending into the burning forest like I'm just another flame.

Leaving nothing but chaos and destruction in my wake.

19
Silver

|???|

After who knows how long, I finally stumble out of the Broken Citadel and back into the hot desert.

I feel different. I feel... raw. Like every inch of my skin and every single nerve in my body have been rubbed with sandpaper.

But I stare down at myself and I don't *look* different. At least, not that I can see. There will be no way to know if my eyes have changed color or my face has any new markings until I can get ahold of a mirror.

At least I'm alive, I suppose.

The sky is still a clear blue, which means that perhaps I've only been in there a matter of minutes. But for all I know it could have been days.

As I stagger forward, my legs feeling somehow heavier than usual, I scan the area.

The other people gathered around the Citadel drop what they're doing and eye me warily, and their conversations turn to hushed murmurings. Most likely, they're wondering what I'll do now that I no longer have vines in my eyes. Or perhaps their caution is because they don't know what manner of magic I might have come out with.

For that matter, neither do I.

I stop in place, the Citadel at my back, the magic tingling where it hits my skin in a way that it didn't before.

Until this very moment, I haven't spent much time considering what I should hope for. "Live through it" pretty much topped the list, but now that I've done that, I'm not sure what else I want to have happen.

I could be one of the ones who comes out with no power at all. Like some of the less-talked-about sons in the Jungle Realm. Like Mara was thought to be at first.

That would be a relief, right? The powers are often dark and always twisted. They weigh on their wielders. Mance sometimes speaks with longing of the way she was before. The way her father and her sister were before. It's probably best to just avoid the whole thing altogether.

But the thought of that ignites a gnawing sensation in the pit of my stomach, one I recognize. It's that familiar nagging feeling that I'm not good enough. Insufficient somehow, not meant for anything important. It tells me that if I came out of that ordeal with nothing then I'm really *not* worthy. Not even for the Citadel.

And I don't know how that feeling would sit with me long-term.

I swallow, dry air burning my throat, as I try to bludgeon those feelings with logic.

After all, at least that option is known. Disappointing, but in a familiar way. In a way I'm sure I can handle, because I've been handling it all my life.

If I had magic ... who knows how that would change me? Who knows if I would even still be *me* anymore?

All these thoughts flit through my mind in a matter of seconds, and then movement to my left derails them. Someone is approaching, and I whip toward him.

As I suspected, I know this man. He's the one who met the carriage just outside the gates of the Desert Realm, the one Kiar slipped something to.

Probably a seed to subdue me with when I came out.

Sure enough, I see him reach for his pocket, though he's moving slowly, watching to see what I might do.

And I realize that if I do have magic, I need to figure it out fast.

Because in mere seconds, I could be under their control again. I could become a soldier fighting mindlessly at their command.

Has Mance suffered the same fate?

Did she figure out what happened to me? Did she follow? Did they stop her? Is she hurt?

Or did she carry on without me? Is she married right now?

The fact that I don't know, that I'm not there with her, makes fear swell in my chest in a way that's almost physical. So tangible that I look down, almost expecting to see it leaking out of my skin.

And then I do.

Fear, as it turns out, looks a lot like smoke. White and wispy and insubstantial, but undeniably there, becoming more and more solid the more I stare at it. Does that mean my fear is growing?

Probably, because my hands are sweating and my heart is pounding and I'm having trouble catching a breath.

I glance around to see if anyone else is alarmed by my skin suddenly emanating smoke, but I don't see any changes in expression, and I don't hear any alarmed cries. Which means I'm likely the only one who sees me as a human chimney.

Okay.

All right.

So I do have magic, then. I can see . . . my own fear.

Is that useful? Or just creepy?

The man withdraws his hand from his pocket and my fear smoke billows larger, even though he's still sizing me up. I know I don't have long. I have to figure out a way to make this work for me. *Now.*

Wincing slightly, I poke at the smoke with one finger. To my surprise, it winds eagerly around my hand and starts to feel almost solid, like silky threads or spiderwebs. I swirl my fingers deeper into the smoke until it's wrapped tightly around my skin. And then I pull.

It doesn't hurt. It feels like bleeding, but without any cut. Just the disappearance of some substance inside me.

But as soon as it's not connected to me, it evaporates into thin air, and my actual subjective experience of fear evaporates with it.

My breaths come easier, my heart slows down, and the tension I didn't even realize I was carrying in my back releases.

More importantly, the Citadel behind me doesn't seem to loom so large anymore. And the people flanking me, my enemies, don't feel like such a threat. They're just people, after all. Even the one slowly approaching me with a seed clutched in his hand, gaining confidence now that it's been several seconds without me showing any visible sign of violent powers.

As he gets closer, I feel something like a furnace in his chest. Actually, now that I'm focusing, I can feel a furnace in everyone's chest, every single Forest Realm citizen staring me down. Most of them aren't burning too brightly now. The embers dim the more time passes without me fighting back.

But instinctively, like the magic wants me to use it, I suddenly realize that I can change that. I could stoke their fires if I wanted to.

I fling my hand wide and the man in front of me stops in place, wary of what I might do. His fire burns a little brighter without my assistance.

With a flick of my fingers, I stoke it, and a heightened unease makes his eyes narrow and his mouth thin into a line. I experiment for a moment with increasing and decreasing his fear in small increments until I know I can control it. Until I have a handle on how much I can pull and how fast. Once I have that nailed down...

I clench my fists and I engulf him.

In fact...

I engulf everyone.

All around me, men and women fall to their knees, eyes wide with terror, skittering backward. Some cry, some shake, some cower, and some make a run for it. To my eyes, their bodies are billowing smoke like they're burning from within. Not a single one tries to come after me, too consumed by their terror.

A slow smile spreads across my face as I feel their fear wash over me like waves of heat.

Yeah.

I think I can work with this.

20
Mance, Without Livid

I don't bother running after Livid. The damage is already done anyway. As I stand in the midst of the burning wreckage of my own wedding, I can't help but feel shock that there's some part of me that could do *this*. In the corner of my mind, Alect's memories flare, filling me with his own discoveries of what his different parts were capable of doing. For a minute, my horror and despair blend with his in a potent cocktail that transcends time.

Then a hand grabs my shoulder and I whip around to see Reltas.

"Survived the blast, did you?" I say grimly. "Good work."

He shoves me back, though not hard. "I have to respect the effort," he quips back. "Burning my whole realm to the ground just to get out of marrying me? It's impressive."

I sigh. "Livid is . . . not exactly under my control."

It's an odd thing to say, but as before, Reltas accepts my explanation as though it makes perfect sense. He nods distantly, straightening his sleeves, possibly because the wounds underneath are bothering him again. "In that case," he says, "should we continue? After all, I'm pretty sure all this counts as a violation of the Treaty. Not only did you break the agreement your father made, but you've also attacked my people. I'd be willing to overlook it, though. If you'd just come back to the altar. I don't actually mind committing to each other in the middle of a raging inferno. Seems . . . thematic somehow."

I turn to him, taking in his messy hair and singed waistcoat. The dirt on his cheek. "Where *is* my father, Reltas?" I ask, in a tone that is almost accusation. "You keep saying he won't see me, and maybe he's so angry with me for locking him up that he didn't bother coming to the wedding either. It's possible. But I know Silver was looking for him. And now he's gone." I swallow around the word, and it feels like shards in my throat. "Kiar said it was because he knew too much. So what exactly did he find out?"

I'm trying hard to keep the desperation out of my voice. Trying not to think about the boy I love forced into the Broken Citadel and everything it means. But the idea of him in that awful blackness tears a hole through my heart. I don't want to find out how it will twist him. Don't want to wonder if I'll even know him when I see him next.

If I see him next.

Reltas's expression shifts slightly in response to my question, but it's enough.

"So my father's dead," I say. "Isn't he? I don't have to marry you at all."

He exhales, a long and exhausted sound that would move me to compassion if we were different people in a different situation. "I didn't mean for it to happen, if it's any consolation," he says. "But when my citizens got going, I couldn't stop them. They had so much rage. We *all* have so much . . ."

Wood crackles around us from the burning of my own rage, and there's a part of me that understands. But there's also a lot of me that doesn't.

I feel numb.

I feel *sad*.

Not because I lost my father, but because I lost the potential to ever have any kind of redemption in our relationship. Now it will always only be what it was. A struggle for power. Control instead of love. Painful memories and scarred hands.

"Well," Reltas says. "I had hoped it wouldn't come to this. But I suppose it's where we are now."

He draws the sword from his waistband and plunges it into the ground next to me. It's similar in shape to our Victory's Herald, but with a pommel of twisted, polished wood instead of stone. I don't have to ask what it is or what it means. I understand fully that he's just made a formal declaration of war. The only thing I need to ask is, "*Why?!*"

He shrugs stiffly. "So you didn't break your father's agreement. But all this"—he waves his hands around at the burning wreckage—"can still easily be considered an act of war. So I'm within my rights."

"Yes, but . . . But *why*, Reltas?"

His eyes grow cold. "Because my people need justice," he says. "And they're not satisfied yet." He snaps his fingers and a small but not inconsequential squadron of soldiers emerges from the smoke and flame behind him.

Alarm bells ring in my mind, but as I start to split, hoping to get myself far away quickly, Reltas flings a lengthy chain necklace around me, and my attempt to teleport through it only creates a jarring sensation that has me holding my head.

"Where did you get one of Mara's necklaces?" I ask through gritted teeth. We aren't exactly handing them out.

"Your father's cell," he says casually. "I thought it might be useful later, so I pried it off when I freed him. I had a hunch I might need it today."

The forest lurches, but at least the throbbing in my head starts to subside after a few calming breaths. "All right," I say finally, lowering my hand. "So you've got me. Now what are you going to do? Kill me? Do you hate me that much?"

"I don't hate you," he says softly, like a confession. "I tried to, and I couldn't. But that doesn't mean I can stop all this. We've come too far to . . ." He shakes his head sharply, as though physically flinging away the thought, and his voice hardens. "I'm thinking hostage. I've had a recent vacancy in my prisons."

His flippancy makes me sick. Mere minutes ago, I thought I'd reached my lowest point. At the altar. But that was before this threat of imprisonment, this declaration of war. Before I knew about my father.

About *Silver*.

Suddenly it's all too much, and I open my mouth, not even fully knowing myself what I'm about to say.

And then something forceful rolls through my body, snatching the words from my throat.

At first I think it's another wave of nausea. But, no, this is different. This . . . doesn't make any sense.

In the wake of it, my entire chest is gripped with a terror that I have never felt before, not even when I was dying. Not even when I killed. But the feeling has no logical root, it's just surging senselessly within me, aimed at nothing.

Somehow, the baselessness of it frightens me even more, and I find myself on the ground, cowering against the border of Mara's necklace. This one must be made from blood, because I feel the smooth, congealed moisture of it against my face, and it only stokes my fear hotter and hotter until I feel like I might explode. A whimper escapes my lips, and I'm trembling violently, my mind shutting down completely in the face of such all-consuming, irrational panic.

I don't realize at first that everyone else is on the ground, too.

Not until the fear twists like a snake in my belly and everyone starts running.

I try to run also, but there's no escape for me. I claw at the invisible blood that circles me, but it won't give. It only leaves me feeling slimy and repulsed.

And so, so scared.

The more I feel the fear, the more my mind provides reasons for it. I've failed everyone. Hundreds will die because of me. I'm no better than my father. I might even be worse, because at least he made all his bloodshed useful. But me, I'm only a victim. Unable to save myself or anyone else. All I amount to in the end is fodder for someone else's plans. Again.

Livid is still on the loose.

The boy I love is in the Citadel.

Everything is falling apart.

The sense of doom and helplessness consumes me, and I start to cry. Cold, harsh sobs of pure terror. It's *awful*.

Then a man appears in front of me, arms stretched out to the sides. It doesn't take me long to realize that this person is the cause of my torment.

The thing that's harder to wrap my mind around is that the person in front of me, the person putting me through all this . . . is Silver.

21
Silver

I've never felt so powerful in my life.

In the middle of the chaos I created at the Broken Citadel, I enlisted the man making spectral doors to create one that opened into the Forest Realm.

And by enlisted, I mean that I made him so afraid of me that he had no other choice but to comply. Trembling, he cut a glowing rectangle into the sand, and when I stuck a hand into the dark void that opened up, I felt the scratchy needles of fir trees. So I jumped, and the magic carried me, and it felt like riding the wind itself. It was exhilarating.

I mean, not at first. At first it was terrifying, and my own skin started to bleed fear like mist, there in that shadow tunnel of incorporeal magic. But I pulled the wisps out of my chest and I let them slip away from me, and all that was left was sheer joy and jagged exhilaration.

Until I landed in a burning city. More fear billowed in my chest, and I ripped it out, too, even more viciously this time. Because I had to focus.

I had to find her.

Fortunately, it didn't take long. And I had the power to drop down in the middle of the conflict and make our enemies scatter.

I saw the whites of Reltas's eyes before he fled in panic.

I heard Kiar cry out in terror, the handful of seeds she'd been clutching falling to the ground from limp fingers.

And then there was nothing left but an empty square, because everyone had run before *my* awesome power, leaving only the fading wisps of their fear behind them.

With a grin, I look back at Mance.

Only to find her contorted into a ball, scrunched up against the boundary of Mara's necklace, gasping and whimpering, her eyes flung wide with panic.

I swear, rushing toward her, trying to apologize, unclasp the necklace, and pull away her fear all at once. Doing a clumsy job of all three.

For a brief moment, I wonder how my magic even got through Mara's barrier, but then the clasp gives and I'm focused entirely on coaxing the smoke from her body, letting it dissipate into the air. When the last of it is gone, I pull her into my lap and she moans.

Then she pushes away from me and throws up in the dirt.

"Sorry," I say again, gently gathering her hair away from her face and holding it back for her as she lurches and vomits a second time. "Sorry, sorry, sorry. I'm still figuring out range and control. That won't happen again, I swear."

She looks up at me, face pale, eyes direct and probing. "So it's true," she says, voice wavering. "You really went into the Citadel."

I tense. "Kiar forced me to," I tell her, weirdly defensive. "She has seeds that can control your body if she plants them under your skin."

She accepts this without question, a testament to how bizarre things have gotten in the last few days, but her eyes are raking my face. "Are you... okay, though?" She puts a hand up to my cheek but stops just short of touching me, as though afraid I'll dissolve on contact.

I lean into her hand, pressing my skin against her fingers. "I'm okay," I tell her.

She blows out a breath, though her expression is still conflicted. Then she throws herself back into my arms and I gather her against my chest. I'm probably squeezing too hard, but she lets me, burying her face in the crook of my neck. Her breath feathers against my throat, harsh at first, but as she gradually relaxes against me, it evens out, and it's only then that the tension starts to leak out of my own body as well.

"Why would Kiar do that, though?" Mance mumbles against my throat. "Send you to the Citadel, I mean. It seems like a huge risk and I can't understand what she thought she had to gain."

I grimace into her hair. "Well, her first plan was to kill me. This was a fallback."

Mance nods again, this time brushing against my jaw, and I swallow before hurriedly filling her in on the rest. The growing magical army. The plot to enlist Cliff Realm citizens to make the army even larger. How Reltas's marriage to Mance would give him the power to do it.

When I get to that point, I falter. "Speaking of which... You're not, uh..." I clear my throat. "... already married, are you?" I try to make the question sound casual, but my heart is beating out of my chest. Reflexively, my arms tighten around her.

To my relief, though, she shakes her head right away. "The wedding kinda went up in smoke," she tells me.

"*That's* what this is?" I ask, looking around at the wreckage.

Now that I've scattered all the people who were trying to put out the flames, they're spreading faster, leaping from branch to branch and rooftop to rooftop at alarming speed. "Who started the fire?"

She stills, seemingly unwilling to answer. I bring my gaze back to her face just in time to see something almost imperceptible close off behind her eyes. Then she merely says, "I need to go."

I shake my head. ". . . What?"

She extricates herself from me, and hot, dry air fills the space she just left. "I need to go," she repeats. "Now. Reltas may not care about the myriad ways in which he's flagrantly breaching the Treaty, but the other realms *will*. They may not have offered me support when it was just about my marriage, but a plot like this will be enough to force them to act. This is good. Or, well, not exactly good. But manageable. We can manage this."

"By starting the very continental war you've been trying to prevent this whole time?"

"He's initiated the war already, and it sounds like continental conflict is impending even if I do nothing. But I can get ahead of it. We can control it. Contain it. I have to get back to the Cliff Realm and get a plan together."

She makes like she's about to leave right then, but I grab her arm. "Hold on!"

She only speaks faster. "I don't have *time* to hold on, Silver; time is of the essence. Once he's regrouped from the fear you struck in him, he'll make his own move. We have to act first."

"Just tell me why you don't want to answer my question," I push, because that look in her eyes is still bothering me. "What aren't you telling me? Who started the fire?"

She goes silent, clearly weighing something. Her lips press into a thin line and she stares at me as though willing me to just drop it. She even tries to pull her hand away from me, but I hold on tighter, waiting. Finally, she drops her head. "It was . . . another part of me," she says, voice small.

The words hang in the air between us for a moment, confusing and absurd. And then, suddenly, they hit me square in the chest.

Mance burned down the town square? People's homes and livelihoods? That makes no sense. I can't see any of the parts of Mance that I know doing something like that. Which means . . .

I flex the hand at my side, trying to keep my voice level. "Why haven't I met this part?" I ask.

"We didn't want you to." Again, she speaks distantly, as though she's not even present in this conversation.

I stare at her. "You *hid* her from me?"

"It was a group decision."

I grit my teeth. "And how long ago did you make this decision exactly?"

"It was . . ." She swallows. "It was actually the first one we made. Together, I mean. Can I go now? We can talk about this more later. I have things to—"

"Mance," I say firmly, as the last few months of feeling like something was missing start to take a different shape. "I want to meet her."

"No."

The response is so immediate, so decisive, that it takes me a couple seconds to process it. "*No?!*"

"As I just said, we don't want you to. Trust me. It's for the best." She puts one hand on her chest, almost compulsively, and grimaces. "Look around you. Look at what she did. She's out of control. She needs to be *contained*, not trotted out for a meet and greet."

"I don't care if she's out of control. She's still *you*. You said you wanted all the broken parts of me, why would I not want the same?"

"I said I'd take all the broken parts you're *willing to give me*," she clarifies. "I'm not willing to give you this. You can't just force me to."

My shoulders hunch. "No one is trying to . . . force you. It would be one thing if you were up-front about it, told me it was something you were struggling with and you weren't ready to share it. I could be patient if that were the case. But you *hid* her from me. We can't be in a relationship if you're deliberately hiding parts of yourself from me, Mance. It's not going to work."

Everything I'm saying is true, but there's more that I'm not saying. A desperate clawing in my throat that I'm shocked I can even speak around.

Because I hear what *she's* really saying. That she doesn't feel like she can trust me with all of herself. That I'm not worthy of it.

That even now, with all this power, I'm not enough.

"Don't say that," Mance says, her face paling and her eyes going wide. "It's not—it's not that I was trying to shut you out, I just . . . I just want to give you the parts of me that are good. The best parts!"

"I've never wanted your best, though!" I explode. "I want your all, I want your everything! I don't just want to stand next to you when it's all going great; I want to hold you when it's hard! Why won't you *let* me?"

"I—" Her face screws up like she's about to cry. "I can't, Silver! I just *can't*!"

"Then *I* can't!" The words echo around us, bigger than I meant them to be.

She goes still. Hazy fear leaks from her skin, making her appear to be clothed in wispy tendrils of smoke. "You don't mean...," she whispers, and even more smoke spills from her mouth.

I expect fear to leak from my own skin as well, but it's not coming. I must have pulled at it too hard.

And honestly, I can't seem to bring myself to care. What has fear ever done but get in the way? If she doesn't want me, then that's fine. I don't need her. All she does is make me feel like I'm not good enough, and I've had plenty of people in my life making me feel that way as it is.

"I do mean it," I say harshly.

Her face crumples, like I've slapped her. Then her desperate eyes go distant and she splits, flinging herself as far away from me as she can.

In another second, she's gone.

Leaving nothing but curling smoke behind her.

22
Mance, Without Livid

I split and merge over and over and over, not even stopping to rest between, so by the time I'm back in the Cliff castle courtyard I am doubled over and gasping for breath. If there were anything left in my stomach, I'm sure it would be coming up now. My head is swimming, and everything hurts.

My heart most of all.

I struggle to rise, black spots in my vision, and stumble toward the palace, long before it all stops spinning. I don't even know where I'm going until I get there, but some need drives me. And then I am standing, panting, in front of my sister's room.

She tried to help me before. Tried to step into my mess. But she didn't know how and I didn't know how to let her and to be honest, I still don't.

Even so, a deluge of memory floods my mind. Sleeping in Mara's room for a week after we came out of the Citadel. Mara holding me while I cried over the animals I killed, their blood still on my clothes. Or, once the fights got bad enough that they ended in unconsciousness, Mara waiting by my bedside for me to wake up. My sister has always been the one who was there for me in the aftermath.

Just never during.

She wants to be, though. And maybe right now the wanting is more important than the knowing how.

So I knock.

"Come in," she replies, and I swallow again, hard, before pushing through the door.

Only to come up short.

It's been a few months since I've been in Mara's room. Last time I was here, there were full-color murals on the walls. The Citadel, in shades of orange and vibrant green. The magic on the horizon, against a cheery blue sky. Only one of the walls was painted in the color of the Citadel's core: a deep and layered black.

Now they all are. The other murals are gone, eaten up by that darkness. And not just the walls, but the ceiling, the floor, and the furniture, too. Her messy array of knickknacks. Even the sheets on her bed. Everything has been painted, dyed, or colored in black, black, black.

"What's . . . all this?" I ask.

Mara looks up from where she sits in the center of the room, her face the only point of pale color in the midst of the darkness. "It helps me think," she says, her voice oddly distant. "Something's wrong. Can you feel it?"

It takes me a minute to will myself to step over the threshold, but I do. I join her in the darkness. Then I sit down facing her, right at its center. "Yes," I say. "Only it isn't something. It's *everything*."

At my words, or perhaps my tone, she seems to come out of whatever stupor she was in and focus. Her one eye fixes on me, and when she speaks her voice is sharp. "Are you hurt?"

"Not physically."

"Are you married?"

"Fortunately, no."

"Then what is it?"

My lip quivers, some part of me still wanting to hold it all inside. To keep my chin up and pretend it's all perfect. But it's not. I'm not. And when she puts a careful hand on my knee, it all comes out at once.

"Father's dead," I start. Mara stiffens but doesn't speak, and I'm talking again before she has a chance to. I fill her in on how the Forest Realm has declared war, how my relations with every other realm have worsened in the last week. How Silver broke up with me, in the middle of a raging inferno that *I* started. "I'm failing, Mara. At *everything*. I'm trying so hard and I care so much and I only ever seem to make it all worse. Because the only example I have to follow is Father's and I don't want to be like him, but I don't have a clue how to be anything else. I don't know how to be a leader. I don't know how to make the other Primes understand. I don't even know how to have a normal relationship. I mean, I *love* Silver, but no matter how I try to show it, somehow he always ends up hurt. How can I be so bad at every single thing I do?" My voice cracks on the last word. Tears are dripping down my chin, and I swipe at them harshly.

And now that it's all out there, the silence that follows is heavy. The black walls feel like they're pressing in.

Mara's hand is still on my knee, but she doesn't move to hug me. She doesn't murmur placating assurances. Instead, she studies me, and it makes me feel as though she's about to render a judgment. The longer the silence stretches, the tenser I get.

"Failure," she says finally, "is one of the things Father never taught us how to do. I'm learning how to sit with it as well. And it's . . . hard."

I blink at her. "Do you fail?"

She barks out a startled and unladylike laugh. "Me? How can you even ask that? You're only doing any of the things you're doing because I *passed* on ruling, remember? At least you're out there *trying* to fix things. Meanwhile, I'm such a failure that I let my little sister take my rightful place on the throne because I legitimately couldn't be bothered."

I sniff, surprised. I'd never really thought about it like that. It felt right for me to take the throne when I did because it was the result of my own personal battle, but I didn't spend a lot of time thinking about how it really should have been hers. She seemed fine with it then, and so it didn't occur to me to wonder whether her feelings about it ever got more complicated.

We sit in that knowledge together for a moment. The fact that neither of us really knows what we're doing, no matter how we pretend.

"So how do you . . . handle that?" I ask finally.

"Not always well," she admits. "But I try not to focus on what's been done and turn my attention instead to the things I might still be able to make a difference in. Like . . . the magic."

I shake my head, not following. "The magic?"

"Yes." She fingers the floorboards, all covered in black paint, and when she raises her hand again, the skin is stained. I realize suddenly that the paint on the floors is fresh, which means it's all over my shoes, all over my dress. I shift and, sure enough, the silk now looks shadowed. "The magic is changing. Have you noticed it? It's gotten so much . . . darker."

I suck in a breath. Because as soon as she says it, I realize that I *have* noticed, I just chalked it up to other things. But splitting and merging has started to hurt more and more. Alect's memories have begun to seal off. My animals suddenly sprouted wounds that they never used to have. Heart's bruises won't fade.

There are even signs in the others. Mara's necklace didn't keep out Silver's magic the way it was supposed to. Azele's power is developing beyond her control. And Reltas seems closer and closer to giving in to the hands that want to pull him under.

"But why?" I wonder aloud. "Why would it change on us after all this time?"

"Why does darkness ever get worse?" she asks. Her gaze goes distant again. Absently, she runs her fingers across her lips, leaving sooty streaks behind. "Because someone is feeding it."

23
Silver

The trudge back to the Cliff Realm takes most of the rest of the day. Mance probably made it in minutes. I hate that even if she had wanted to take me, I would have slowed her down.

My fear is gone, but a sadness still festers in my chest when I think about all I've lost in the last day. If only I could rid myself of it, like I can my fear. In this moment, if I had the option, I would pluck up every negative feeling that swarms in my chest and crush them all, one by one, like bugs beneath my heel.

But I guess the magic doesn't work that way.

It's not until I get to the Outskirts that I remember I don't really have anywhere to spend the night. I've been staying in the Forest Realm since this area turned into even more of a wasteland than it was before. My newly reconstructed home is sunken half into the mud, dirty, broken, and uninhabitable.

I skirt around the edge, painstakingly avoiding the newly dug graves, heading into town instead.

I don't want to go back to the palace. How pathetic would that be? She'd let me in, but right now, I'd rather sleep in the gutter than show up bedraggled at her door. It's not like it would be the first time I've spent the night on cobblestones.

I do have one friend left in town, though, and my feet know the way before my brain even registers the decision. When I look up, I'm right in front of Vie's apartment. So I climb the rickety stairs to the back entrance.

Her place is a glorified attic space, crammed above a pub. Probably one of the ones she fights in. But it's hers, which means it isn't Mance's, and that's pretty much everything I'm looking for in a living space right now.

At my knock, the door whips open then slams shut again, and to my surprise, a dagger comes flying toward my face. I duck reflexively, just in time for the knife to sail over my head and stick in the wall behind me.

"What was that for?" I demand.

The door creaks open, slower this time, and Vie appears in the crack, giving me a flat and unimpressed stare. "You didn't use the friends' knock," she scolds.

I roll my eyes. "You only told it to me one time, months ago."

"And whose fault is it that you never once visited me in all those months?"

I duck my head, chagrined. "Sorry. What is it?"

She taps a rhythm onto the wood, two short, one long, and then two short again.

"Got it," I say. "Can I come in?"

"Uh..." She looks over her shoulder and has a hushed conversation with someone I can't see. My shoulders tense. But then she swings the door wide and it's Rooftop, sitting at her dinner table. My tension evaporates. "Sure," she says, somewhat unnecessarily, because I'm already halfway inside.

"Did she throw a knife at you?" Rooftop asks as I settle beside him.

"Yeah," I say. "You too?"

"Of course not; I used the knock."

Vie sits in the third chair and we all stare at one another, the silence stretching.

I don't know why this is awkward.

We've sat around a table together many, many times before. Most nights that I can remember, in fact. Is it my fault? Have I spent so much time wrapped up in Mance and her problems that I started neglecting my own friends?

"Rooftop and I are seeing each other," Vie blurts out.

Or it could be that.

Rooftop's face erupts in a blush, and despite the brashness of her tone, Vie is avoiding my eyes.

"What?!" I ask finally. "Since when?"

"Since he got a fancy new job and the ability to ply me with sweets whenever I want," Vie answers quickly. "It's purely transactional."

"Shut up, Vie; you like me."

"I do not," she mumbles into her hand.

"Wow," I say, unable to think of anything else to fill the silence. "Wow. Okay. Uh, congrats."

"Try not to pull a muscle jumping up and down in excitement," Vie says dryly.

I shake my head, trying to get rid of the fog that's keeping me from being present. "I'm sorry," I say. "I'm just surprised. I am very happy for you both." And I am! But I also suddenly feel like a third wheel, and among the people I've come to view as family. It stings a little bit. "Why didn't you tell me?"

"Rooftop wanted to," Vie admits. "But you know I'm not so good with the feelings. I made him jump through a lot of hoops before I was willing to call this what it is."

"Why tonight, then?"

She gives me a look. "Because you're in my house and you look like you're not here for a short visit, and I kept thinking about how I would have to not kiss Rooftop for however long you were staying and that didn't sound fun at all."

Rooftop's blush gets even deeper, but his mouth twists to the side in a lopsided smile.

"So the expressing-your-feelings thing ... It's getting better, huh?" I ask wryly.

"I'm working on it. So am I wrong about you staying the night, or do I need to get out another bedroll?"

I hang my head. "No, you're right. There's a lot I need to tell you guys."

Vie gets out some kind of sourdough molasses bread and we chat, tearing off pieces and passing the loaf back and forth. The bread is much more decadent than our traditional fare, probably something left over from dinner at the castle, but the action at least is familiar, and I start to relax, the weight on my shoulders gradually easing. I can even ignore the way Vie and Rooftop hold hands under the table, because they're talking to me like they always have, and whatever awkwardness there was when I came in fades away. Rooftop is sympathetic and comforting. Vie makes sarcastic comments about how she told me the relationship was doomed anyway and how it's simply *awful* that I have godlike magic powers now. By the time I crawl into Vie's spare bedroll, hard floor at my back like old times, I feel considerably better.

But I should have known not to get too comfortable.

Because, as they say, every magic has a dark side.

I don't find out what mine is until the sun sets.

24

Mance, Without Heart, Asset, Poise, and Livid

I stay up all night. Between Reltas's plans for domination and the knowledge that his actions at the Citadel have been corrupting the magic for everyone, I have two solid reasons for every single realm to join me in declaring war. I split and send each part of myself to a different realm, all at once, and then I even drag myself to the last one so that no realm is left uncovered. We meet back in the war room at dawn.

It's beyond excruciating to merge all of us back at once. It's so clear now that the magic is worsening, because every split and merge feels like being ripped apart and smashed back together, and that pain goes deeper and lingers longer than it ever did before. Unsure if I can stomach the merges one after another, I elect to do them all at once and end up flat on my back, the room spinning around me as I scream hoarsely through the pain.

But when it all settles and I catch my breath, a slow smile spreads across my face, even through the ache that still sears across my skin.

Because every single realm said yes. They're all coming. They will *all* take my side.

Shakily, I haul myself up and approach the Victory's Herald where it now hangs on the wall, intending to do something silly and symbolic, like hoist it into the air in triumph.

But as I reach for it, I falter.

I remember stealing this sword, months ago, with Silver. I try not to dwell on the secrets we shared that night, or the way he reached for my hand, because those memories only bring on a fresh wave of anguish. But I do let myself linger on how desperate I was to avoid bloodshed back then. The efforts I put into keeping my father from doing exactly what I'm doing now.

After everything . . . is a war between all the realms really how we end this?

I understand that it's a just and necessary one, that we are trying to prevent atrocities. But when I look out the window at the walls that surround my castle, all I can think about is standing in front of them and making vows to my realm when I took this crown. I told them that I would seek peace for them.

Yet here I am leading the whole Continent into war only three months into my reign.

Was my father right?

Is it all just inevitable?

I wrap my fingers around the hilt of the sword and lift it, feeling its weight. Through the window, the first tendrils of the sunrise gasp for life on the horizon, grim and wan. They pale next to the vividness of the green magic that looms above them, and my heart sinks as I watch that sickening light rally against the pale morning.

It's getting bigger. I can see that now. The magic has stretched farther, reached higher, than it ever has before. It even looks deeper. Darker.

Insurmountable.

I sit with that for a minute.

But only for a minute. Because if I go too far down that train of thought, I'll end up gasping for breath on the floor again, and I don't have time for that.

So I sheathe the sword at my waist and stride out of the room, tucking all my negative feelings away. The ones about the war, the ones about the breakup, all of it.

I'll do what I have to do.

Like I always have.

25
Silver

The sun disappears behind the horizon, and it starts as a whisper. Fears tickling the back of my mind.

You'll never be good enough.

No one really likes you.

Happiness is for other people, not for you.

At first, I don't think there's anything weird about it.

The whispers are something I'm used to, and a lot has happened today to trigger them. The Citadel, the breakup, the fact that my two best friends seem to be a unit without me now.

I try to pull the fear out of my chest, just like I've done a few times now.

But my magic fails me.

And then other thoughts start leaking in, ones that don't belong to me.

The Forest Realm will never be what it was.

If they find out how much my leg hurts, they won't let me fight.

With all this violence, we're going to lose the baby.

I have enough time to be confused, and the briefest of moments to be alarmed, to realize that there's something foreign in my own mind and to feel a violent revulsion at the very idea of that.

And then, an onslaught.

Fear, so potent that I can feel it in my bones, like being hit with a sledgehammer.

"Silver?"

I'm on my knees. I might be screaming. I don't know who spoke.

"What do we do? Silver, what do we do? What's going on?"

I'm not even sure if their voices are outside my own head. There are so many. Thoughts, feelings, images, sensations, all revolving around fear.

The fears that *I* stoked today. This is what I made all those people feel.

My breaths are rasping. My eyes are bulging. My entire body is shaking. I can't tell if I'm screaming or crying. Maybe both. My pulse is racing and my jaw is clenched so tight it feels like it might shatter.

But worse than the physical sensations are the terrifying scenarios that I live, all at once. The blackness of the Citadel rushing in. Water closing over my head. My spouse leaving with someone else. Beetles crawling on my tongue. The inability to find a friend. An explosion in the middle of my home. Blood on my hands. A slamming door. A rib cage made of twigs. On and on and on and on.

And this continues . . .

All night.

I'm pretty sure the mind isn't meant to stay in such a heightened state of fear for such a long period of time. Aside from the emotional anguish, my head is pounding, my muscles ache from the prolonged tension, and I can't stop hyperventilating. It feels like my body is shutting down around me. Or maybe that's just one of the fears I'm living, playing out so realistically that I can't differentiate it from my actual physical sensations.

I'm certain I'm dying.

I'm certain I'm dead.

The onslaught never pauses, not even for a moment.

Not until the gray light of the morning reaches over the horizon, and then, suddenly, it all disappears at once, and my mind is startlingly, blessedly empty.

There's a weightlessness to that moment. Reality takes a few seconds to catch up, the memory of the smorgasbord of anguish that I experienced still lingering, blending with the very real aches and pains of my body as the tension finally sags out of it and I slump against the floor.

Actually, the floor feels weirdly soft. I must be in a bed now. I don't remember being moved, but that doesn't surprise me.

Rooftop is dabbing something cold and wet on my face, and his eyes widen when they catch mine, the cool cloth stilling against my forehead. "Hey," he says softly. "Are you back? Is it over?" He's trying to sound casual, but I hear the catch in his voice betraying how awful the last few hours must have been for him.

I didn't experience his fears last night, but I know him well enough to know that being unable to stop the suffering of the people he cares about is one of them. I reach up and squeeze his wrist, croaking out a reassurance before my attention is pulled beyond him by the sound of something shattering.

Vie and Mance are screaming at each other, locked so deeply in an argument that they haven't noticed yet that I'm awake.

I prop myself on my elbows, taking them in.

It's jarring to see Mance here.

Not just because it's here.

Not just because we broke up.

But also because her fears were among those I lived. For the first time I felt the pressure of rule, how badly she wants to do the right thing and how scared she is that she is too broken to figure out how. There were a fair amount of fears around losing me as well. And it was odd to experience losing . . . myself.

I wonder if the different parts of Mance have different fears, or if her fears are core enough to who she is that they translate across her selves.

I blink at the Mance in front of me, trying to figure out which one she is, and my brain must still be foggy because it's taking longer than usual.

Her hair is down like Heart wears it, but instead of being breezily free-flowing, it hangs in her face and she glares through it, in a way that Heart never would. In a way that I haven't seen Mance glare in a long time. *Months.*

I sit up suddenly.

Rooftop tries to ease me back down, but I brush him off, instead getting up and shouldering my way into the middle of their argument. They both break off at the sight of me clearheaded and Mance doesn't hesitate to shove me in the chest with two open palms, making me totter backward.

"Don't scare me like that!" she berates me.

She goes to shove me again, but I catch her hands and use them to pull her closer. "It's . . . you," I say, studying her face. "You're the one Mance didn't want to tell me about."

She bares her teeth in a way that is oddly more defensive than aggressive. "They call me Livid."

I flash back to when Mance took down her father. I was in and out of consciousness, swimming through a haze of cold pain. But at one point I surfaced long enough to see Mance pulling a string of beads tight against her father's throat. Looking like she wanted to keep them there.

"Yes . . . ," I say slowly. "I remember you. Where have you *been*?"

She sneers, pulling out of my grasp and crossing her arms over her chest, rocking backward on her heels. "Mance locked me in the prison initially. I broke out about a week ago."

"*What?!*" The idea of Mance doing something so drastic to *herself* is shocking. How could she trust herself so little? "And where have you been since then?"

"Here mostly."

I turn to Vie incredulously. "*Here?*"

"What?" she asks. "She's the only part of Mancella I actually like."

"But you didn't even *tell* me?"

"Once again, it's not my fault that you never visit."

I shake my head and refuse to engage in the argument, my gaze instead drifting back to Livid, trying to place her. There's a fire in her eyes that I haven't seen in what feels like so long.

She returns my gaze in full force and I feel the breath catch in my throat. She takes a step closer to me, and for a second I sway toward her, drawn in somehow by the force of her. But then I break eye contact and take a step back, a weight settling into my chest. "You should know . . . ," I say. "Mance and I kinda ended things."

She scoffs, angry. "Which one? Did Poise think you were messing up her image? Did Asset think it was the best tactical decision? Did Heart think she was sparing you from something? Or was

Mance just too tired to put in the effort to keep you?"

Her voice is harsh and I can't help flinching at each guess, wondering how close to true each of them might be. How very nearly every single part of her could have walked away from what we had.

I open my mouth to answer her question, but she cuts me off. "I actually don't care. Because *I* didn't break up with you. I am the one who fights, Silver. And *you* are one of the things that I will always fight for."

Before I know what's happening, she crashes her lips to mine.

Adrenaline sears through me, dulling the aches and pains I felt just a moment ago and lighting me up from the inside. I try to fight it for the barest of seconds, but my willpower is shot, and I reach for her like a starving man, plunging my hands into her hair. All the passion, all the feeling I've been missing from her, is here in this kiss, and it's like waking up from a dream. There's stark, desperate emotion in her fingertips as she presses them into the sides of my face. There's yearning in the tilt of her body as she pushes closer to me. And I return it all in kind, meeting her with the same fervor, holding her so tightly against me that I can't tell where I end and she starts.

Our tongues tangle, our breath is hot, and then she whispers something against my mouth. I think it's "I've missed you."

I say it back, knowing immediately how true it is, and every inch of my skin is on fire.

When we finally break for air, I'm panting. She grins at me and leans up to kiss me again, but—with the supremest of efforts—I hold up a hand to stop her. Though my traitorous gaze lingers on her lips for another moment before I manage to wrench it away.

"We have to get you back to Mance," I tell her.

Her smile evaporates, a scowl sliding into its place. "It's not like she doesn't know we're apart, Silver. She doesn't want me, and she won't be happy to see me."

"She may not want you, but she does need you. She just doesn't realize how much."

I make for the door, but she grabs my arm, her expression suddenly desperate. Almost scared. "Can't we just... run away together? You get me in a way that she doesn't. We could be good together."

"We *are* good together," I say, putting my hand over hers. "But it's like I told Mance. I don't want just part of you. I want *all* of you. Every single bit."

Livid grimaces, but her eyes are vulnerable. "Even if she doesn't want all of herself?" she asks.

"Especially then," I tell her. "Come on."

26
Mance, Without Livid

Silver finds me on the parapets of the Lonely Tower. Despite its name, I'm only up here because it's the best view of the surrounding area.

Certainly not because Silver and I had one of our first conversations on this rooftop, one that I have been replaying in my mind so vividly that when I see Silver emerging from the door that leads to the stairwell I initially think him only an extension of the memories I've gotten lost in.

When I realize he's real, my creatures tumble over each other in a rush of emotions, embarrassment being only one of them. Seeing him now and here, so soon and in the middle of so much, is overwhelming. I want to run to him. I want to punch him. I want to cry. But instead I only clutch the chain at my throat, then regret it when his eyes follow the movement.

"You're still wearing it," he says. I can't read his tone. Is he happy? Disappointed? Judgmental? Amused?

I close my fist around the metal, as though to shield it from his view. I want to say that of *course* I'm still wearing it. That I tried to take it off, but I couldn't bear to. That it's still a testament to how I feel even if it's no longer a testament to what we are.

But as before, when I try to put into words all the tumultuous, vivid things that I feel for the boy in front of me, my throat goes dry and I can't get them out.

So finally I say, with both a sense of stubborn self-preservation and a sincere reluctance, "Listen. Now's not . . . really a great time."

He tenses and sticks his hands in his pockets but doesn't stop striding toward me. "Why's that?" he asks, voice low. Intense. Like quietly burning embers. Like the last time we were here, because we were enemies then. He didn't trust me. He didn't know me. Does he feel that way again now?

Instead of asking, I respond to his question. "Take a look," I say, turning away from him and bracing my hands against the parapet.

He comes to stand next to me, and I get goose bumps on that side of my body at the feeling of him so close and yet not holding me. At the fact that I don't know how he would react if I reached out to touch him. What I *want* is to kiss him. But I also want to run. There's even a small part of me that wants to throw him off the roof. Mostly I just want to not feel this weird.

Rubbing my arms, I force my attention to the landscape below us.

There are four armies marching into our realm at once, all on different winding roads that skim the cliffside and end at the palace gates. By some whim of chance, they are all arriving at the exact same time, each Prime bringing a modest retinue to symbolize the larger forces they are willing to contribute. I've been studying them through a small pair of binoculars, which I now pick up and pass to Silver.

Our hands brush and I flinch.

He notices but pretends not to, and I keep my gaze forward, on the Primes traversing the cliff paths.

On the far left is the Grasslands Realm, dressed in tones of gray. Ash on their cheeks.

Next over is the Jungle Realm, wearing their magical armor, iridescent as a beetle shell. They wield spears with glowing heat rocks on their tips.

The Swamp Realm has uniforms hung with rope, and I have no doubt that rope will leap to life and strangle any enemies within reach.

Finally, all the way to the right, the Coast Realm comes with its own symphony, drifting on the breeze, tense and dramatic. Even from this distance, I need to fight to resist its pull.

I'm feeling plenty tense and dramatic as it is.

"I think . . . I think maybe I want to try to talk to them," I force myself to say, hoping he'll understand that I'm making an attempt to open up more, *trying* to include him. Hoping the gesture will mean something to him. "Before any fighting starts. Maybe it's not too late for a peaceful resolution. With all this might . . . maybe we won't have to actually use it. What do you think?"

He's unnaturally still beside me, and I don't know if it's because of what I said, because of what he's looking at, or because of the enormous emotional weight that stands between us. Unbidden, my eyes burn and I have a sudden, awful fear that I'm going to start crying.

"Mance—" he says, and the word is urgent. Frightened.

I turn away from him and try to keep my voice steady, resisting the urge to wipe at my face. "Y-yes?"

He starts to answer, but a commotion at the gates draws my attention away. My head snaps in that direction and I stare, not understanding what I'm seeing.

Because the armies have reached the glass trees.

And they aren't stopping.

With a single uplifted finger, Azele turns the glass to ash, marching through the resulting flurries with a singular recklessness.

The Prime of the Jungle Realm uses the oversized heat rock on his spear, which must be blazing, to melt the trees into misshapen, glowing orange puddles.

The Prime of the Swamp Realm unleashes ropes like tentacles, bringing trees down and tipping them until they emerge from the earth, dirt-encrusted roots exposed.

The Prime of the Coast Realm's song reaches a crescendo, one loud and jarring enough to shatter the trees in her immediate vicinity to pieces.

"Wh . . . what is happening?!" I gasp.

Silver yanks on my arm, pulling me down and out of sight. I land hard, my hip throbbing. "Mance," he starts again, somehow even more frantic than before. "They have vines in their eyes. Every single one of them. Kiar got to them; she must have implanted some kind of order. And if I had a guess as to what it is?" He looks back, through the arrow notch, and whatever he sees makes his face contort with anguish. ". . . I'd say they're coming for you."

27
Silver

They're here to kill her. They won't stop until it's done. A bleak wave of horror washes over me, leaving the tips of my fingers numb.

"We need to hide you."

She leans closer, to look through the same arrow notch that I am, even as the sounds of jarring battle music and shattering glass assail us. "I'm not sure that will work," she notes, her voice weirdly distant. "I don't think any of them have seen me, but they still seem to have a pretty accurate sense of where I am."

And it's true; they're all aiming for the section of wall nearest us. I remember suddenly how well the magic knew how to get to the Citadel when I was ordered to enter it and I curse.

She turns her head toward me, hair framing her face, and her eyes are inscrutable. "Is there any way to stop them?" she asks.

There's a burning in my chest as I wish, fervently, that I could tell her yes. That I could be her hero right now and avert what's coming. But, slowly, painfully, I shake my head. "If I knew that, then I never would have gone to the Desert Realm," I say, voice grim.

Her eyes go from inscrutable to completely blank, and she turns to the arrow notch again, stoic except for a slight trembling in her hands. I glance back to see what she's seeing, only to find her courtyard flooding with soldiers rushing to engage the threat.

She surges to her feet. "Don't attack them!" she yells. "They're not in their right minds!"

"Get *down*!" I hiss, pulling her back to the floor.

She looks at me with a kind of quiet dismay. "Why? It doesn't even matter. None of this, nothing I've tried to accomplish, will end up mattering at all. The least I can do is limit casualties."

My stomach lurches at the detached tone of her voice. At the conclusion she's implying. "Don't talk like that."

"I thought you didn't want me to keep anything from you."

The bitterness that leaks into her tone makes me wince, and my hand tightens around her arm. "Fine," I say. "Talk like that. Talk however you want. Just don't give *up*, Mance. There's gotta be something we can do. *Something*."

"I just wanted peace," she says faintly. Her head thunks back against the stone and I flinch at the sound. "How could something like wishing for peace create so much bloodshed, so much lying and manipulation, so much *war*? It doesn't make sense."

Her words make me feel cold. I get to my feet and start pacing, brainstorming. "I'll increase their fear. I can make the armies flee."

"The Primes seem to be plenty afraid already and it's not stopping their actions." I look again and it's true. Their expressions range from angry to frantic, but their bodies keep moving with that stiff purposefulness that is all too familiar to me.

"Then we'll run," I say, coming to a stop and crouching in front of her.

"Forever?"

"If we have to!"

She lays a hand on my leg, and I want to rip it off, because I can feel what she's about to say before she even says it. "Maybe it's time to stop fighting, Silver."

"No!" The word resonates in my mind, but I'm not the one who spoke it.

We both whip around to see the door to the stairwell slamming open, so hard that I hear it splinter.

And in the doorway stands Livid. Fists clenched.

With all her predators behind her.

28
Livid

I stand before Mance unshackled, my animals fanning out around me, snarling and snapping. Emulating with every hair on their bodies the all-consuming rage that I feel.

She scrambles to her feet as they advance on her, making a helpless noise and pressing her back against the wall, though there is nothing but a sharp fall and a set of murder-bent Primes behind her. She glances back, as though remembering this, and then returns to the scene in front of her.

Face pale, she takes in the sharp claws and bared fangs, possibly remembering what it was like to grapple with these beasts in the arena. Slowly, deliberately, I sink into a fighting stance, the same one that we took in each and every one of those battles right before going in for the kill, and I can see from the widening of her eyes that she recognizes it.

"All right," I say. "I think it's time you and I settle this thing."

"Now?" she screeches, casting another glance at the advancing armies. "You could not *possibly* have picked a worse time."

"Oh, I'm sorry, is it not convenient?" I clench my fists. "You've had *months* to talk to me, Mance. You never tried to. So you don't get to pick an opportune moment anymore. We do this on my terms." I hold up a wrist, displaying the painted black bracelet I got from Mara's room on the way here. Making it clear that she can't call me back into her, and I can't call my animals back into me. She's gonna have to deal with all of us, right here and now.

She bites her lip, her head whipping from side to side as she braces for one of the predators to attack, flinching at every movement. "This is ludicrous," she hisses. "If you kill me, you'll kill yourself, too. I . . . think."

I open my mouth to answer, but before I can get a word out she takes advantage of an opening between the shifting creatures and makes a dash toward the stairwell.

But just as she reaches it, Silver steps in her way.

She crashes into him and he catches her around the waist, but she startles like she ran into my grizzly bear instead. "Silver!" she gasps, as though she'd only just remembered he was there. Her head whips toward me, frantic, and then she starts tugging against him, fighting his grip. "You have to run, Silver. *We* have to run. Don't you see now? Why I didn't want you to meet her? I mean *look* at her!" She slams her palms against his chest, half to underscore her statement and half in a genuine attempt to get him to move. My lip curls in a snarl.

He gently catches her wrists with one hand. "I see her, Mance. Do you?" She stops struggling, confused, so he continues softly. "This isn't the first time that she and I have met."

Mance's shoulders slump at his words. "It's not?" she asks, voice small. "Then it really *is* over between us."

I wish it didn't, but that stings.

"Actually," I snarl. "Silver isn't as horrified by me as you seem to be."

He gives her a tight grimace but then meets my gaze, his eyes burning. "Quite the opposite, actually. Livid is the one who first made me think of you as something more than a mark. I met her in the glass gardens. Remember?"

I do. Me, fighting a wisteria. Him, shattering my worldview and a glass bonsai besides. Us, making whispered promises in the moonlight.

Mance shakes her head, disbelieving, her back still to me.

Silver places a hand under her chin, raising her eyes to his. "Do you know what I think?" he asks. "I think you're not afraid of me seeing her at all. I think you're afraid of seeing her yourself. But you need to, Mance. If there's anyone who can help you now, it's her. And she's a part of you, just like any other."

"The worst part of me," she snaps, and I flinch.

Silver looks over her shoulder and then spins her, holding her against his chest. "Look," he says. "Really look."

Slowly, her brows draw together in confusion.

At first I don't know why. But then I realize that the animals around me are no longer snarling. They're hunched like I am, cowering away from the harshness of Mance's words.

As soon as I realize it, I'm embarrassed, and embarrassment turns right back into fury. My beasts rise up again, growling. But it's too late. She's seen what the fury is hiding.

"I didn't know you could be hurt," Mance says. "You're always so . . . so *angry*!" Her words are underscored by the sounds of crashing and shattering glass, getting closer. She starts to look, but I move in front of her.

"Of course I'm angry!" I explode. "I should be! Have you been paying attention? Our father was cruel to us! He made us kill animals, over and over. He made Mother into a shell of herself. He stabbed Mara in the stomach and then told her not to tell anyone about it. He slaughtered nations, started senseless wars, turned us into a weapon—"

"Yes!" Mance cuts in. "He did all that. And you just can't get over it. You dwell there, stewing, reliving it all over and over again in your mind, working yourself up. But I don't want to do that! I want to move on; I want to move *forward*! I don't want to be like Reltas, devoting my life to revenge and spreading more and more hurt just because I can't get past the hurts that were done to me!"

"So you'd rather just forget?"

"*Yes!*"

"You'd rather shove it down, shove *me* down where you can't see me anymore, just so you don't have to think about it?"

"If that's what it takes to keep myself from turning into a monster, then *yes*, I would!"

"A monster," I repeat. Around me, my beasts are not growling anymore, but their hackles are raised, their heads are lowered to the ground, and their eyes are latched onto Mance, ready to strike. "Do you know . . . what was often the worst part of dealing with our father? For me?"

She doesn't respond, her gaze on the beasts, and her hand clutching Silver's. Over her shoulder, his eyes encourage me to keep going, even as shouts echo up from below.

I pace closer. "It was that he would do all these awful things, but he would never say they were awful. He would talk in this calm and measured voice about how necessary they all were. How justifiable. He made me feel unhinged and irrational for the feelings that I had, as if they were the problem and not the things that he was doing to cause them. He never listened. *No one* listened."

"I know," Mance says. "But now—"

"Now you're doing the same thing," I tell her. "You're not listening either. You're acting like I'm just as irrational and overly emotional as he did."

Mance's mouth drops open. "N-no! It's different! I'm just trying to—"

"I don't care what you're trying to do. The result is the same. If you recall, it didn't work out well for him. Because of me. Because it didn't matter that no one else fought for me; I fought for *myself*. I carved something out for us that was safe. So if you push me down, too, then you'd better understand that I won't go quietly. If you lock me up, I will break out. And I'll come for you with a *vengeance!*"

My animals roar around me, echoing and underscoring the rage that laces every word.

Mance goes pale, but her fists tighten, and I can see that her convictions about me haven't wavered. She's probably thinking of better cages, better magic, more locks to keep me away from her. And for a second I consider taking her on. Having the fight I'm promising, right here and now.

It would feel *good*.

"But there's another way," I say, speaking just as much to myself as I am to her.

"What's that?" she asks through gritted teeth.

"Maybe if you *did* listen, maybe if you let me in again, then we could do something with all this anger. Something better than unleashing it in a blind rage. We could hone it. We could apply it.

Asset could help me use it effectively, Heart would help me to use it *kindly*. Poise will keep me from screaming and spitting in people's faces. I'm . . ." It pains me to admit it, but I press on. "I'm not meant to act alone. You say you want to move forward? I do, too! But I don't think something like forgiveness comes from just pretending the pain doesn't exist. It comes from working through it. Help me do that. And in exchange"—I stand taller—"let me help you fight. You were about to give up a minute ago. *I* am the part that won't let you. Take me back, and let's fight *together*. Aren't you tired of only fighting yourself?"

When I finish speaking, the silence is thick. Not even my predators are making a noise, and the commotion at the gates seems far away.

Mance still looks unsure.

But sometimes fighting means surrender.

So I make the first move.

I unclasp the bracelet on my wrist and let it clatter to the stone between us. Her eyes flick down to it and then back to mine.

She can call me back in now. And she may still decide to lock me up. Perhaps nothing that I've said matters.

But before she does, she'll have to live my memories. She'll have to experience all the things I've been through. And maybe, just maybe, she'll understand and she'll make a different decision.

Silver unwinds his arm from her waist, giving her the freedom to run, the freedom to choose, even as his shoulders tense.

But she doesn't flee.

She takes a step toward me, hesitates, but then takes one step more and lays a hand on my shoulder. The moment stretches long. My animals barely seem to be breathing, and the fighting below has dulled to only a background hum.

Then, finally, after months apart, she pulls me back in.

And it feels like going home.

29
Mance, Whole

It's the worst merge yet.

Months of pain and rage hit me all at once, and I am brought to my knees.

A seeming lifetime of memories, all the ones that I've tried to ignore, barrage me until I am gasping for breath. Even ones Livid wasn't involved in, like Heart's death in the Outskirts, take on new meaning and new emotion when relived through Livid's view. It's like being ripped apart and smashed together over and over until I am a completely different shape. A completely different person.

Yet, somehow, I feel more myself than I have in a long time. The pain isn't pleasant, but it's honest. Letting it in is almost like the aching relief of unclenching a fist. The stitch in your side when you finally stop running.

When I come to, I'm lying on the ground. Silver is holding me half in his lap, looking like he's doing his best to pretend he's not panicked.

"You okay?" he asks, voice hoarse.

I nod slowly and prop myself up. "I think so."

I expect him to relax at my words, but he doesn't. "Great. Well. No pressure," he says, "but the armies have breached the walls. They're almost here. I give it, like . . . I don't know, three minutes before they're on us?" He twitches, as though flinching at his own words. "You didn't happen to come up with any ideas while you were writhing on the ground in pain, did you?"

I purse my lips in thought, feeling eerily calm. Strangely... ready. "Actually, I think I did."

His face lights up in relief. "Really? Because I would absolutely love to hear it."

"Right," I say, sitting up. "I think... I am going to have to die."

His face falls immediately, and he shoots to his feet and away from me, running his hands through his hair and pacing in angry, stilted strides. "No!" he says forcefully. "That's the plan you had *before* you merged, Mance! I hated it then, and I hate it now. I can't just let you—"

"No, stop," I cut him off, grabbing him by the shoulders to halt him in place as a desperate plan comes together in my mind. "We don't have time. Just... trust me, okay? Trust me."

Silver's muscles stay tense beneath my fingers, his eyes sweeping across my face in worry. But he must see something in the intensity of my gaze that reassures him. Finally, he blows out a breath. "I... *do* trust you."

"Good." I look over the wall and swallow. "Then let's do this."

"Okay...," he says, still hesitant. "How can I help?"

I swallow again, my throat suddenly incredibly dry. "Actually, can you... Um, can you just—" My gaze drifts to the door.

Silver closes his eyes in pain and puts his forehead against mine. "Don't ask me to leave, Mance. I won't be able to stand it. *Please.*" The anguish in his voice nearly undoes me.

I lean into his touch, cupping his face and pressing the pads of my fingers into the angles of his cheekbones. "I was actually just going to ask if you could hold me through it."

He covers my hands with his, then pulls his head back, meets my eyes, and nods. "That I can do."

I get up and lock the door, one final tiny barricade for anyone who makes it that far. Then, side by side, we stand at the parapet and look out on the destruction unfolding beneath us. The glass forest is completely destroyed now: shattered, disintegrated, melted, and upturned. And the hasty fortifications my soldiers erected are, too. The Primes are in my courtyard, almost at my feet.

I steel myself.

Then I send out all four parts at once, one in front of each Prime, and I immediately feel sick and empty with them gone, knowing what I sent them to.

"Oh," Silver whispers, as he understands. "Oh, Mance..."

He wraps his arms around me and pulls me down, tucking my head into his chest. We sink against the wall until we're sitting, me between his legs and the stone at his back.

Then we brace for it.

The first to fall is Asset, and the memory slams into me, harsh enough to take my breath away.

※✻※

"You deserve this," Tibits snarls at me. "This is what comes from trying to take on someone more powerful than you. From trying to throw flowers before giants."

There's no point in arguing with him, not now. I can feel the blaze of the heat rock on his spear from here, as grass withers beneath it, a vibrant orange and then a burnt black. Sweat beads on my forehead. I wonder if there's a way to stand that will make it hurt less. Most likely, what I want is to make the event as quick as possible.

So when he thrusts his spear through my chest, I fight my body's urge to flinch away. I lean into it, into the furnace consuming me from the inside out. And it's so much hotter than I thought, so much more consuming.

So much more... terrifying.

Death just doesn't feel rational, and neither does the scream that wrenches itself out of my mouth.

✤

I gasp, clutching my chest, as Silver tightens his arms around me.

"It's okay," he whispers. "You're okay." But I can still feel the heat, even though it isn't there. I start to sweat as though it is.

And the next to fall is Poise, all too soon.

✤

I stand before my aunt, back straight and chin high, refusing to bow to the discordant notes playing around her.

"What evil have you brought to our realm?" she spits at me. "Why couldn't you have just gotten married as I advised? You could have contained all this. But instead you're displaying the whole mess for everyone to see. You should be ashamed of yourself."

"I used to think that the path you walked was easy," I muse aloud, even though I know it isn't the time for speeches. "You make it look that way. I thought I was the only one who struggled to keep smiling. Who had so much ugliness hidden behind the mask. But now I think we all have darkness, whether it's out in the open or not. You doomed my mother by marrying her to my father. Then you tried to sell me off in the same way. But I'm not going to dance to your tune any longer. I know this doesn't feel like a better choice right now . . ." I take in the destruction around me, the once-perfect trees ruined forever. "But I have hope that after pain there can be healing. And I know that will only happen if we acknowledge the pain first."

She opens her mouth, and at first I think it is to scream at me. But no, it is to hold a note. An awful, jarring note that slices through the melody around us and causes a splitting, awful pain in my head.

Blood leaks out my ears.

"I hope you find healing, too," I say.

And then everything goes searingly white.

※ ✻ ※

I clutch my head in my hands, moaning. The tower seems to swim. Silver presses a kiss to my temple, and it reminds me of my mother, kissing away my pain when I was a child.

I lean into him, comforted.

Until Livid's death slams into me next.

※ ✻ ※

"You thought hiding away in your net of ropes would protect you forever, didn't you?" I scream. "Your safety mattered most, even if it hurt others. Well, look at you now!"

Even as I speak, his ropes wind themselves around my body, pulling tight.

"I don't want to do this!" Prime Artro growls.

"But you're going to, because when it comes down to it, you can never build walls high enough to keep out every threat. And you're a coward for trying! Some fights are worth it!"

Then the ropes go taut and I can no longer form words.

I keep struggling, thrashing and straining, and it takes several minutes for unconsciousness to claim me.

To his credit, Prime Artro doesn't look away.

�֍ ✱ ֎

I cry out, almost startled to hear noise finally escaping my throat. Silver inhales sharply, rubbing slow circles on my back. He looks like he's going to be sick, but he only holds me closer.

And then it's Heart's turn.

�֍ ✱ ֎

"It's not your fault," I say as soon as I manifest.

"Mancella," Azele cries, clearly struggling with herself. "Please run!"

"It won't do any good," I tell her, shaking my head sadly.

Rift stands, as always, at her side, trying to restrain her. His gloved hands are wrapped around her long sleeves, none of their skin touching.

"At least we can find out now," I say. "Whether your touch will really kill a person."

"I don't want to learn like this!" *Tears flow down her cheeks and*

Rift flinches as though they cause him physical pain.

"I know," I tell her. "I know. But you were right. Idealism can only get us so far. Sometimes hard things are unavoidable. For what it's worth, I forgive you."

She makes a choked noise as I ease her gloves off her hands.

"Are you sure?" Rift breathes. I can only nod.

Then he releases her and with a cry of despair she presses her hands to either side of my face.

It feels a lot like splitting myself into two, but instead of every bit of me tearing apart, it all just unravels into nothingness. It hurts, but it's also quick. Like a handful of snow melting in the sunlight.

"I forgive you," I repeat, just before the awful disintegration reaches my lips.

The last thing I hear is the broken way she whispers, "No . . ."

✴

"No," I whisper, too.

My body feels incorporeal, barely stitched together. Like if I move at all, I might just crumple into ash again. My limbs lock up, and even swallowing feels terrifying. I go as still as a statue.

Silver holds me through it all, rubbing life into my limbs, coaxing warmth into my body. He's relentless in his gentleness.

And it feels so good. I don't know why I fought this so hard. Yes, I'm a mess. Yes, there are hard things I go through that he may never understand.

But there are hard things he goes through that I can't understand either.

And it doesn't mean that we can't be with each other, comfort each other, while we endure them.

Just like this.

"Is it over?" he whispers finally. "Are they all . . . back?"

I nod against his chest.

He tilts my chin up and kisses me, and I feel the depth of the kiss brushing every part of my soul. As his hands wander my skin, convincing me that I'm alive by making me *feel* it, I can sense his acceptance of every bit of me, and I lean into it, craving more of the feeling. I forget how stiff my arms are, because they're already wrapped around him. I forget the burn of the rope on my neck because he's chasing the sensation away with soft kisses along my throat that make my head spin. And I respond to his fierce care with a ferocity of my own, desperate to convey my own feelings back to him. I need him to know, through the pressure of my lips, the lack of space between our chests, the way my fingers tangle in his hair, how grateful I am that he's here. I want him to feel, through the way I curl myself around him, the way my heart is pounding, that I accept every part of him, too. That I'll never let him go again. That we are an *us*, together in anything, able to weather any storm as long as we're doing it together.

In the midst of so much pain, who knew there could be kisses like this?

In the wake of my own destruction, in the halo of devastation that surrounds us, this moment feels so good. So perfect and whole and right.

Right up until the door explodes on top of us.

30
Silver

"Cool trick," Reltas sneers, stepping through the wreckage. Half the stairwell is rubble now, and there's a sizable hole in the wall below it. Black liquid flames hover in the air around him from the bottled explosion that he threw, and Reltas weaves through them. Then he notices us on the floor, fully wrapped around each other, and scoffs. "Cute."

I struggle to my knees and tuck Mance behind me, trying not to let Reltas see the rough shape she's in. She can't take another confrontation right now.

"We beat you, Reltas," I say desperately. "The seeds are gone, Mance lives, and you're surrounded by five armies. It's over."

But he just rolls his eyes, looking annoyed. "As if this stunt was my only move. This was merely one person's power. Did you forget that I have *scores* of magic citizens at my disposal now?"

He takes out a knife and I reach for mine, but he's not coming for me. He throws it behind him, toward the wall, and it zips along the entire barrier around the castle, turning sharply at each corner, seemingly directed by its own power, before finally sinking into the side of a guard tower as easily as if the edifice were made of soft flesh instead of hard stone.

For a second nothing happens.

Then the path that the knife traveled ripples and distorts, forming a split in the air.

I swear and push Mance farther back against the crumbling half wall before a multitude of people start emerging from the slice in the air, like bugs crawling out of a corpse.

"However many of my traps you outmaneuver, I've got a hundred more ready to deploy," Reltas says, sounding bored. "Thanks for summoning all the Primes to one place for me, though. Makes the whole thing a lot easier."

Behind me, Mance goes rigid.

In the crowd of magic users, weapons are readied. One man starts giving off sparks, like human lightning, though he grits his teeth like it costs him. A young girl conjures a whirlwind in her palm, and her eyes get duller the faster it spins. There are so many different types of magic that it's impossible to follow or comprehend. All of them somehow twisted, somehow wrong.

Below us, the Primes of each realm ready their own weapons, and what is left of Mance's army by the gates does the same.

Mance struggles to her feet, bracing against the wall, but she slips and collapses back to the stone with a cry, clearly still not recovered from living through her own death four times over in the last several minutes.

I have to do something.

Now.

Because we are seconds away from the bloodiest battle since the Treaty, one that will have consequences in every single realm and will perhaps change the face of the Continent forever. If this plays out the way Reltas wants, then *every* realm will be a wasteland, as broken and abandoned as the Outskirts, or the Forest

Realm. Leaving so many survivors starving for revenge—like him.

And so many orphans like me.

I flash back to one of the first times I felt this desperate, this overwhelmed by stronger forces. When I escaped the Academy and had to make a life on the street, had to steal from the very people I was afraid of.

I learned that they had fears, too. And if I knew what they were afraid of, then they were much easier to manipulate, no matter how much more power they had.

And I realize suddenly that I know what Reltas fears.

In the deluge of nightmares, the swamp of terrors that I spent the night drowning in, I remember the ones that belonged to him.

"You're not saving them," I say. "You're ruining them. You're ruining *her*."

I don't know where Kiar is in this mass of people, but I assume she's here, and as soon as I finish my sentence, Reltas's eyes find her for me. At the look on his face, she scowls and whispers something to the man on her left. Without thinking twice about it, he raises his arms and lifts the earth, creating a jutting ridge in the middle of Mance's courtyard, which Kiar promptly strolls across, even as every step causes a painful-looking footprint to appear on the man's chest.

"Whatever he's saying about me, don't listen to him," she scowls when she reaches us. "I'm *fine*." Even so, Reltas takes a beat too long to return his gaze to me, and when he does there's an edge to it.

"You don't know what you're talking about," he snaps, stance turning protective.

I raise an eyebrow. "Don't I? Tell her to show you her stomach, then."

This time when Reltas's eyes shoot to Kiar, her face is alarmed, and she reflexively folds both arms over her abdomen. She drops them again just as quickly, but the action was a giveaway, and Reltas knows it.

"What does he mean?" he demands.

"Nothing."

"Then show me."

She raises her chin. "No."

Without another word, Reltas backs her into the wall and reaches for her shirt. She fights him, drawing her blade, but hesitates just short of actually hurting him, long enough for him to grab the hem and raise it for the briefest of seconds.

It's enough.

Enough for all of us to see that her skin has been replaced by a tangle of ivy, and her exposed rib cage is turning into branches, some of which have snapped and started oozing sap. It's even worse than it was in my nightmares, which makes sense because she's implanted at least four more people since then. There's a gaping hole where several of her vital organs should be, and it's unclear how she's even alive. The magic must be sustaining her somehow, but it won't forever. I know she feels it.

"Her power is killing her," I tell him. "And the more she uses it, the faster she dies."

He inhales sharply, eyes boring into hers. "Why didn't you tell me?" he whispers. "Why do you continue to—"

"The same reason you keep using yours," I tell him, "even

though the hands are turning on you. Even though they're trying to drag *you* down into the dirt with them, and *even though* there's a part of you that wants them to succeed. A part that is getting stronger by the day. Even though you can *feel* your magic getting more and more corrupted."

"Strictly speaking," Mance says behind me, "*everyone's* magic is getting more corrupted."

Reltas rounds on her, fists clenched. "What do you mean?"

She pulls herself up, slower this time, brushing off her skirts before approaching. "Mara's been doing some research. On the Treaty. She found out that it was never signed to keep the power limited, as we were told. No one really cared about stopping all the wars, not if they thought they might win them. It was signed because everyone noticed that the more people were put into the Citadel, the darker everything got. The more the magic was fed, the more damaging and painful it became, until everyone's godlike powers turned into debilitating weaknesses. They agreed to stop, for all of their sakes, but they also agreed to keep the real reason quiet so as not to appear weak before their citizens. And that worked for a while. Until you"—she jabs a finger at Reltas's chest—"started throwing all your citizens in by the wagonful, and it all started up again. The magic is reacting the same way as before. You've noticed, haven't you?"

Reltas's jaw is so tight it looks like it might crack.

I step forward. "You have," I answer for him. "And so have they." I gesture around at the walls, at all the people poised to fight, and I know the fears of their hearts. "Your hate and vengeance are destroying *everyone*—"

"What if I don't care?" Reltas cuts in. "You're right, it *is* getting harder and harder not to let the hands pull me under. But what if my plan was always to let them? What if I just want to make sure I take the rest of you down with me?"

He bares his teeth, but I'm not fooled. This wasn't the plan. Reltas is as scared of this happening as the rest of his realm is. I see the smoke blooming in his chest, and I know he cares about his people. But now that we're here, looking at a tidal wave ready to crash over our heads, his instinct is to open his arms and drown. It's easier that way. And it doesn't hurt his *pride*.

"I'll stop you."

I was about to say the words myself, but a quiet voice beats me to it, and I shut my mouth in shock. Because it wasn't Mance, either.

It was Kiar.

The silence after her words is charged. The promise of battle hangs in the air, all around us, ready to ignite at the slightest spark.

"*You'll* stop me?" Reltas repeats. His tone is incredulous, but his expression is hurt. Then furious. "After everything we've been through? You'd abandon me now?"

"No," she says firmly. "I will always support you. I will *always* seek your good. And I thought what you needed was revenge. I thought maybe once you had that, you'd go back to the way you were before. When we were younger. But the further we go into this plan, the less I recognize you, Reltas. I don't think you can ever go back. Now you tell me you're thinking of giving up your own life? Pushing the magic and yourself so hard that the end of all this, all that we've worked for, is just losing yourself completely? No. I won't let it happen. I would fight *anyone* who means you harm. Even if that person is you."

His eyes narrow, but Kiar meets his gaze resolutely, firm in her conviction.

"I think," Mance says quietly, after a pause, "that you, too, have parts of yourself that you've suppressed. I locked up Livid because I was afraid of my anger and hate, afraid to admit that I even felt those things at all. But I understand her now. I understand why she's part of me and why I need her. And maybe you did the opposite. You locked up your version of Heart because you were afraid it would make you weak, like you think your father was. But you need that piece of yourself just as much as I need Livid. No part should ever act in isolation, and no part should ever be completely ignored."

After one loaded breath, Kiar nods, reluctantly, like she doesn't enjoy agreeing with Mance. Or maybe like she's realizing there are parts of her she needs to listen to better as well.

"We may not get to choose the beasts that our parents—that *life* buries in our hearts," Mance continues. "But we do get to choose the beasts we raise." She unfolds her hands, and a dove appears between them, perched on her open, scarred palms. "Choose to let this vengeance go, Reltas. Not because it was right that it happened. Not because my father deserves forgiveness, or because yours didn't fail you. Choose to let it go because it is destroying you and everyone around you. And letting it do so means you are still giving it power. Take that power back, not by picking up a sword . . . but by putting one down. Be *free*." She lifts her hands and the dove takes flight, spiraling toward the sun.

Reltas watches it for a moment, but his expression doesn't soften. When he responds, it is through gritted teeth. "Free," he scoffs. "It sounds pretty. But there's no way to undo what the magic has already done. Even if I stop attacking now, if what you're saying is true, then its darkness will still destroy us all anyway. I've already poured too much into it. What do you propose that we do about *that*?" He spits the word, and his attitude is still confrontational. But there's a desperation behind the words. Perhaps even . . . hope?

"I think," Mance says, "It's going to take more than just you and me to figure that out." She turns, making her way back to the parapet, and when I see how much she's swaying, I hurry to prop her up. Spread below us, four foreign armies still wait in a wreckage of glass trees, and Mance leans heavily against me as she stands at the edge to address them.

"Primes," she calls out, and I'm proud of how strong her voice sounds, even though her hand is shaking in mine. "I formally request a counsel. There is much that we need to discuss . . . All of us."

31
Mance

Sometimes when you visit a place you haven't seen since you were a child, everything looks so much smaller than you remember it.

Not the Citadel, though.

The sky crackles with green energy above us as we approach. The magic has swelled, spreading like disease across the horizon. It's darker, too. Still that vivid, poisonous green at the top, but a deeper, shadowier green near the base, like the magic is burned or rotted. In the Citadel itself, the green is so dark that it's almost as black as what lies within. I shiver.

The other Primes walk beside me, their expressions stiff. No one is excited to be here, and tension is thick in the air. Reltas told his crowd of magic users to stand down, and they did. But they also followed us here, through that awful rift in space, and they keep looking at their Prime like his words might be a bluff. One he'll take back at any minute.

I'm not even sure they're wrong.

And even if Reltas does behave, I can't shake the feeling that one wrong move could set them all off anyway. Given the staggering array of unknown magics they possess, that would be very, very bad. We're not on the other side of this yet.

Plus, if I'm honest, I'm not sure I can count on any of the other Primes either. Their magic may be known, but that doesn't make it less dangerous. Especially considering the fact that it's *all* gotten darker in the last few weeks. It could push any one of us to our breaking point, even if we weren't in such a tense situation.

It feels like we've all been crammed into one of Prime Gore's bottled explosions, ready to go off any moment at the flick of a cork.

"So," Prime Azele asks quietly, "what now?"

I take a deep breath, steadying myself, before taking a step forward and turning to face the gathered leaders. They look back at me with varying degrees of guardedness and apprehension.

"I think this event has shown," I start, "that the Citadel's existence is more of a danger to our realms than a benefit. Perhaps it is time for a new Treaty."

"What good will that do?" Prime Artro grouses, pulling at his unkempt beard. "Prime Reltas's actions are illegal under the Treaty we already have, and it didn't stop him."

"It's true," Prime Tibits interjects, voice booming. "And we should dispense with its justice first. It is within our rights to strip Prime Reltas of power. Even to execute him."

There's a stirring in the crowd behind us and Reltas smirks. "Try it," he taunts. "See what happens."

I shoot him a "you're not helping" look.

"Perhaps if we had more truth around the purpose of the Treaty, then Reltas wouldn't have broken it. Instead of pretending it was something noble like the end of the wars, we should have been honest that it was more about our own survival. More about not losing ourselves to the darkness than it was about protecting anyone else from it. Maybe then he would have thought twice."

I'm hoping Reltas will take this opportunity to back me up, as doing so would make him look more sympathetic, but he only shrugs, like he might have done this either way.

I am beginning to regret not chaining him up.

"As the only one of us who was there when the Treaty was signed," Prime Artro pipes up again, "I can tell you that *I* never had any intent to deceive. I have been truthful about it in my own realm. What your parents and grandparents told the lot of you is not the fault of the Treaty itself."

"Then perhaps there is no Treaty that can protect us," I snap angrily. "Not even if we all vowed never to use the Citadel again. Perhaps this level of power is too great a temptation to exist at all."

"You speak as though it could be otherwise," Prime Apea says coolly, her expression as impassive as ever. "The Citadel *does* exist."

"Well, has anyone ever tried to take it down?" My words are met with a heavy pause, as though even the suggestion of it has stunned them all into silence. There are a lot of pursed lips and rolled eyes.

"Such a thing is . . . a monumental undertaking for any one person to consider," Prime Azele says gently, after a beat.

"Well, what if it wasn't just one person?" I press. "What if it was all of us? The only thing that can affect magic is other magic, right? We all know that. And, yes, the Citadel has a lot of magic. But we have a lot of magic at our disposal now, too." I gesture around at our circle, and then beyond it at the hovering crowd. "We could work together."

My words are yet again met with hesitance. Primes eye one another, give sideways glances at the restless magic users behind us. I can see that no one is going to be the first to trust. The first to believe we could all be on the same side for once.

So I'll do it.

I break off from the group and summon my predators, lingering a moment on how good it feels to have their ferocity accessible to me again. The roar of my grizzly reverberates through my body and when I summon the wolf, he comes out howling.

I look up at the Citadel, intentionally dwelling on everything that it's put me through. The way it twisted me, twisted my family, twisted the world until nothing felt safe anymore. The way I hate it. The way I fear it. The way I want it gone.

As I let my feelings for the Citadel swell within me, my animals react. They fall on the sandstone walls, claw at the wisps of magic in the air. They attack with all their strength.

It . . . doesn't seem to make much difference. The sandstone doesn't crumble, and the magic only grows brighter in response.

One of the Primes behind me scoffs, and my heart sinks. My creatures sit back on their haunches, looking dejected.

But then Azele steps up beside me, laying her hand against the walls.

She closes her eyes like she's trying to focus, and I hold my breath, waiting. When she opens her eyes again, though, her expression is disappointed, and the wall remains solid.

Even so, it's enough to inspire the other Primes to step up.

Prime Tibits hurls a heat rock spear through the open door.

Prime Apea sings a haunting battle cry.

Prime Artro summons ropes and casts them at the side of the building.

Even Prime Reltas, though he rolls his eyes, scribbles the names of some citizens from his realm who never came out of the Citadel and buries it, unleashing a couple hands to claw at the sides of the ruins that killed them.

The Citadel seems to swallow it all.

Bile rises in my throat as the attacks slow down and then stop completely, everyone breathing hard and wearing expressions that range from frustration to despair. No one looks surprised, though. Not really.

I hang my head.

"It was a cute idea," Prime Tibits says bitingly, adjusting his iridescent armor. "But hopefully you see now how foolish it was. The only thing that matters in this world is power, and the Citadel is the most powerful thing there is. Don't you see? Someone like you can never stand up to a power like this."

I glare at the sand, feeling like a child. No older than the last time I stood here, and with no better idea of how to handle the problem in front of me.

His words are enough to awaken my old fear that my father was right. That I *am* naive for thinking I can stand up to things that are so much bigger than me.

Silver comes up next to me and holds my hand. I think at first that he's just trying to give me comfort, so I squeeze his fingers without looking up at him. But then he leans over to whisper in my ear. "I have an idea, but I don't think you're going to like it."

I give him a side-eye, measuring his expression. He seems serious. Solemn. So I turn toward him. "What is it?"

"I think . . ." I can feel him weigh his words. "I think we have to go back in."

"What?!" I drop his hand, taking a step back. "I can't go back in there, Silver. I don't even like *looking* at it."

He folds his arms over his chest, regarding me quietly. "How did it go for you when you didn't want to look at or think about Livid?" he asks in a low voice.

"That's different," I protest. "She's a part of me."

"You don't think the Citadel is a part of you?"

"Of course not. It's something that happened to me. It's not *me*."

But Silver only shakes his head. "For better or for worse, you wouldn't be who you are without the experience of going through that door. Right?"

Fear coils in my heart. There is a bitter truth to his words.

"I'm not saying it won't change you again," he continues. "But it's like what you said to Reltas. The Citadel is always going to have power over you until you stop letting it. Power over *all* of us." He looks around at the others. "Every single one of them is as scared as you are. Some even more so. Probably not the ones you'd expect to be." His gaze lingers on Prime Tibits, who scowls, even though he's too far away to hear what's being said.

"You can see his fear?" I ask.

Silver nods. "And there's a lot of it."

This makes me feel better, but I'm still unsure. Attacking from the outside didn't work. It only made me look foolish. There's no real reason to think that attacking from the inside would go any differently. And there are much more serious potential consequences.

I've never heard of anyone going into the Citadel twice. Would it twist me again? Even further? Would it break me this time? Would I come out with a *third* dark magic? And if so, would the combination of the three be too much to handle?

Or would I not come out at all?

"The Citadel has fear in it, too," Silver says.

I start. "What do you mean?"

"It's not alive, so it doesn't feel things the way we do. But fear is a part of it. Part of what created it. I can *see* it, Mance. Smoke in the magic."

I look up at the Citadel in awe, futilely straining to see what he does. Then Silver turns toward me again.

"Trust me, okay?" he asks, holding out a hand. Echoing what I said on the tower.

And for all my other doubts, *that* is something I can answer without question. "I do," I say, taking his hand.

We hesitate for a minute, looking at each other and entwining our fingers. Holding on to this moment as though it is our last.

Because it might be.

Then, without any further deliberation, we approach the Broken Citadel together.

32
Silver

It's funny, looking at the Primes—with all their weapons and armor, all their magic, all the soldiers ready to die at their command—to think about how unworthy they used to make me feel.

Right now, they're all terrified.

They hide it behind different veils—brawn, perfection, gloves, and walls—but they can't hide it from me.

I'm scared, too. But I'm realizing that power doesn't lie in how well you hide that. It lies in how well you can face it, and what you're facing it for.

What we're about to do is probably the most reckless thing I've ever attempted, and I've set a pretty high bar. I know that the Citadel can change, because it's bigger and it's darker than it was even a day ago. So if it can change in one direction, then surely it can change in the other.

But do I know what to do once we plunge back into its heart? Not entirely. Do I know whether we can even survive it a second time? Not at all.

My skin buzzes with the familiar jolt of adrenaline I get before I do something ill-advised. There's a white mist rising out of my chest, and there's even more haloing Mance. I take a moment to appreciate the fact that she's feeling all that fear and she still put her hand in mine and chose to walk beside me. Her trust makes me feel unconquerable.

We explain our plan to the other Primes and they look worried at best, and disdainful at worst, but even through all of that Mance doesn't waver. And neither do I.

All too soon, we're standing in the doorway, still and solemn. We lock eyes, memorizing what it is to be with each other in this moment.

Then...

We step into the darkness together and let it envelop us.

Mance's grip tightens around my fingers and I hear her gasp, but otherwise I can't see or feel her at all. It's like she's been stripped down somehow to only a breath and a softly applied pressure on my hand.

"It's okay," I say, rubbing the back of her knuckles with my thumb. I have to assure myself that she's still there, still connected to the fingers I can't actually see.

I've only just started to believe it when the darkness rushes in.

Even though we expected it, the force of it still hits like a hurricane, pushing and pulling us from every direction. We scramble to hold on, only to be torn apart.

"No!" I cry as her grip slips. "Mance!"

If she forms any reply, I don't hear it. And I'm not sure my own words actually make it out of my mouth, either. It feels like the darkness snatches them from my throat as it rushes in to coat every bit of my insides.

Again, I get the sense that it sees me, *knows* me, more than anyone else ever has. Like I can't hide a thing from it, even those things that I hide from myself. I feel its perception of me, like eyes on every bit of my being, watching, knowing, seeing, breaking me apart for study.

Only this time, I look back.

The Citadel feels different now than it did before. It takes effort, but if I focus, I can still sense the wisps of fear that stitched the Citadel together. Even though I can't make out its color, I can feel its shape. Through the oppressive force of it, I can find pockets of insubstantial smoke.

And I can grab hold of them.

I feel my own smoke dimming. Because the darkness having any kind of shape at all makes it less scary somehow. Less like an all-consuming and terrible supernatural force and more like something tangible and real. Something that can be understood. Something I might be able to affect?

In being aware of the shape of the darkness, I also become more aware of my own body. Of the fact that it can move. And I press forward, toward where Mance was ripped from my side. I lean into the fears I sense, letting them guide me, and as I touch them I feel a misty impression of the ancient terrors that built this place.

It's almost like last night. It's more muted, but I'm still wading through so many layered fears from multiple sources that it's hard to keep my own identity straight. They are all so different and yet also somehow, at the very core, they are all so very much the same. Fear, I realize, is truly universal.

Then, with a jolt, I find Mance's fear, and it's almost like finding myself.

I've felt her fears before. I know them. So it's easy to latch on to them and let them pull me in, so much more real than anything else in this oppressive milieu.

I lean into them, living her failure, knowing her weaknesses, experiencing her regrets and worst-case scenarios. And then all of a sudden I'm holding her hand again, one single point of connection in the immutable blackness, and from that single point, sense and reason flood back in.

Mance

For a moment, I'd forgotten I wasn't alone. When the darkness overwhelmed me, it did so completely, and I was nothing but torn-apart fragments. The world was nothing but invading shadows.

And then . . . Silver found me.

The moment I feel his touch, everything else becomes grounded. I respond immediately, clawing at the air in an effort to get to him, and at the same time he's pulling me close to his chest. I smell pine smoke. I feel the familiar curve of his arms around me, and it's like finally catching a gasping breath of air after struggling underwater. I bury my face in his neck, crying into his skin, and he doesn't let me go.

Even as we cling to each other, the darkness still doesn't let up. It feels like we're in the middle of a hurricane, the force of it whipping around and through us. But we hold on. And I suddenly realize that I can see Silver as well as the darkness can. We are laid completely bare, not just before the force of the magic, but also before each other. I see him and he sees me and for all the ugliness that that intimacy reveals, it only makes us hold on tighter.

Until, at last, the magic goes still. As one, we brace ourselves for the twisting. I feel the muscles of his arms tighten at my sides, and I am holding myself so rigidly that I feel almost about to break.

But it doesn't happen this time. There is no new wrenching in my soul, although the memory of it echoes deeply.

And then the door reappears, tempting. A way out of the blackness, a way out of the fear. We don't have to linger here; we could run and never look back.

But the sunlight on the other side of the doorway shines on Silver's face, and he cups mine, and I remember that we came in here for a reason. We came to understand the dark, and to change our relationship to it. "What do you think we do now?" Silver asks. "Attack?"

"No," I say, suddenly sure. "That didn't work. It could never have worked."

"So then . . . ?"

"We need to heal."

Silver

When she says it, it feels right. Her expression gets serious, and her fingers clench the back of my shirt as she looks around. "How, though?" she muses. "How do you heal something so much bigger than yourself? How do you even start?"

"Understanding." I reach out, keeping the connection between Mance and me open, and I tap into my link to the magic, letting her experience what it feels like for me. At her sharp intake of breath, I know it's working. She sees the wisps of smoky fear that I do, and she presses closer to my side.

But I can see more than just the fear now.

"When I first came in here, I was afraid," I say, although I'm not sure whether I'm talking to her or to myself, because it's almost like I'm only realizing the truth of things when I put them into words. "I thought what I needed was power. Over the situation, over other people. Over fear itself. I don't think the Citadel gave me magic. I think I pulled it for myself from the depths, according to what I thought I needed. And when you first went in—"

"I thought Alect was dead," she whispers. "I thought Mara was dead. All I wanted was a way to bring them back."

"You reached out and claimed the power to resurrect," I confirm. "Even though you didn't realize you were doing it."

She shakes her head slowly. "But it's so twisted. It's so wrong. It didn't protect me; it only brought me more pain."

"That's because it came from something built in fear and darkness. You took what power you could to survive, but you took it from a dark place."

She tilts her head back, looking up, almost as though she can see the sky above. "It's only dark because that's what we've been feeding it, though. The Citadel was created in war and that's all we've been using it for since. How do we break that cycle?"

"The only way you can," I say. "One bit at a time."

I pick out one specific tendril of fear and I pull it toward me. Instead of stoking it into something bigger, I lessen it. I let it ease.

Not the same way that I pull fear out of my own chest, because that's just ignoring it. Refusing to feel it. Instead, I listen to the fear and console it gently, until it dissipates between my fingers on its own.

Mance

I stretch my hand into the space that the strange, wispy fear just occupied, awed to find only emptiness. Stunned by the implication of what Silver just did.

Then I straighten my back, determined to join in the effort. I can't do exactly the same thing, obviously, but there must be a way to use my power, my twisted, fierce power, to do something positive, too.

Fear is not the only thing that festers here. There are also memories of those who have entered the Citadel. Either ones they came in with and left behind or ones created right here. With a hitched breath, I reach into the stream of magic and pull out these memories, these consciousnesses that the different parts of myself can see and understand. And I let those different parts of myself step forward and relate to them. Livid sees anger. Poise sees the urge to hide. Asset sees plans gone awry.

But Heart sees a yearning for something better, too. And I respond to all of it.

The emotions I find that are too dark, too far gone, I kill with my bare hands and resurrect into something new.

Amazingly, as we work, side by side, tiny sparks of light appear in the darkness, like starsprouts in the night. They glow green at first, then lighten to a buttery yellow, as clear and bright as the sunshine streaming through the door.

We continue like this for several minutes, together in the darkness, coaxing tiny points into light and celebrating each other's successes, however small. Then Mara appears in the doorway, framed by the light and squinting in at us. "Something you're doing is working!" she calls. But she's not looking directly at us and her voice is too loud for the proximity.

She must not be able to see us.

I pull Silver forward, toward the door, until I am able to grab Mara's hand. She shrieks and pulls back, true terror in her cry, and with my connection to Silver still strong, I can see fear billowing from her skin like there's a forest fire blazing through her. But I thrust my head out to reassure her.

"It's okay," I say. "It's just me. Come inside." Mara's expression sets into something hard and cold, and she tries to pull back, but I stop her with a gentle pressure on her wrist. "Be *with* me in the darkness this time, Mara," I urge. "Let me be with you."

Her face crumples, but even so she wraps her fingers around my hand and visibly forces herself to take one step toward me, fear still thick as fog. I could pull her in, but I wait, letting Mara take each deliberate step herself.

Until she's past the threshold.

The second she crosses it, she doubles over with a scream, and the darkness around us rushes toward her. I catch her, and Silver hurries to hold her up as well, probably afraid the darkness will rip us all apart and Mara will be lost in it.

But the darkness doesn't affect us the same way anymore. It

doesn't tear at us the way it tears at her. We can still see her, and it, and each other clearly. Which means we can hold her through it.

Before long she is standing next to us on her own strength, no longer gripped by the darkness. Like it was before, her vulnerabilities are ripped open like a raw wound, displayed for us to see, and Silver drops his hand and steps away, offering privacy. I lose the ability to see the wisps of fear, but even so, I am grateful for his consideration.

I take her other hand in mine as well and I hold on, as we truly see each other for the first time in years, wordlessly sharing similar memories from different perspectives. Mara cries stoically, with quiet tears flowing across her scars, and I cry unabashedly, collapsing against her. Because underneath all the hard memories, all the distance between us, all the ways in which we struggle to know how to support each another while trying to protect ourselves as well, there is love. I feel her love for me and she feels my love for her, and in this moment that is all that matters.

I show her what we've been doing, how we've been trying to heal the magic, and after a few moments, Mara steps back, considering the darkness around her and how her own magic might affect it.

She creates boundaries within the shadows, sectioning off the parts that feed and bleed and darken, and she breaks the walls around the parts of the magic that long to be free. Light sparks beneath her efforts, too, and I smile, proud to see her shine.

With three of us working, the pinpricks of light appear faster, like a starry sky emerging from behind the clouds.

And then I reach a hand out the door again, and this time it's Azele who takes it, like she was only waiting for the chance.

After enduring the consumption of the shadows, she uses her

power to pluck up the deepest corners of the darkness, the ones Mara contained neatly in little boundaries, and turn them into ash that flutters harmlessly into the rest.

And the work carries on.

Silver

❦✣❧

We continue this pattern, reaching back in invitation, pulling someone into their own personal darkness, holding them through it, and then showing them how to use the gifts the darkness gave them to make it brighter for everyone else.

Each and every person brave enough to enter the place that haunts them was also brave enough to look at their darkness directly, see it for what it is, and then use their power to heal instead of hurt.

It's easier for some to figure out how to do this than others. But easy or not, everyone finds a way.

I am shocked when Kiar comes in, following some members of the Forest Realm she must know well. After getting through the storm, she plants seeds that urge the magic to mend itself, and the vines on her chest don't grow further when she does. When she sticks her hand out the door, it's Reltas who grabs it. Only he tries to pull Kiar back out, to him.

They wrestle with each other, whispering harsh words. Kiar stands stubborn and firm, but Reltas fights with an unexpectedly vulnerable desperation. The flinty anger I'm used to seeing on his face is stripped bare at the prospect of Kiar going somewhere he can't follow.

When he finally surrenders, more falling in than walking, it is with a cry of grief.

But he makes the choice nonetheless.

The storm he endures is intense, but Kiar is relentless in holding him through it, and when it passes and they stand emotionally exposed before each other, neither one speaks for a long, long time, their eyes locked and their arms trembling even as they grip each other hard.

I look away, focusing on my own work, and when I look back Reltas is summoning hands to bury the ashes that Azele left scattered on the ground. He and Kiar are no longer looking at each other, but their fingers are still entwined, a small gesture of intimacy in the middle of the dark.

Once their Prime led the way, the Forest Realm at large plunges inward, so many at a time that those already inside have to scramble to be there for all of them through the initial rage of the magic. But once they're through it, once they understand what it is that we're doing, the atmosphere turns almost jovial, with so many sparks of light floating in the air that it feels like a holiday. There's laughter, the kind that comes on the other side of a tragedy, when you suddenly and unexpectedly realize that you've somehow made it through all right.

Not everyone enters. Prime Tibits never shows, nor does Prime Apea. But I'm happy to at least see Prime Artro enter with the last of the Forest Realm citizens, his aged head bowed. Mance holds his hand personally, as he braces against the darkness that has haunted him for decades upon decades. He looks lighter once he's finally through it.

Of course, we don't heal the whole Citadel in one day. It will take time. It will probably take generations to undo the darkness, because it took generations to build. But we toil until we're spent, and then we parade our daisy chain of people back out the door, spilling onto the sand and collapsing in exhausted relief. When we turn around to see what we've done, there's still a twisting body of magic crackling above us.

But the light has changed. The darkness at its center is not so deep. And the green mass at the top now boasts a gorgeous fringe of yellow and orange at its tips.

It reminds me of a spring leaf slowly changing color in the fall.

Mance

EPILOGUE

Not everything will change at once. Even with the evidence in the sky, some Primes still refuse to be a part of the transformation effort. My aunt, Prime Apea, prefers to pretend that the problem does not exist, even as her songs get more violent in their control, and Prime Tibits has holed himself up in his throne room, though the heat rocks in its walls keep blazing hotter.

On the other hand, the Swamp Realm has taken down its nets and opened itself up to travelers for the first time, and Prime Azele sent word that, with focus, she and Rift are now able to touch without gloves.

Everyone who reentered the Citadel has noticed changes in their magic. At minimum it has stopped declining, and for some, through hard work and by degrees, it is even starting to heal. My animals are no longer reenacting their own deaths without warning, although they have retained some scars that weren't there before, and while splitting and merging my parts too quickly still causes me pain, it has stopped getting worse every time I use it. The pain is now a predictable thing, one I can prepare for.

Still, the progress is slow. My fellow Primes and I haven't yet been able to agree on a new Treaty. As it currently stands, anyone who wants to rule a realm must still go through the Citadel first. But at least Prime Reltas has adopted the current agreement and has committed to stop sending in his citizens in droves.

In the meantime, Silver and I will go back regularly to coax light out of the dark, and Azele and Rift have stated that they will, too. Reltas and Kiar didn't say anything one way or another, but my hope is that they may join us someday, as well. I haven't heard from them much since the Citadel, but at least their realm in general seems calmer.

It could be a while before we truly know the effects of our actions, but we're dedicated to the cause anyway.

I lean back against Silver's chest and he wraps an arm around my waist as we look out at the velvet night. The yellow and orange streaks in the magic hanging on the skyline remind me of the morning sun peeking over the horizon. And below us, spring is blooming. The first starsprouts of the season appeared tonight, soft and small. But still glowing.

I tilt my head to look up at Silver, my smile serene, and he holds out a small bouquet of dawn-colored flowers, even more vibrant than the first because of the starsprouts that make the whole arrangement glow. He's been taking seriously my request to pick me new ones every day.

As I accept them, he leans down to press his lips to mine.

My eyes flutter shut, and I lose myself in him. It's almost like being in the magic again, with all our deepest secrets laid bare. Because the kiss is everything all at once. It's vulnerability and acceptance, a question and an answer.

The pressure of his lips on mine says, "Yes, I want you."

My fingers in his hair say, "Yes, I will fight for you, whenever you need it."

The way he pulls me against him says, "No, you're not alone."

Every caress, every heartbeat, every inch we close between us says, "Yes. Yes. Yes."

Yes, you are enough. Yes, you are mine. And yes, I am yours, too. Yes . . .

"I love you," he breathes, and my eyes fly open.

We're still breathing hard, still close enough that any small movement would send us colliding again.

So when I smile, it's against his skin.

When I say, "I love you, too," it's a whisper into the corner of his mouth, the one that always raises when he smirks at me.

And I find that those three little words aren't hard to say at all anymore. In fact, they may be the least complicated thing I've ever said.

He kisses me again, more passionately, and I feel like I am lit up from the inside, brighter than the starsprouts, brighter than the sunrise, brighter even than the magic in the sky.

I think about the girl I used to be, on my knees in the arena, wondering when I would finally be strong enough.

And I know now that I am strong enough for anything.

Even healing.

Even love.

ACKNOWLEDGMENTS

I have to thank Brian Geffen first for this sequel, because it genuinely wouldn't exist if it weren't for the fact that he wanted it to. I put *The Beasts We Bury* on submission as a stand-alone, and one morning my agent forwarded an incredibly kind note of interest from an editor (Brian) that made me giddy with excitement until the final words: "Additionally, I was wondering if there's a synopsis of Book 2 available? This is a planned duology, correct?"

Reader, it was not a planned duology. And in that moment of panic, I had absolutely no pitches for a second book. Worse, I was a practicing attorney, and I needed to get to court. I had a hearing that morning that went all the way until lunch, and how I managed to present my case professionally over all the panicked screaming in the back of my mind I will never know.

But the second person I need to thank is Catherine Cho, my agent, because over the course of the next twenty-four hours or so I sent her a series of stream-of-consciousness emails filled with ideas, and we brainstormed back and forth until, somehow, I had a concept that I loved and felt passionate about. Then she took that pitch back to Brian and sold him on it, too. I am forever grateful for her wise insights and her amazing advocacy on my behalf, not just in this instance but many different times over the course of the last couple of years we've worked together.

I am also deeply grateful for the editing process with Brian Geffen, Emma Jones, and Carina Licon. It's been such a pleasure and a privilege to work with all three of them. Their edit letters are so encouraging and inspiring, even (maybe especially?) when they ask for major changes, and it's been such a joy to watch this book in particular come to life under their guidance.

Of course, there is an entire team of people at Holt and First Ink who deserve thanks as well: art director Aurora Parlagreco, editorial director Ann Marie Wong, production editor Kristen Stedman, production manager Jie Yang, and copy editor Emily Stone. As always, I'm sure I don't even know half of what they all do, but it genuinely means the world to me that they do it.

I want to especially thank Kate Forrester for another absolutely gorgeous cover. It was so cool for me to see how you brought so many different elements together, and the final result is stunning!

In addition to all the phenomenal professionals who made this book happen, there are quite a few friends and family members who deserve my gratitude.

First and foremost, I want to thank my mom. She is the reason I love books, and she's been an incredible cheerleader throughout this whole journey. When I told her about my first book tour, she immediately and without a thought volunteered to fly across the country to watch my kids while I was gone, and that's just *one* example of her selfless love. It's been an honor to have her by my side in life. *Especially* when she expresses her affection through cooking.

I am also grateful to my brother, Joe, for brainstorming some of the new magics in this book with me. He is one of the reasons I value imagination so much in the first place, as he spent our whole childhood encouraging it in me. I wouldn't be who I am without him.

And then there are the many people I am blessed to call friends. I don't think I even realized how many true friends I had until I published a book and then turned around to see a veritable *tidal wave* of love coming my way. I would be remiss if I didn't include the unfailing support of my writing group, VS, in these acknowledgments, because they have been with me from the beginning and are such an incredible source of steadfast fellowship. I am thankful for all of them. For this book in particular, I want to especially honor Jenni Howell, Elisse Hill, Charis Buckingham, and Kelsey Epler. They are some of the best women I know and are always down to hear about my latest plot snarl or help me problem-solve a kiss scene. More than that, though, they've each offered me an endless amount of love and understanding, always checking in on me and bolstering me up when I need it. I'm so honored to have them in my life.

Honestly, there are quite a few people I'm honored to know. To be frank, acknowledgments sometimes stress me out because I have far too many supportive and wonderful people on my side to list, and I am grateful for all of them. But I have to give a special shout-out to a couple more: Rebecca Chinery, for her constant, passionate belief in me, as well as her unparalleled and always impeccably timed baked goods, and Stephanie Sousa, for always reminding me of what's most important, and also for being one of the funniest and most genuine people I know.

And now for my very favorite people: the ones I'm privileged to share a home with. I want to thank my kids, for being so proud of me and so excited about every silly video I post on social media and every little milestone I reach. Their precious wonder and joy have helped me feel more of those emotions myself, and no matter how many mentions in prestigious publications I may get, nothing's ever going to beat seeing my daughter's third grade "get to know you" form, where she proudly wrote *my* name next to "favorite author."

Of course, none of this would be possible at all without the incredible support of my husband. He's so proud of me it's embarrassing sometimes. But even when I want to hide behind a fruit display while he talks me up to strangers at the supermarket, I am so deeply grateful for his encouragement and love. I said in the dedication that he accepts every part of me, and I cannot express how healing that is. How much I needed it when I first found it in him, and how grounding and freeing it has been ever since. For the record, I accept every part of him, too. I love this man so much that I'm trying to get into *baseball*, you guys. He's that great.

Lastly, and most importantly, I give the glory to God. I would not be where I am today without Him. My feelings are best summed up in Psalm 100:5, but the bottom line is this: I am so, so grateful.

**If you enjoyed *The Beasts We Raise*,
why not try these First Ink books...**

A Tempest of Tea
Hafsah Faizal

Of Flame and Fury
Mikayla Bridge

The Sleepless
Jen Williams

Legend of the White Snake
Sher Lee

@firstinkbooks